DEAD FOR NEW ORLEANS

Also by
Rodric Edward Cascio

Solange
Madame Solange Deshotel ... Damned for all eternity,
imprisoned in an endless time-loop

Dead for New Orleans

The Story of Vincent Jacola

Rodric Edward Cascio

Sense of Wonder Press
JAMES A. ROCK & COMPANY, PUBLISHERS
FLORENCE • SOUTH CAROLINA

Dead for New Orleans: The Story of Vincent Jacola by Rodric Edward Cascio

SENSE OF WONDER PRESS
is an imprint of JAMES A. ROCK & CO., PUBLISHERS

Dead for New Orleans: The Story of Vincent Jacola
copyright ©2015 by Rodric Edward Cascio

Special contents of this edition copyright ©2015
by James A. Rock & Co., Publishers

*Explanation of tarot card (The Magician) by James Rioux, Copyright 2000 James Rioux
(The Black Shadow) bshadow@nbnet.nb.ca.*

Address comments and inquiries to:
SENSE OF WONDER PRESS
James A. Rock & Company, Publishers
1937 West Palmetto Street, #248
Florence, SC 29501
E-mail:
jarrock@sprintmail.com   larrock@earthlink.net

Internet URL: www.rockpublishing.com

ISBN-13/EAN: 978-1-59663-864-8

Library of Congress Control Number: 2013932602

Printed in the United States of America

First Edition: 2015

This book

is dedicated

to my parents

Ed and Belle Cascio

Acknowledgments

Many heartfelt thanks go to my test readers: Shirley and George Cummings, Joey Feltri, Loretta Rivers, Fran Parker, Amy Weatherly and Darryl and Karen Shelton. Also, I am deeply indebted to the late Frances Brister for sage advice, and to the late Vera Lee Mansfield for character inspiration. Both are gone but will never be forgotten!!

PROLOGUE

It had begun with an embrace. He'd gotten lucky tonight—or so he thought. Bitch must've given him the flu or something. He felt cold. The sex was great—this chick took him places he didn't know existed. Something's different since she's left, though. He felt cold ... empty. He just wanted to get in bed and pull the covers over his head. Maybe he'd do that. Perhaps some rest would help him to feel better in the morning. Trouble was, there'd be no feeling better for him anymore ... he was dead.

CHAPTER ONE

I had never heard the term chakra before. I had no idea what it meant. Little did I know, knowledge of that six letter word marked the beginning of the end of life as I'd always been accustomed. From that day forward, I'd traded my life for an existence.

A little later than most, I attended college in New Orleans. Deciding to settle there, I invested in an unassuming white-framed house in the older, established neighborhood of Gentilly. Well cared for and modestly updated over the years, the home belonged to a lovely old lady who'd become infirmed and could no longer maintain the place.

Gentilly was the latest and greatest of the post-war housing boom. Remnants of early twenties to mid-century living abounded everywhere. Even though I'd lived in New Orleans a mere four and one-half years, I somehow felt a part of this neighborhood. The moment I'd settled in, I felt an instant sense of belonging.

Written in script across faded signs, obsolete store fronts bore local names such as Espinoza, Scramuzza and LaLu. Streets with delightful labels such as Harmony, Serendipity, and Painters all contributed to the ambience of 'Old Gentilly.' The French Quarter was a mere two mile drive toward the Mississippi River, while Lake Pontchartrain was a short walk north on Franklin Avenue.

It was no secret that I had joined a community well into its waning years. Nevertheless, all of the red tiled roofs, forgotten, jagged streets of white concrete and tiny neighborhood restaurants entranced me. Only the locals knew that these off-the-beaten-path establishments housed the true secrets of New Orleans culinary magic. Not in my wildest dreams would I have imagined that Boliviee's Restaurant—a local soul food eatery directly across the street from my home—would house the meeting place responsible for my ultimate demise.

And I loved that place, dammit to Hell …

CHAPTER TWO

How do I describe Boliviee's Restaurant? Like most of the neighborhood, the small building is painted white. A black sign—reminiscent of the art deco era—hangs from the front of the structure. Holes strategically placed throughout the front of the sign give clues to a long defunct mechanism of neon illumination. The days of neon are long past, though, with an amateur paint job advertising the current restaurant proprietors.

Like the sign, the restaurant's interior is Art Deco. Encased in black lacquer frames, etched glass partitions define the bar area. Smooth lines, curved walls and indirect lighting all help to provide an architectural glimpse into the past. The look of Boliviee's typifies local drinking establishments of days gone by.

My name is Vincent Jacola. I'm thirty-seven years of age and work as a dental laboratory technician. I work most evenings until six-thirty, after which I usually make a beeline home to grab a beer and eat some supper across the street. I'm not much of a cook these days; I know how to cook but don't particularly enjoy it. I hate the residual mess of the whole endeavor; therefore, Boliviee's serves as a handy solution to the mealtime dilemma. Although usually the only white face in the restaurant, I'm a local there. My Caucasian presence, however, no longer stands out much in the crowd. I know all of the regulars and have befriended most of them. The proprietors, Mozetta and Pierre Conerly, have practically adopted me.

Most weeknights—in front of my customary seat at the bar—a dinner place setting awaits my seven p.m. arrival. My favorite dishes are stuffed bell peppers and fried chicken. Mozetta always places a call to remind me chicken will be hot and ready at seven-thirty; seven-thirty 'chicken time' gives me a few minutes to unwind and perhaps have a drink or two. Too bad if a customer gets a bit disgruntled about the late suppertime, as 'Fried Chicken Night' for the most part is just for me.

Even though I'm now just a face in the crowd, a beautiful, green-eyed red-head sitting alone at Bolivee's bar is a different story. Six months ago, while traipsing through my daily supper routine, I met Solange Deshotel. Perfectly attired, matching alligator purse and shoes complimented an expensive dress of brown silk. In a rich 'V' formation, her hair raced toward the middle of her back. She was the most beautiful woman I had ever seen. I had to meet her.

"I don't really have a line for you. I'm in here every night and I've never seen you before."

Barely acknowledging that he had mustered the nerve to approach, her glance never faltered. Still fixated upon the cocktail in front of her, she simply smiled and said, "OK." She then returned her attention to her drink.

Yeah … that went really well … He smiled at her again. "I'm Vincent."

"Hello, Vincent."

… And you don't give a shit. "Can I buy you a drink?"

"Hey Vince!"

Across the room stood Felton Andrieus. Resident bartender at Boliviee's, Felton was also my confident and closest friend.

His attention diverted toward the end of the bar, Vince made a face as if to say, *Lay off!*

"Get yo' lily white ass down here, boy!"

Walking toward him, in mock protest Vince threw up his hands. "What! I'm trying to score a few points down there, you know?"

"Don't mess with that."

"What up?"

"She's trouble … bad trouble. You do not want a piece of that. Find you somethin' else—that ain't for you."

"You know her?"

"No, I know of her."

"Shit, Felton, don't give me a bunch of crap. I've got a chance to get some red-head booty and you're going to advise me based on the latest gossip?"

"Ain't no latest gossip, Vince. I'm tellin' you she's no good for you. Leave it alone. I think it's time for you to get yo' ass back across the street where you belong."

"I haven't eaten yet!"

"Order it to go. I'll have Mo bring it over when it's ready."

"Man, you suck. What makes you think I'm going to do what you say?"

"Because I'll whip yo' sloppy, white butt if you don't get the hell out of here."

"Crap. Guess they'll be big and blue tonight, thanks to you … And thanks to me, too, because for some strange reason I'm doing what you say to do. Big and blue, Felton, hope I get to return the favor one day, asshole!"

"Better than dead, boy. Now go!"

Dead?!? What the hell did he mean by that? "I haven't paid yet."

"Settle up tomorrow. Mo's cookin' Bubble and Squeak. Got some fresh Peralta's bread comin', too."

Vince grabbed his wallet and keys off the bar. "Night, dick-face."

"Sleep tight, big boy. Supper'll be over in about thirty minutes."

Walking past her, Vince leaned toward Solange and whispered, "I'm headed home. I hope I'll see more of you."

Solange turned to return the whisper. "Be careful what you hope for, Vince. You may get your wish." Bringing her perpendicular to the bar once again, her stool revolved clockwise.

Sentiment is expressed in many ways. Something as simple as a furrow of the brow may convey frustration, while a mere twinkle in the eye can signify mischief. There is no more effective method, however, to induce fear than a deadpan stare. A lifeless look in the direction of the intended victim can elicit feelings of dread as well as doom.

The void of emotion which accompanied her last glance did just that. Maybe it was time to end the visit … maybe Felton really was on to something.

Visibly shaken, he reached for a cigarette. Lighting it, he inhaled deeply and began his departure. Demarcating his path of exit, a trail of smoke followed closely behind.

CHAPTER THREE

There was a knock on the door. Vince walked across the house to answer it.

"Hey, Mo."

"I heard what happened."

"Ain't that some shit?"

"More shit than you realize, Vince. Felton was right. You need to stay away from her. There's some talk about this woman that don't get into yo' culture."

"Culture? Mo, you're talking in riddles."

"That woman comes with a curse."

"Hey, you have a minute or do you need to get back to the restaurant?"

"I have a few minutes."

"Come in. I'll eat my supper while you fill me in on this. You want something to drink?"

"Got some sweet tea?"

"Just made some."

Returning to the kitchen, he made his way toward the refrigerator. "Have a seat, Mo."

He placed the Styrofoam box of food onto the table and proceeded to fill two glasses with ice. Bringing them to the table, he then filled them with tea. "Now ... tell me."

"You know there's such a thing as Voodoo, don't you?"

"Of course ... I don't know anyone who practices it, but I've heard of it."

"Word has it that woman ain't natural, Vince."

"Who said that?"

"It's well known in the community."

"I've never heard it."

"The black community, Vince." As she shook her head, Mozetta closed her eyes. "You know, when it comes to common sense, sometimes I think you got the short end of the stick."

"You ain't the first person that's said that, Mo. I don't give a shit …" Shifting positions in his chair, he continued. "Now that we've established the fact that I'm a dumbass, tell me more about this woman. She's about the best looking thing I've ever seen."

"You ain't no dumbass, honey, you just don't connect the dots sometimes. Rumor says this woman's over a hundred years old."

In an attempt to process what she'd just said, he fell silent. Staring at her, he took a deep breath and exhaled. "I don't feel so stupid anymore. I've heard some ridiculous things in my life, but this takes the cake. That woman looks barely thirty, Mozetta."

"I'm tellin' you what I know."

"If she's over a hundred, then we need to call Ponce de Leon. There's some serious fountain of youth action going on somewhere …"

"She made a deal with the devil. That's the only action goin' on." Intentionally not blinking, Mozetta returned the stare.

The steadfast gaze made him uncomfortable. "C'mon, Mo, you've been watching too many movies. You don't believe that, do you?"

"A lot of stuff out there don't make it into yo' world, Vince. Some of my people used to practice Voodoo in the West Indies."

"Did they know this woman?"

"Sure did. My mother said that woman murdered her aunt … drank her blood, too."

"For God's sake, Mo, I'm eating." Vince dropped the chicken leg onto his plate and drank some tea. He then pushed away from the table. "That blood comment about did it. I think I'm done."

"I didn't mean to spoil yo' dinner, honey, but you need to listen and listen good. Stay away from her. She's not for you. We got plans for her. We will handle her in our own way."

"Do you think this chick has any clue her ass is about to be in a sling?" Vince made a melodramatic facial expression to exaggerate the comment.

"It's kind of a face off. Solange has come to do battle. She ain't scared of us at all, but we ain't scared of her, neither. We plan to avenge my Aunt Angelique's death. She knows that and intends to take care of it. She thinks she gonna put us in our place."

"Shit." Pausing a moment in thought, he then looked up and continued. "This is too rich for my blood. Maybe you guys across the street need to heed some of your own advice. This sounds serious."

"It is." She arose to leave. "Bubble and Squeak tomorrow night, you coming?"

"As far as I know... I don't see any hot dates coming my way."

"You need to get out more. You need to get out of this house and around some people yo' own age."

"I do, don't I? Well, as of now, I have a date with you tomorrow night."

"What do you want me to fix you?"

Raising his eyebrows in anticipation, he said, "Stuffed artichokes?"

Mo sighed. It was a long, exasperated sigh. "You don't ask for much, do you? OK, baby, I'll pass by Pap's tomorrow and pick up a few. You do know I don't make those for nobody else?"

Vince grinned. "I'm 'bout in the mood for some red beans and rice, too."

"Monday, baby. I already got 'em in the freezer." Opening the door to leave, she continued. "You heed what I say, boy. You hear?"

"I heard every word. I'm listening. I'm heeding and running like hell. How does that sound"

"Like maybe all of that alcohol you pour down yo' face has not completely fried yo' brain."

This made him laugh. Following her toward the door, he further opened it. "Love ya, Mo."

"Love you too, baby." As she left the house, he closed the living room door behind her.

CHAPTER FOUR

Let's face it: I was a creature of habit. Sunday mornings were always the same. I'd wake up about eight and get dressed. Being the weekend, I didn't bother to shave. A baseball hat usually took care of the hair. I'd slip on a pair of jeans as well as my cleanest, wrinkled tee shirt and head off to P.J.'s Coffee Shop. P.J.'s was the perfect way to spend a lazy Sunday morning. Typical fare usually consisted of ambient classical music, the Times Picayune and a delicious slab of homemade pound cake. Served with a sack of powdered sugar and fresh butter, a hunk of P.J.'s pound cake lasted well past three cups of strong chicory coffee.

Around noon, morning ritual complete, I'd jump on my bike and head for the Quarter. Although a bit confining at times, the French Quarter was always the perfect place for mindless occupation. Anything goes and a festival is ever present somewhere in those few blocks of downtown New Orleans. It was there that I saw that woman again.

On Decatur Street, about halfway into the French Quarter, an amphitheatre of sorts sits against the backside of the Mississippi River levee. I'd decided to spend my afternoon there, as I'd just read that sometime between two and three o'clock, Skat Riddles was holding an outdoor mini-concert. As I passed the theatre, I noticed it was fast becoming full. Hurriedly, I chained my bike to a pole near the Jackson brewery and jogged back up the street to the stands. Settling in to people watch, I managed to grab a seat near the top of the concrete bleachers.

In a crowd that size, there is no way that woman could have spotted me, and yet I would swear at one point we made direct eye contact. I know I did not imagine it; I did imagine, however, how much I'd like

12

to bounce a quarter off that firm ass of hers. For a moment we exchanged glances. Then, as quickly as she'd come into view, she disappeared among the artists, tarot readers, and mimes of Jackson Square.

Twice in one weekend … what are the odds? It was too coincidental to be a coincidence—something was up. Mozetta's warning rang through my head. Surely I wasn't in the middle of some shit I had nothing to do with, was I? I remained distracted throughout the rest of the concert, opting to ride home afterwards in search of Mozetta Conerly. She'd have some real input into this. Mo would have a definite opinion on this situation.

✳ ✳ ✳

"So anyway, that's it."

"Sounds like that's enough."

"Maybe so …" Pausing for a moment, he changed positions in his chair. "But I just find it coincidental—as well as a little alarming—that after you've given me all of this 'hoo-doo' background information, I see this woman twice in one weekend."

"Mmm-hmm."

"Mmm-hmm, what?"

"Mmm-hmm now I know that wasn't no accident— you meetin' her in my restaurant."

"Yes, it was."

"No, it was not." Mo had a look of unbridled conviction spread across her face.

"Alright, then, what the hell does she want from me?"

Her syntax had become deliberate as well as distinct. In order to add emphasis to her comments, Vince also noticed that she was no longer using contractions.

"I do not know. But I can assure you that I will find out." She belted out *will* about fifty decibels louder than the rest of the sentence.

"You know, I'm just minding my own business here, fucking up my own life. I don't need any supernatural shit piled on top of it. It's fucked up enough, already."

"Vincent, there's a story behind this woman you do not know."

"Yes, I do; you told me Friday night. She's old, but doesn't look it. She's a fuckin' ghoul, for Christ's sake, a brick shithouse ghoul."

"You ain't never used no shithouse or you'd know they wasn't made of brick."

"It's an expression, Mo."

"This woman is able to travel through time."

"And you been smokin' crack."

As he said this, Mozetta bristled. "And you fixin' to be lookin' at the back of yo' face!"

"Maybe so, but before you swing, perhaps you ought to see things from my point of view. So far, since Friday, I've heard about Voodoo, and draining some chick's blood …"

"That was my aunt," Mo interrupted.

"Whatever … And now you say this red-headed vampiress can leap across the ages. This is like some low-rent, spooky campfire tale."

"She's wreaked a lot of havoc, Vince. I'm tellin' you she knows somethin', and somehow you fit in her plan. You better watch yo' step, boy. Right now, things are not what they should be."

"She may as well not jack with me, then. I don't want any part of all this. Hell, next thing you know, there'll be a dead chicken on my front porch."

"And you better learn not to make fun of things you don't understand. That alone can get yo' ass killed. I know you mean well, but I will say this to you one more time and I want you to listen real good. You have embedded yo'self right in the middle of a culture that you do not belong to. I truly do not know if it was an accident or if it was meant to be. That being said, you need to understand that there's a lot goin' on that you do not know about. I suggest you keep that big mouth of yours shut and those wisecracks to yo'self."

"Damn … I didn't mean to offend …"

"Well, you did. Not everybody loves you, Vince. Not everybody down here's taken you in as one of their own. This is New Orleans, and things are different here. Understand?"

Vince smiled. "Yeah, I understand. I'm sorry, Mo."

Mozetta returned the smile. "It's OK, baby, you just be sure to let me know if you see her again." She arose to leave. "Now, I have work to do. I'd better get back across the road before they burn the place down."

As the storm door closed behind her, Mozetta began her descent down the front porch steps.

Realizing he'd forgotten something, Vincent hurriedly made his way toward the doorway. "Hey, what are you baking for tonight?"

Turning to face him, she answered. "Not baking anything. We ordered stuffed king cakes from Frances'."

"Chocolate?"

"Chocolate, cream cheese and strawberry."

"Sounds good."

Leaving the doorway, he made his way back inside. In search of the telephone, he walked toward the rear of the house. As if somehow accentuating the second exit, the storm door once again slammed shut.

***

"Hey man."

"Dude … What's happening?"

"Don't ask. I have a feeling my shit's headed straight south."

"Wow, man … sounds like you've had a rough week or month or something …"

Race Vidrine was my token hippie friend. As a rule, my friends were labeled as queers, whores, alcoholics, and the occasional bitch. In order to be a friend of Vince's, a severe personality disorder was required. If I actually took inventory of these friendships, I'd probably realize that they were right.

Although my circle of friends did include all of the aforementioned categories, none of the gang was in prison or anything … There were worse things in life than drunken whores, weren't there?

Probably entering the field in order to self-diagnose, Dr. Race Vidrine practices psychiatric medicine at Louisiana State University Medical Center . I met him at Forty-One Forty-One, a bar in Uptown New Orleans. Forty-One Forty-One features a three-for-one happy hour on Wednesdays; we both are mid-week regulars there. Usually solving the world's problems in nine beers or less, over the years we've become good friends.

"What's headed south, Man?"

"Race, there's some weird shit creeping into my life."

"Dude …"

"I met this chick at Boliviee's."

"Boliviee's … Cool. Man, we need to hang out there again. I feel like I'm in an alternate reality in there. We get to step into another existence …"

"Damn, you just said a mouthful."

"Tell me about the chick."

"She's not really a chick. She's a woman."

Race laughed. "A female … that other species …"

"Sophisticated, Race."

"You can handle sophisticated … might have to tune up the vocabulary a bit." Race slapped a hand across the back of his shoulder. "My sophisticated friend!"

"Some scary stuff surrounds this ho."

"A ho! Did you get any?"

"No, man, I was told to run like hell."

"Another alpha male claiming his turf …"

"Actually, Race, that's not it. There's some cult shit going on. We're talking a war of the netherworlds."

"Wow … you've slid into a supernatural cataclysm, man …"

"I ain't slid into nothin'. That bitch is hot, but if she's a ghoul, vampire or whatever, I'm out of here. I don't fuck dead shit."

Race through his head back in laughter. "Man, you're not right. You kill me!"

"Mo said to go!"

"Mo's the man, dude. The 'she-man' … aw hell … you know what I mean."

"Means I'm listening to Mo, dude."

"I hear ya."

"I need another beer."

"Well, let's get the bartender over here so we can imbibe."

"I'm thinking shit-faced, Race."

Race laughed again. "I've walked down Claiborne Avenue a few times under the influence. One more won't hurt."

Vince smiled. Forty-one Forty-one may wash his fear away tonight, but somehow he knew it would be waiting on him tomorrow morning. Depending on how fucked up he got tonight, hopefully there'd be a tomorrow morning.

CHAPTER FIVE

The world of dental laboratory technology is not exclusively male. In fact, Delia Melancon has directed the DLT program at LSUSD for more than seven years. Her last name is actually pronounced Meláwnsawn; her Cajun roots reach deep into the bayous of coastal Louisiana. Delia is actually from the small fishing village of Cocodrie. Virtually detached from the outside world, the folks of Cocodrie exude a warmth and hospitality unique to their isolated culture. Although Delia shares in the kind, Cajun demeanor, her program is run with strict adherence to policy and protocol. She takes the job seriously. Rules are followed to the letter.

As he left the clinic floor, Vincent grabbed a spot on the elevator and headed for the basement.

"Hey Mel!"

Eyebrows raised, Delia turned toward him.

"Joubert wants anatomy in this bridge."

For more than eight years, Dr. Thierry Joubert had been on staff at the school. He'd recently been promoted to head of the Fixed Prosthodontics Department.

"It has anatomy in it."

"The student ground it all out trying to seat it."

"Then let him carve the anatomy into it. We're busy."

"Please, Delia. Do it for me."

Delia felt the familiar looming presence behind her. Apparently, once again, Joubert had appeared. "I'd rather not. The students are supposed to do it."

"I'd consider it a personal favor." In a gauche attempt at charm, he smiled at her.

"Dr. Joubert, let's get one thing straight. If this were an isolated incident, I'd be glad to do it. Unfortunately, you have too many 'personal favors.' Now, I will put some anatomy in this bridge, but realize that your students are being graded on my work. Third year dental students should have no problem carving anatomy into porcelain, so I would appreciate your not asking me to do this again."

Joubert smiled at her and planted a kiss on her forehead.

"That's another thing. If you value the rest of your face, keep those lips off of me."

"You're too cute." Dr. Joubert dropped the bridge into a laboratory box and left.

"That French mother f…!" She stopped herself mid-sentence. After a moment, she began again. "I'm gonna rack his slimy butt next time he even thinks about throwing a kiss my way."

"I don't think he gets it. Seems to me, he's getting some different vibes."

"What do you want, Vince?"

"You."

"You must want to get hurt …"

"Maybe … I'm always game for new things."

"I don't need this. I have a lab to run. What's up?"

"Want to grab a bite after work? I have a little scenario I'd like to run past you. I ran it past Race."

Delia interrupted. "Like that's any help. What'd you decipher between the 'Cool!' and 'Dude, that rocks!'"

"That's about all."

"Got a date tonight, how about lunch tomorrow in the courtyard?"

Vince sighed. "You're missing the best red beans and rice of your life."

"Bring the leftovers. We'll eat 'em tomorrow."

"Damn … red beans two days in a row. Tomorrow, the lab might just go boom!"

"You are gross; you know that?"

"You didn't like my onomatopoeia?"

"No, I didn't. In fact, I don't even know what you just said."

"Get yo' quarter round out and start carving, Mel, Joubert awaits."

"He awaits a boot up his rear end."

"Don't give him any kinky ideas. He might like that …"

✳✳✳

Several weeks had passed before I saw her again. Really, I'd almost for-gotten about her when our paths crossed once more. That's a lie; I had not forgotten her. I well remembered what Mo and the others had told me. I just hoped that maybe I'd escaped a horrible scenario that was slowly developing around me. No more Solange, no more Voodoo talk … out of sight, out of mind. It's that 'knowing look' that creeps me out. The chick stares a hold right through you. You'd think we were friends or something.

Understand this: most would think I'm a loser. My credit cards are maxed out with shit I don't even own anymore. I have no savings and barely have enough money to pay my mortgage. Why, you ask? Let's see … alcohol, Boliviee's, cigarettes, casinos, cocaine, and an occasional bag of pot tend to eat up most of my profits. As for women, I'm friends with a few and fuck what I can. I'm usually able to find something to go home with in the wee hours of the morning; the Quarter's been good to me in that way. So, based on what I've just said, you can understand why I'd be a little tempted to give a second look to someone who looks like Solange. I mean, after all … how do I know all that 'undead' shit is true? The story is pretty incredible if you ask me. Trouble is no one asked me …

✳✳✳

"What can I do for you? The name's Tim."

"I heard you're supposed to be the best."

"I do what I can."

Luna Azul sits Midway down Royal Street. The door is demarcated only by a small wooden sign hanging above its doorway. Painted an irides-cent blue, a small raised crescent is carved into the center of the sign. Tim, the resident card reader, runs the paranormal parlor most weekdays.

"I have a problem."

"Well that's interesting. I'm usually not in the problem solving business. My end is more toward the avoiding problems business?"

"Can you read my cards?"

"I can read my cards ... I don't know about yours."

Vince smirked at this. "Can I just get a fucking reading?"

"Since you put it that way, have a seat. What brings you in here, anyway? You're a tourist?"

"I live in Gentilly."

"I don't get many locals."

"Does that mean you're a *quack*?"

"Never been called that before. Here ... choose three crystals. I'll deal."

I chose two green stones and a violet quartz. He dealt a Celtic cross pattern onto the table in front of us.

"Hmmm."

"What does 'hmmm' mean?"

"I see some changes on the near horizon."

"Good changes?"

"Well, there's a woman in your future, and there's longevity. Yep, I see a long life ahead of you."

"OK ... those are good things." As if a light bulb had gone off in his head, he refocused his gaze. "Hey, man ..."

"What?"

"How about that Death card?"

"Don't let it spook you. The Death card symbolizes change as well as transition. What's your name?"

"Vincent Jacola."

"Vincent, I find this a little befuddling."

Whatever befuddling means ... "How so?"

"I see transition ... but it's interfered with somehow. Something's not quite right."

"Oh, cool. My tarot reader sees a fucked up transition. Imagine that ..."

"You need to watch your back. You have some deep water in front of you."

"What deep water?"

"You don't need to make a change anytime soon. It won't be a good one."

"What kind of change?"

"That's all I have for you, man."

"Come on, Tim, don't leave me hangin' …"

"Follow your gut instincts, Vincent. They're right."

"Thanks, man."

"Forty bucks, Vince."

Oh, so now I'm Vince? Forty bucks to confirm I'm fucked, Tim. I already knew that. Well … fuck you, too!

With that thought complete, I paid the man and left the parlor. Feeling totally defeated, I headed for Boliviee's.

CHAPTER SIX

Roberta read the letter before her.

Conerly
9811 Dreux Avenue
New Orleans, LA 70122

Dear Dr. Staten:
I'm sure that as you read this letter, you're greatly disturbed. I know that I am. The thing that we most fear has come to pass. The evil that has transpired before us did not die with your father; it is upon us once again, and has come to do battle.

Dr. Staten, we both know that in your possession you have the means to fight this demon. I am asking you for it; with God's help, and enough ammunition, we can send this vile force back to the Hell from which it came. Please help us. We must succeed in defeating this evil enemy.

Sincerely yours:
Mozetta Conerly

CHAPTER SEVEN

How do I describe Miami? Salsa? Latin? Or maybe just tropical. From New Orleans, it's easy to get to there. Hop a plane, and in a little over two hours, you've arrived. They fly over the Gulf, for Christ's sake; it's a straight shot. Depending on where you end up in Miami determines in what decade you'll spend your vacation. Retiree fifties architecture abounds everywhere in Pinecrest, while thirties Art Deco has been scrupulously preserved in South Beach. On Eighth Street you can catch up on all of the latest happenings in Cuba. Truly, something for everyone exists in Miami.

I'd had enough 'weird' in my life for awhile, and decided a bolt and run was in order. Race couldn't leave his practice long enough to come with me, so I rang my nephew and told him to clear off the couch.

Some twenty-odd years ago, my sister married a Cuban. A child soon followed. Although I may be eighteen years older than my favorite—and only—nephew, amazingly, there doesn't seem to be a generation gap. Maybe it's because I'm stuck in adolescence ... I don't know. What I do know is that he can party like a son of a bitch and I can almost keep up with him.

As for my sister's in-laws, I love them. No matter how long I may stay in Miami, I have a place there. Their culture is different. They actually cherish family instead of dreading it.

Just past the security zone of Gate 23, I saw my nephew Luis. Waving at me, with three of his friends he was awaiting my arrival.

"Damn, boy, are you a sight for sore eyes! You don't know how glad I am to be here."

"¡Tío! ¿Que pasó?"

24

"¿Que pasó? You got all day?"

Luis smiled. "Yeah, actually, I do have all day." He then turned his attention toward the other three men. "Hey Tío, these are my friends, Eric, Cristobal and James."

"Nice to meet you. Hey guys, I need a Mojito."

"Kinda girlie, Uncle Vince. Why don't we get a beer?"

"How about some grub, too?"

"Mom's got black beans, rice and fried pork chunks waiting on us."

"I want bar food. I want a cigarette, some cheese sticks, lots of alcohol and a good ear."

As he said this, Cristobal laughed aloud. "Dude, your uncle's cool!"

"Yeah, he is cool, isn't he? You know, if we're gonna have bar food, the best place to eat might be The Rack in Kendall."

Cristobal smiled again. "Yeah, definitely. They hand cut their own cheese sticks and make homemade ranch dressing."

"Why don't you and Eric go over there and get us a table. I'll hang around here and help Uncle Vince get a rental. As soon as we get his luggage loaded into the car, we'll meet you."

Taking car keys from him, Eric then turned toward Cristobal. "OK, we're gone. Tío, it was cool meeting you."

"You, too, man. We'll call on the way so you can order for us. I'm hungry as hell."

As Eric, Cristobal and James made their way out of the airport, Luis refocused his attention toward his uncle. "Hey, Tío, we need to head down the escalator toward baggage claim. While we're on our way over there, I want you to tell me what's up with you."

"You'd never believe it."

"Yes, I would."

"OK, how's this: I think I got a ghoul after me."

"That ugly, huh? Man, that's bad."

"No, actually she's not ugly at all. You'd cut off your right nut to fuck her."

"What? ¿Estás loco en la cabeza?"

"No, that's the sad part. I'm not crazy." As if he'd forgotten something, Vince suddenly stopped walking. "Hey, nephew, is Shelly gonna be pissed if we don't eat her pork tonight?"

"She probably won't be pissed, but you'll be able to bounce it off the wall tomorrow. It doesn't age too well."

"Hmmm."

"So, Uncle Vince, why don't you stay down here for awhile?"

"I have a job, remember?"

"We'll find you a job here."

"If I wasn't so freaked out, I'd say that sounded pretty stupid."

"We can do it …"

"I'll think about it. You may not have to twist my arm too hard."

As Vince finished the statement, they both became aware of a ringtone.

"Tío, that's your cell phone ringing."

Looking downward toward his coat pocket, he realized his device was illuminated. "Damn, it sure is." Subsequently retrieving it, he pushed the button demarcated by a green telephone handset symbol.

"Hello?"

As Vince answered the phone, the color literally drained from his face.

"I can't breathe!"

"What's wrong with you?"

"Oh God … I … I … get me out of here! I can't breathe!"

"There's a door over here. Hurry! Don't pass out!"

As fast as I could, I headed for the exit. The last thing I remember was falling toward it. My cell fell ahead of me, and concrete came screaming toward the side of my head. Before I closed my eyes for good, I remember seeing Luis running toward me. I could hear him yelling, "Hello? Who is this?" *Faintly, I then heard a voice yell,* "Call 911!" *That was it. Fade to black—I was out.*

CHAPTER EIGHT

"El despierta."

"Yeah, yeah, I'm awake."

I awoke in Baptist Hospital—Bay five of the ER. Aracély, Luis and Tomas were standing over me. Now, you have to realize that even though my sister's given name is Shelley, the Cubans have called her Aracély so long that it stuck.

"Thank God!"

"What the hell are you thanking God for, Shelley?"

"Watch your mouth, Vince. Something's bad wrong. I can feel it."

"You can't feel shit. You have no idea what's going on. Your brother's in trouble, and this time it's not my fault."

"Just like the other five hundred times, huh Vince?"

"Fuck you, Tomas. Damn … I said that way too loud." My head felt like it was about to explode …

"Tío, who is Delia Melancon?"

I was about to answer when a man entered the room.

"We'll have to save the question for later on, folks. I need to examine the patient."

"Who are you?"

"I'm Dr. Acosta."

Dr. Juan Acosta was the attending physician. Apparently, he was called onto the case after I was admitted into the ER.

"I hope you're here to help; my head feels like it's in a vise. What the hell's wrong with me, anyway?"

"You have a concussion, Mr. Jacola."

"Do you need to shoot me?"

"Hardly … You'll need rest, some anti-inflammatory medicines and more x-rays. We want to make sure there is no hematoma."

"What's a hema—whatever you just said?"

"A blood clot on the brain."

"No … we don't want one of those. When will we know?"

"You're here for a couple of days. We'll know by then. What happened, Mr. Jacola?"

"Vince."

"As you wish."

"I uhhh … had an anxiety attack."

Turning toward the others in the room, he continued.

"Señores y Señora: Ustedes hagan el favor de salir del cuarto."

"Sí, Doctor." *With that, they all left.*

"Why'd you throw them out? And, by the way, yo hablo Español. So don't try and pull any language bullshit on me."

"What do we have here, Mr. Jacola?"

"A hematoma."

"You drug tested positive for marijuana, codeine and methamphetamines. You came in here drunk, high and scared to death. If it weren't for that nasty bump on your head, I'd have you in community rehab rather than on my floor. So, I'll ask again. Why did you pass out?"

"You tell me. Sounds like an overdose to me."

"Keep playing games and I'll have you committed."

"If only it were that easy." Staring straight ahead as he said this, he then refocused his gaze toward the doctor. Breathing in deeply, he exhaled and began again. "I'm in trouble, Doc."

"I figured as much."

"Big trouble."

"Wanted by the law? ¿Usted necesita un abogado?"

"I don't need an attorney. I may need a freakin' exorcist, but I'm OK on the attorney front."

"Hmmm … maybe the fifth floor is not such a bad idea after all, even though somehow, Mr. Jacola, you do not strike me as crazy."

"Again, if that were the case, things would be much simpler. As circumstances now stand, Doctor Acosta, I'm not yet crazy. I can't, however, promise anything in the near future. While in the airport, I received a phone call. I haven't told my family any details about it, but it was from a close friend of mine in New Orleans."

"Your girlfriend?"

"No, just a co-worker. Something terrible has happened back home. Something horrible."

"¿Que pasó, Señor?"

"A buddy of mine was murdered."

"Are the police looking for you?"

"They are. Felton Andrieus works across the street from my house. He's a bartender at the restaurant." *I sat up in bed as I said this.* "His throat was slashed. Someone slit his throat and dragged him onto my front porch."

"¡Dios mío!"

"I'm scared I'm next, Doc. Someone's after my ass."

"Have you told the police?"

"There's lots more to the story."

"¿Podemos entrar?"

Tomas, Shelley and Luis had reentered the room.

"Yeah, come in."

"And, to answer your question, Dr. Acosta, no, I haven't told the police."

"Police?"

"Long story, Shelley, have a seat."

"I must inform the authorities of your whereabouts."

"I don't care. I didn't do anything. I was here when he was murdered."

"Oh God, Vince, who?"

"Felton Andrieus … a friend."

"You have a lot of explaining to do."

"If you want to hear this, you may as well sit down. We'll be awhile."

As I began to explain, I realized how complex and bizarre this situation was becoming. Felton was one of my best friends. Here I am laid up in a hospital, not even knowing the details of his murder. I had to call Mel … I had to get them out of here and talk to her soon. Did I want to? Hell no! Did I have to? If I wanted to keep my ass on the dull side of that blade, I'd better do it soon—real soon!

CHAPTER NINE

10:00 A.M.

I packed my shit and headed to Key West. Much to the dismay of my family, I had to clear my head—what was left of it, anyway. I had a buddy with a small condo off of Duval Street. Close to all of the festivities, the condo was just far enough off the main drag to warrant some peace and quiet.

Yeah, I know the police want to talk to me, but I'm not ready to talk to them. No luck in contacting Mel. Where the hell is she? I guess my next haul is Cuba. There's nowhere else to run. I promised my family I'd return in a couple of days. My head hurts all the time; if I had some shit right now, I'd smoke it. I could use a break from reality.

"Hey, dickhead, let's get some beer and take the boat out. You look like you could use some fresh air."

My friend's name is Doug Adair. Not as fucked up as I am, he's just lazier and a bit more independent. I don't have the cojones to pack up and head for the islands. I guess I'm a little more responsible ... yeah, right.

Just then my phone rang. "Hello?"

"Vince! Where the hell are you? I got your message. What's going on?"

"Mel! Oh shit, Mel! I don't know. My whole life has gone to the dogs. I'm in trouble, Mel, and I haven't done anything!"

"You better call in or something. I've covered your tail as much as I can. You're about to be fired if you don't check in and tell them how sick you are. Where are you, anyway?"

"Key West."

31

"What?!? Vince … have you lost your freaking mind?"

"Mel, somebody's trying to kill me, and I have no idea why."

"If you're feeding me a line of bull, I'll tell them to fire your butt right now. Why would someone want to kill you? Who did you not pay? How much do you owe, Vince?"

"It's not that, Mel. I swear it's not that. Some supernatural bullshit …"

"Oh, I see. You're already messed up for the day. Call me when you're straight."

"Look, you're wrong. I'm not messed up at all." Swallowing hard, he took a deep breath. "You gotta do me a favor."

"No, I don't. I'm all favored out."

"Call this number: 555-2538."

"Who is that?"

"Mozetta Conerly."

"Why don't you call her?"

"Mel, I'm scared I'm gonna be traced. Tell Mo to call Adair. She's met him a few times."

"Does she have the number?"

"I'll give it to you."

"When can we expect you back? You better call Joubert and do some fast talking. I've been covering your lab work. I'm getting sick of doing two jobs, by the way."

"Mel, if I can't fix this, you won't have to worry about me much longer."

"Now, Vince, you're scaring me."

"I'm not shitting you."

"You can't hide in Key West forever. What are you going to do?"

"I have to get back to Miami. I'm hiding here a few days in case the police question my sister and family."

"Did you kill that man, Vince?"

"God no! He was one of my best friends."

"Then why are you running from the police?"

"To stay hidden. The police aren't trying to kill me, Mel. That Solange bitch has some business with me."

"Who?"

"A woman in … I don't have time to explain it all. Have Mo call me. Tell Joubert I took a fall and am in the hospital in Miami. I've suffered a concussion but should recover. I'll call him as soon as I'm able. I have some doctor's reports and shit; I should be able to snow him and save my job."

"OK, I'll do what I can. Call me and try to keep in touch."

"Later, Mel."

As I hung up that phone, I realized that Mo really did know what she was talking about. But why me? I'm nothing. They must be trying to teach Mo and her Voo-crew a lesson. (She'd have my ass if she knew I called them that.)

Putting his face in his hands, he inhaled deeply. As if in imminent defeat, he then brought both hands to the sides of it and forcefully exhaled.

I should be safe down here. They can battle that shit out among themselves in the Big Easy. The dust will settle and the 'red-head queen of Hell' can kill someone else for revenge. I'll wait a few days and talk to the police in Miami.

Wiping his hand across his brow, he winced in pain. Refocusing his gaze toward Adair, he then shook his head 'no.' *Screw that, I'll wait a few days and then wait a few more. I ain't goin' home.*

CHAPTER TEN

Key West—Old Key West—could actually be labeled a sister city to New Orleans. Other than the streets being a bit wider, the French Quarter and the historic district of Key West actually have a lot in common. With wide porches, tall windows and massive shutters, the indigenous architecture is similar, and like the Quarter, the atmosphere in old Key West is electrically charged. Strangely enough, the similarities between here and home bring some comfort. Inhibitions and worries seem to dissolve here as most anything goes at the tip of the good old U.S. of A.

By land, the only way to get here is via the Overseas Highway. Even though I'm a mere three hours from Shelley and the rest of my family, mentally I've made another huge escape. Whatever works ... it's all about the mind thing.

"Can we get cell phone reception way out here?"

"Sure. We're not that far out. There's a tower on Key West."

"Can they track us?"

"I don't know. You rob a bank or something? If so, I'm charging rent. You can pay the gas for this boat, too."

"We're sailing, Doug ... and fuck you!"

"I think I can get you a job at Jake's on White."

"Bartending?"

"Yeah. You may have to clean the place after hours ... get it ready for the next day and crap like that."

"I can do that ... by the way, thanks for driving up and getting me."

"No prob." Bringing the boat about into the wind just a bit, he turned toward Vince. "You know, down here you can get around pretty well without a car. I got a couple bikes behind the condo. It's actually easier to use those."

"Man, this is all too much to take in. Adair, if I stay here, I have to make some arrangements. I have to talk to my neighbor, and get her to send my bills and stuff."

"If someone is trying to murder you, having your mail forwarded is the least of your worries. In fact, it's pretty damn dumb. And I didn't say you could move in permanently, by the way."

"And you can kiss my ass, Doug ... I'm a friend in need."

"You also tend to be a friend in 'mooch'."

"For now."

"It's cool. So, when am I gonna hear the story?"

"I'll tell it now if you want ... it doesn't make any sense, though."

Doug handed him a handful of pills. "Here, eat these. If the story's fucked up, we may as well be, too."

✳✳✳

"I picked up a load of stale donuts from Lawrence's. I figured I'd make a bread pudding for the dessert menu."

"Mmm-hmm."

"Did you hear me?"

"Yes, Pierre, I heard you."

"Then, what's ailin' you?"

"I got a call from some woman."

"It ain't none of my women." He chuckled after he said this.

"Better not be. Some woman from the dental school called me. She gave me a number to call and get in touch with my baby."

"He ain't yo' baby. He's a grown man—a sorry excuse for a grown man."

"Never you mind about all that."

"I just find it strange that he ran his ass out of town right before Felton got hisself a second smile."

"Somethin' has spooked him. You know he ain't killed Felton. You and I both know that. We know who did this."

"Yeah, we do."

"Maybe it's better that he's out of the way."

"Especially now."

"What do you mean?"

"Look who's comin'."

Mozetta turned to see none other than Solange Deshotel walking through the restaurant doors.

"We're closed."

"This is not a business call."

"This ain't no kinda call. Get out!"

"You may be interested in what I have to say."

Mozetta said nothing.

"I thought so. Terrible thing that happened to that bartender, wasn't it?"

"Yeah, I thought you could have done a better job. Yo' work is sloppy."

Solange laughed. "How have you been, Mo?"

"Oh no you didn't!"

"Didn't what?"

"Let's get a few things straight. First of all, my name is Mozetta. Only my friends have the privilege of callin' me Mo, and you certainly ain't no friend of mine. Second, how I am doin' is none of yo' business. Say what you got to say and get out of my restaurant. Better than that, go on and get out now! I don't care what you have to say!"

"I plan to make him like me. You can't stop me. I plan to relish the look of pain on your face as I destroy his mortality."

"Why would you do that? There ain't nothin' special about that boy."

"Hmmph … you got that right."

Mo turned to Pierre. "You better shut up yo' face!"

"Your people better back off. I'm not afraid of you, but your persistent antics are interfering with my plans. Mozetta—I trust you deem that title more appropriate—I'll kill everyone remotely close to you. I'll turn them into forlorn immortal creatures who will beg your God to release them from their bonded existence. I'll defy every law of life and death as you know it. I never stop, Mozetta. You also will beg for mercy before I'm through with you. Think about it."

She turned to leave and then stopped. Turning to face Mozetta and Pierre once again, she began. "And tell 'your baby' even Key West is not far enough to escape Solange."

"He may not have to run too much longer. Maybe you better mind yo' P's and Q's, too."

"We'll see."

She said nothing else. Passing through the restaurant doors, she turned and made her departure.

✳✳✳

"I cannot believe him."

"Since when?"

"Every time he has responsibility, he runs. He needs to face the police and put this behind him."

"He's not a man."

"He's my brother. Whether you like it or not, Tomas, he's still my brother."

"He's a bad influence on our child."

"Maybe we can help him."

"He has to help himself. He needs to learn things like work and responsibility."

"He does work. He has a trade."

"When does he come back to Miami?"

"I don't know; a few days, maybe."

"Tal vez, no va a regresar."

"You hope so, don't you Tomas? You hope he doesn't return."

Tomas let out a defeated sigh. "No … I don't hope that. He's blood. We'll stand by him, just as we're supposed to."

"Well, that makes me feel a little better. At least you acknowledge that I do have a family …" Shelley shifted uncomfortably in her seat. "Tomas, go around."

"What is this? Something's going on?"

"Our street is blocked … and there are three police cars in front of the house."

"¡Dios mío! ¿Que pasó?"

"I guess we're about to find out."

"This has something to do with Vince."

"And I don't think it's a good thing."

"You don't think? I know, Aracély. I know it's not a good thing. Nothing with your brother Vince ever is …"

A policeman approached the car. "You live here?"

"I'm Tomas Levy; it's my house."

"Do you know the whereabouts of a Vicente Jacola?"

"My brother's name is Vincent—Vincent Jacola." Shelley crossed her arms in protest.

"My apologies, Señora. Can you tell me where he is?"

"What do you want with him?"

"With all due respect, Mrs. Levy, I'm asking the questions."

Once again, acting as if Shelly were not there, the policeman focused his attention on Tomas. "Mr. Levy, do you know the whereabouts of Vicente Jacola?"

Oh, as if I don't know you just did that on purpose …

"No, Officer, I don't."

"And we don't have to tell you, either. Do you have a warrant?"

"Again, with all due respect, Mrs. Levy, we do not. We can easily get one if needed. If you have knowledge of this man's whereabouts, and keep it from us, you're obstructing justice. If a warrant is issued for his arrest, and you're hiding him from us, you're aiding and abetting. ¿Comprende Usted, Señora?"

"I understand perfectly. The man has not done anything. Why are you looking for him?"

"He's now a 'person of interest' in two murders."

"Two? For God's sake, who?"

"The New Orleans police want him for questioning concerning the murder of a Felton Andrieus." His pronunciation included every vowel sound.

"It's pronounced Andrews."

"So sorry. The Miami police want him for questioning concerning the murder of an Eric Balancia. I assume I pronounced that last name to your liking?"

Shelley fell against Tomas. "Oh my God …"

Suddenly, the officer was aware of her. "Do you know him?"

"I have to find Luis! I have to find my son!" She frantically began calling Luis on her cell.

"Where are you?"

"I'm inside, Mom. You have to get home fast. There are police, here. They want to question me. Mom, Eric's been murdered!"

"I'm out front. I'm coming inside. Do not say anything! Wait until your father and I get there."

She snapped the flip phone shut.

"I must get to my son."

"May we come in? We have many questions."

"Do we need an attorney?"

"I don't know. Do you?"

Tomas turned toward Shelley. "Llamele, ahora."

"I'll call him. You may come in, Officer, but we'll say nothing until our attorney arrives."

Shelley realized it would be a long, long night. She loved her brother, dammit, but trouble seemed to follow him everywhere. She didn't need any of his trouble—none of them did. Now it was too late to say that. *Looks like Vincent had brought a big batch of it … some of his finest!*

CHAPTER ELEVEN

"But why would she murder an innocent kid?"

"Do you really think she cares who she kills? This woman ain't got no morals or conscience. What we have to figure out is where this little Cuban teenager fits into her evil plan. Why take him? My baby is not even in Miami anymore."

"He ain't but three hours down the road, Mo. She sent him that signal she warned us about—in the restaurant."

"And I think it's past time our people teach this redheaded bitch a lesson. I've had enough of her intimidation, and I'm tired of waiting."

"Maybe we need to show her what we are really made of."

"Yeah you right, we sure do."

✳✳✳

He'd never been to Key West before. He'd always planned to spend a Christmas there with his wife and family, but this trip was anything but a vacation.

She'd made a promise to murder his wife—Jennifer told him that— and she'd followed through. She was kind enough, however, to provide intimate details of her untimely demise. She laughed as she intimately described the systematic and categorical method she used to rip the silver chakra from her soul. Ironically, there was no evidence of physical injury; aging ceased and earthly maturity came to a screeching halt. It was as if at that moment, the individual became suspended in time. As a result of eternal punishment, long ago she'd experienced this same life in death abandonment. Through a cataclysmic series of events, she'd managed to acquire the power and destruction capabilities with which to administer the same destructive force.

After the spiritual connection is severed, like batteries in constant need of recharging the human remains must be continually replenished from the living. For awhile after the transition, not yet overwhelmed by the need to survive, recent human emotions remain with the being. Jennifer realized that if she remained, she'd bring her family over to her state of existence. In hopes they would escape the same terrible fate, she chose to leave forever.

With aspirations of saving her husband, she'd challenged Solange Deshotel. No match for her immense power and connection with Hell, she'd sacrificed her own mortal destiny for his. A noble ambition, yes, but one which condemned her for eternity, she was now subservient to the same evil force she'd dared to confront. Perhaps God would save her? Perhaps ... but for now she existed among the damned.

✳✳✳

Patronized mostly by tourists, he didn't stand out much as he entered the building. The Bar was on White Street. Perched on a corner, French style doors lined both the front and right sides of the structure. Accented by three narrow, horizontal green stripes, the building was painted mostly white. An alley down the side of the building led to two small dwellings, which had been recently converted to condominiums.

Tables lined the front of the watering hole. Spying a waitress taking orders, he made his way toward her. He then asked had she seen him. Occupied with a large group of drunken businessmen, she appeared a bit annoyed at the intrusion.

"He's over there at the bar."

"Kind of heavyset fellow?"

"Nice ... real nice." She then turned her back to him and continued taking orders. Her inebriated customers took the liberty of an occasional backside rub as they ran up a hefty alcohol tab. *As long as they were buyin' booze, they could think they were sneaking a little ass pat. They knew, she knew and with money as the common denominator, they let it work.*

"You're Vincent?"

"Who are you?"

"I'm Brad. I'll ask again. You're Vincent Jacola?"

"Who the fuck are you? I've never seen you in my life. Are you a cop?"

"If I were, you'd be the one that was fucked, now wouldn't you?"

"What do you want?"

"For one, I want you to answer my question. You're Vincent Jacola?"

"Yeah, Brad, I'm Vincent." After he'd said this, he stood there staring at him."

"Can I buy you a drink? We can sit at one of those tables by the sidewalk."

"Just so you know, I don't do dudes. I ain't got nothin' against it, but … I don't …"

"Neither do I, Vincent. That's not why I'm here. You need to talk to me. You need to hear me out without a lot of ears around. You need to be able to concentrate, because I'm about to rock your world."

"Rock my world? *What the f…* What did you say your name was? I think we're done here."

"I know Solange Deshotel."

There was silence. Even though the two of them were surrounded by obnoxious, drunken tourists, at that moment neither of them heard anything.

"Brad Creighton."

Still silence. Staring at him, Vince stood behind the bar.

"Alright, now that I have your attention and we've made nice, get us both a beer and meet me at that table by the door."

"It'll have to be draft. I only have two bucks left to my name."

Brad handed him a twenty.

Vince returned to the table with two frosted mugs. The heat and humidity made them sweat a bit, but they were cold and filled with alcohol.

"Now what's so freaking urgent that you demand my undivided attention. Keep in mind, Brad, that doesn't happen much. I'm usually not even listened to." He took a long drink of his beer. Then, in anticipation of an answer, he raised his eyebrows as if to say, *hurry up!*

"You have to leave here."

"I ain't goin' nowhere. Why do I have to leave?"

"For whatever reason, Vincent, Solange has set her sights on you."

"Damn. How much further do I have to go? I mean … I'm on an island at the tip of America, for Christ's sake …"

"You're three states from home—a twenty-four hour drive. Do you really think that makes any difference?"

"I guess I could swim to the freaking equator …"

"We're talking about an entity which can cross dimensions, Vince. She can travel across time. This is nothing." Leaning in bit closer, Brad changed positions in his seat. "Look, if you don't return to New Orleans, she'll kill everyone and everything that matters to you. I know. I've been there in more than one lifetime." He swallowed hard after he'd said this.

"Dude, I've never seen you before in my life. How do I know you're telling the truth?"

"Mozetta Conerly."

"Pretty boy, I'll kill your ass if you lay one finger on her. Make no mistake, I will kill you."

"The Solange circle is not as wide as you'd think. Mozetta was not lying to you when she said that you have intruded into a world in which you don't belong."

"I ain't done shit."

"Neither did I, but it didn't matter. I still had to suffer the consequences. You're headed down that same road, Vincent, and it's not a good one. It will destroy you."

"Oh, man …" Vince could think of nothing else to say.

"Go home, Vincent, if not for yourself, to protect innocent others."

"I'm not that noble. I'm not into self sacrifice for the common good, Brad."

"You don't go home, you're screwed, Vincent. There's no one here to protect you."

"How am I safer in the Big Easy?"

"You got the magic across the street from your house. You haven't noticed how things have gone straight south since you left? You're out of your circle of protection. And let me add, Vincent, since you've broken that circle, you've put everyone else at risk. Do I need to bring up the name Felton Andrieus?"

Vince swallowed hard. "No, you don't."

"Get home while you still can. I'm done here. There's nothing more I can tell you."

"Yes there is, Brad."

"What?"

"You think I might keep the change from this twenty?"

CHAPTER TWELVE

A ring awakened him. It was the doorbell. Three times, four times and then banging.

"I am coming for Christ's sake! Hold your horses!" He opened the door.

"Quit using Christ as your excuse to open the door, and I don't have any horses. I brought my car."

Vince smiled. "Shell, you're a sight for sore eyes!"

"How are you?"

"Lonely … scared … broke …"

"Can I come in?"

He stood aside as Shelley entered the room. "Vince … this place is horrible."

"It's a roof. It's dry, and the window unit works."

"You're gonna get sick living here—if the board of health doesn't condemn the place first."

"It's cheap, Shell. I'm off the street."

"Where's your roommate?"

"Passed out in his room with some chick he took home two nights ago."

"Nice. At least it wasn't a one night stand."

"Where's Tomas?"

"In Miami, he didn't come with me."

"Imagine that …"

"Look, you left us with a lot of grief. It's been hell since Eric was murdered."

"You know I had nothing to do with that. I've been cleared."

"You may have been cleared by the police, Vince, but I think this is some trouble that followed you."

"You have no idea."

"Yes, I do."

"What?"

"I know more than you think."

"What … what exactly do you think that I think that you know?" *Hey, I got that out and I'm not even fucked up!*

Shelley reached into her purse and pulled from it a book. "You need to read this. It may be your only tool of survival."

Vince took the book from her. "It's old. I mean, it's really old. Where did you find this?"

"I went to see Daria Landry."

"You are kidding me. No you didn't!"

"Where else was I to go?"

"Shelley, Daria's crazy. She's always been crazy. In grade school she was a weirdo. She always followed you around, stalking you and trying to hang out with all of your friends … then came the black hair and out there religion. She even followed you down here, for Christ's sake!"

"There you go again. So what if she did the Lord's bidding."

"You know what I mean. It's an expression. Quit trying to change the subject. What in the hell were you thinking by going to Daria for anything?"

"She knows what you're up against, Vince. She's only trying to help. Knowledge can be a powerful thing. It wouldn't hurt to read about this Solange person."

"Where, or a better question is who in heaven's name wrote a book about Solange?"

"You're awfully optimistic about your afterlife, aren't you? Some priest named Donovan something. This book is about seventy five years old, Vince, and this priest writes like he knows what he's talking about."

"Hmmm."

"You ought to read it."

Still studying the book, he looked up at her. "Not like I've got much else to do except clean tables and sling beer."

"Why don't you clean that table? It's pretty bad."

"Ain't my table. I'm just squattin' here."

"You're not paying Doug anything?"

"Nope. Actually, I think he's glad for the company."

"Seems like he has plenty of company …"

"Oh … you mean that whore?"

"A real prostitute?!?"

"Naw, just a local slut."

Shelley shook her head in protest. "Why don't you come back to Miami with me?"

"Well, first of all, that kid was murdered while I was there. Pretty good reason, don't you think? Second, Tomas doesn't want me there."

"I can handle Tomas."

"You don't need the hassle. I'm fine here. Hey Shell?"

"Yes?"

"Some man from Memphis, Tennessee came to see me. Said I needed to get my ass back home ASAP. He said some weird shit like 'I'd broken my circle of protection.' He seemed pretty adamant about the whole thing."

"How does he know you?"

"Through Mo' of all people … I ain't goin' home, Shell."

"Come to Miami."

"I'm stayin' here."

"Then read the book. Read the book and see if you can gain some insight about this whole bizarre scenario."

"I will read it. In the mean time, why doesn't my favorite Sis take her brother out to lunch? Then maybe we can grab some key lime pie on a stick."

"Let's go to Caroline's and sit outside. On the second floor, they have a deck out front."

"Your carriage awaits."

"Sure it does, because you don't have a car."

"True, but I'll drive. Kind of like your own personal chauffeur."
Kind of like my own personal headache …

***

Ariel Culotta was usually described as a bohemian sort. Owner
of Luna Azul Paranormal Parlor, affectionately known as LAPPs in
the Quarter, she had indeed always marched to the tune of her own
drummer. Luna Azul had been a fairly good investment for her. Usually seeing seventeen to twenty clients per day, she recently had to take
on full time help to handle the walk in traffic. When confronting a
potentially difficult situation, a reading at LAPPs was now in vogue,
and tourists were also making the parlor a 'must do vacation destina-
tion' as well.

With rental of the building space came an upstairs efficiency
apartment; free French Quarter living accommodations were a
persuasive perk when interviewing potential paranormal assistants.
Tim Johnson thought they were, as he'd been working at Luna Azul
for over a year. No doubt he had a gift for the art, seeing that many
prominent clients banked important life choices as well as financial
decisions on the content of his readings. Realizing she had a good
thing in Tim, Ariel had even gone so far as to have tee-shirts with
the logo LAPP Reader printed on the front of them. Tim thought
they were a bit lame, but again, they were free. As a rule, unless you
have worldwide notoriety, the profession of Psychic Reading does
not tend to provide opportunities for massive wealth accumulation.
That being said, a free place to live makes full time devotion to the
line of work feasible.

"Are you done?"

"Got to make change for my last customer, why?"

"I'm headed over to K-Paul's for lunch. Hey, there's an opening
down at Strahan's this evening. They have an awesome exhibit open
house featuring 'you know who'."

"You still hung up on James Coignard?"

"I am."

"You're gonna spend that much on an etching?"

"One day ... maybe not today ..."

"Which gallery is Strahans? I forget."

"At the end of the next block, the one with La Paresseuse in the window."

"That creepy place?"

"Creepy place coming from a paranormal reader? I don't think so."

"I've heard tell that some angry poltergeist will start throwing crap all around the building if you remove that painting from the window. It supposedly has something to do with a proprietor who owned it years ago."

"And you believe that?"

"Do you?"

"I guess if I had some substantiated evidence, I would. That being said, do you want to go?"

"To what?"

"To the opening I just told you about. Are we a little hypoglycemic here, or what?"

"No, not hypoglycemic, just distracted from all the talk about *Gallery Sinister.*" Shoving his hands into his pockets, he shifted positions. "You really want to go to this? I'd much rather grab a drink uptown."

"How about we do both?"

"You're not gonna let me out of it, are you?"

Retrieving her purse from the counter, she began again. "Come with me. It'll be fun. We don't have to stay long and can head uptown after that."

In resignation, he sighed. "OK, sure. Long as I can get a cocktail to keep me entertained, I'll go. I'll visit with Johnny Walker Red while you peruse the art world."

"These events usually serve only wine and beer."

"Then I'll have one of each."

Beginning to laugh, she exhaled in defeat. "It starts at 6:00 p.m."

"Come by here and pick me up. I'll walk down there with you."

As if an idea had just struck her, she refocused her gaze upon him. "How about you have a pitcher of frozen Margaritas ready for us? That should get the party started."

"No can do. I'm all out of Cuervo. You'll have to settle for beer."

"Not as refreshing, but will suffice. Until six, Timothy."

"That sounds so juvenile."

"OK, well then have your skinny butt ready by six o'clock, Tim."

"Until six, boss lady. With cold beer in hand, I'll be ready."

✳✳✳

Located in uptown New Orleans, Brigtsen's Restaurant is actually a converted older home. Chef Frank Brigtsen is among the best in the city. Infusing complex flavors and aromas into succulent game, his food choices feature unique cuisine. With decorative touches making patrons feel as if they've been invited to a small, elegant dinner party, the atmosphere is both intimate and romantic. As Delia crossed the threshold and walked toward the Maitre d', her suspicions as to why he'd chosen this restaurant for their 'meeting' were confirmed.

"Surely you jest."

"What do you mean? You don't like it?"

"Of course I like it. It's a beautiful place. Who's sitting in front of me is the reason I'm not feeling the love right now. Joubert, why would you try to schmooze me with a fancy restaurant? What's up your sleeve? I know you're not hitting on me—you're not that stupid, are you?"

"Guilty as charged."

"You're serious ..."

"It's only dinner, Delia."

"Look, this is not a date. You asked me for a meeting, and then you picked the place. I'll sit here and discuss work issues. I'll even try to come up with some solutions, but it ends there, Joubert. Got it?"

"Do you think you might call me Thierry?"

"No. I don't know you like that. If you need more respect, I'd be happy to back down to *Dr. Joubert*. Take it or leave it, that's the best I can do. "

"It'll have to do. We'll consider it a step in the right direction."

"No step, Dr. Joubert, as we're not going anywhere together." Taking a deep breath, she clasped her hands in front of her. Upon exhaling, she refocused her gaze upon him. "Now let's get down to work issues."

"But of course ..." Motioning for the server, he continued. "So that we're not interrupted, we should order first. I could use an aperitif, how about you?"

"A what? I don't need an appetizer; I'm not that hungry."

"How charming, your little 'down the bayou wit' slays me."

God, how I wish ...

"An aperitif is light refreshment which readies and brightens the palate for dinner."

"Oh look, you must understand since you're painfully aware of my 'down the bayou wit', that my idea of an aperitif is boiled shrimp and beer. You have so missed the mark here."

"Let me order for you."

Delia sighed heavily. "It's your money, Doctor, knock yourself out. In the meantime, I must excuse myself to the lavatory."

"I'm impressed."

"Since we're playing dress up, I felt that might be a better fit." She then arose and backed away from the table. "Actually, I have to piss like a Russian racehorse. That hits a little closer to home. Not to worry, though, I'll be right back to enjoy my new palate."

"Such a tart ..."

As he uttered the demeaning comment, she froze. Slowly turning to face him, she forcefully exhaled. "Ok, that is it and game is over. We're not flirting here, Dr. Joubert, got it? Now, I will return in a moment, and if you like, we can discuss problems at work. If you have another agenda ... well, I hear a cab just calling my name. Are we understood here, Doctor ... Joubert?"

Unfazed, he managed a smile. "Absolutely."

Suddenly, Thierry realized that throughout their exchange of banter, the server had been patiently waiting.

"She's a live one, my little Cajun."

With the slightest hint of condescension, the server smiled. "May I take your drink order?"

"We'll both have Dubonnet and soda."

Maintaining the smile, he simply replied, "I'll return in a moment with your aperitifs."

Tables illuminated by nothing more than single, centrally-placed candles created a muted, soft, restaurant ambience. Noting that it was virtually empty, Thierry looked about the place. This lack of patronage seemed strange to him, until he realized he'd made reservations for a week night.

As the server arrived with the drinks, his train of thought was broken.

"Thank you."

"Will you be having appetizers tonight?"

"We most definitely will."

"I'll give you a moment."

"That would be good."

The server subsequently turned and walked toward the hallway. As he reached the end of it, he turned right, and disappeared through two swinging kitchen doors.

To insure no one was looking, Thierry once again scanned the restaurant. He then smiled to himself. *With the right amount of coaxing, sometimes a girl can be persuaded to change her mind …*

✳✳✳

He had a headache. Lunch was great today, but Shelly washed over him like a tidal wave. She was more like a mom than a sister; as he tried to choke down his baked tilapia, he felt lecture after lecture wash ashore. He'd wanted cheese fries and a burger, but given the present company, he naturally had to settle for baked fish with a squeeze of lemon. *Screw that …* Before she'd even made it off of the island, he'd walked over to Corner Stop N Shop on Whitehead and downed a whole bag of Zapp's Crawtaters. Washing them down with a big ole' Redbull, he contemplated the evening. He then grabbed his phone.

"Well, well, well … so you finally bothered to call."

"God, I miss you guys."

"Wouldn't know it … You done deserted us."

"How are you?"

"I'm OK. And you?"

"I'm ready to come home, just afraid to."

"Actually, baby, it may be better for you to stay gone."

"Oh really …" A little surprised by her comment, he fell silent for a moment. Lighting a cigarette, he took a long drag and began again. "What's up over there, Mo? What's going on?"

"Got a lot going on tonight — things that I cannot discuss on the phone."

Oh God, she's stopped using contractions. "When can we talk?"

"I am hoping real soon. You may be able to come home sooner than you think."

"I'd love that. I just want my life back."

"What are you talking about? You are supposed to be in paradise."

"I miss you guys. I miss my friends, my house … even my shitty job."

"Did not have it as bad as you thought, huh?"

"Ok, that's twice. You're not using contractions which means something big is going down. What up?"

"First of all, you are not black, and sound ridiculous saying things like, 'What up?' You may actually value your own identity one day."

Especially if we fail tonight …

"Do not start on me."

"And now you are the one not using contractions."

"I am serious. I'm in no mood for jokes."

"Stay put. Mo and company may have things better for you in a day or so."

"That would be a miracle." Taking another drag of his cigarette, he then exhaled. "Shelley came to town today."

"She doin' OK?"

"Yeah, yeah, always full of good advice."

"You should listen to her."

"How can you help it? For Christ's sake, she never shuts up … she's constantly running that big, damn mouth."

"That ain't no way to talk about yo' sister. You should be ashamed."

"Mo, she gave me this book to read."

"That was nice. I don't see you much of a reader, but that was real nice."

"Daria Landry gave it to her."

"Oh Lord, oh Lord! All we need is Daria Landry to get up into all this mess. For God's sake, what book do you have there?"

"You know Daria lives in Miami now, don't you?"

"I heard that."

"She's a freakin' stalker."

"She stalks you?"

"No, my sister."

"She gay?"

"I don't really know, but that's not the issue."

"No, it is not. The issue is that even though she means well, Vince, she's like a bull in a china shop. You do not want her associated with anything you do. It will be a disaster."

"Well, I'm not doing anything. Shelly actually called Daria."

"What on earth for?"

"For help, I guess. She said she didn't know who else to turn to."

"She sure as hell jumped out of the frying pan and into the fire on that one …" Trying to digest the situation, Mo paused for a moment. As if a light bulb were suddenly illuminated in front of her, she began again. "On that note, let's get back to the book, baby. What do you have there?"

"*Chronology of an Escape from Hell.*"

"Mmm-hmm."

"I hate when you do that."

"Father Donovan's account of Solange's ascent from Hell, right?"

"I guess … I haven't read it yet."

"Written in 1933?"

"Uh, Mo? Have not read it yet, remember?"

"Go on and read it. There is some valuable knowledge in there. You ain't gonna like what you read, but it may help to arm you in the future."

"Have you read it?"

"I have. It's been a few years, but I have read it. How on God's green earth did Daria Landry get all up in this? Why would she have that book?"

"I don't know, Mo. I find that strange as well. That weirdo seems to pop up everywhere. She's like the plague, and you can't get away from her."

"And that bothers me."

"Why?"

"Don't worry yo' pretty little head about that. Read the book."

"There you go again … as always, leaving me hanging. I hate that, too."

"You don't need to know everything. That could be just as harmful as not knowing enough. Know this: things are soon coming to a head. One way or the other, things are about to change."

"I'm getting drunk …"

"Oh, that's great protection."

"Only way I'll sleep tonight." Vince lit another cigarette.

"You keep yo' wits about you tonight. Stay off the liquor and everything else. Read that book, Vince, and I mean it."

"Two moms. Two freakin' moms. My real one is dead, you know."

"Well, this mom is tellin' you to do what I say. We will talk to-morrow—after you've read some of Father Donovan's book. You will want to talk, then."

"OK … I'm …" He paused and took the last drag of his smoke. "I'm … Hell, I'm going back to Corner and slam down another bag of Zapp's. I have to have some vice tonight …"

"Love you, baby."

"Love you too, Mo. Tell Pierre I miss his barbecued ribs."

"We'll smoke some as soon as you get back here."

"Put my name on 'em. Love ya, Mo."

He pressed the "end" button and headed back to the market. *I hate to read, dammit ....*

CHAPTER THIRTEEN

Putting her cell phone into her pocket, Mo took hold of her basket and continued shopping. After World War Two, the city of New Orleans began to spread eastward. Across America, Downtown U.S.A. was no longer the retail nucleus. Store clusters entitled 'shopping centers' had begun to spring up everywhere.

In the midst of one such shopping center crescent sat Pap's Supermarket. Situated along Franklin Avenue, the 60's era supermarket in its day was considered state of the art. Retail giants such as Schwegmann's and Walmart, however, had greatly diminished Pap's business.

These days, Pap's for the most part is considered a 'quick pickup store.' It is, however, still lauded as one of the best meat markets of New Orleans. Pap Schiro was a second generation Italian; being a depression baby, he'd had the notion of frugality drilled into his persona. The obsessive repulsion to spending may have just been what enabled Pap to weather the trend toward demise of the independent marketer. He no longer had to work; as long as the store broke even, it occupied most of his free time. Loathing idle moments, Pap spent long hours greeting customers and overseeing day to day activities of the waning establishment.

"Evening, Pap."

"Not a good idea to wish your life away, Mo."

"Well, it's almost evening."

"Got some fresh greens in for your salads tonight."

"Mmm-hmm. Why don't you teach me how to make that bruscialoni? I want to put it on the menu."

"Family recipe, Mo."

"I'm family, aren't I?"

Pap broke into laughter. "You already stole my *sugo* recipe and sell the damn stuff every night! I deserve a royalty!"

"I do it my own way, thank you."

"Bruscialoni takes awhile to make, Mo."

"Does it freeze good?"

"Nahhh … need to eat it fresh."

"Then I guess it'll have to be a special, not on the menu."

"When you want to do it?"

"Why don't we aim…" Sensing someone was following closely behind, she paused for a moment. Turning abruptly, she began again. "You are just like Pierre's bad breath. I can't get rid of yo' ass."

Pap said nothing.

"This seems to be a charming store."

"You ain't shopping for nothin'. What the hell do you want this time? I'm 'bout sick of yo' lame, white-assed confrontations."

"No confrontation, Mozetta, just making sure I haven't forgotten anything. Have you forgotten … anything?"

"Just her manners, I'm Nicolo Schiro. Everyone around here calls me Pap."

"Ahh, Greek heritage … How ruggedly masculine …"

"Shows how stupid you are, he's Italian." Mo used a long 'I' with this, making sure she stressed the *Eye*-talian."

"Actually, I do have Greek ancestors, too, Mo. Nicolo is in fact a Greek name."

"Hmmph."

"And your name is, pretty lady?"

"I assure you she is no lady."

"Madame Solange Deshotel."

"Yeah, you got dat Madam part right."

"Nice to meet you, Mrs. Deshotel."

"It's Ms. Deshotel."

"Well, while you two get acquainted, I will finish my shopping."

Mo moved her basket beside Solange. "And you are really askin' for it. I've had enough. In fact, I'm past that point, now." Looking at her watch, she noted the time. She then turned so that she was standing between Solange and Pap. With her back to her, she began. "Pap, any motivation I had to shop has pretty much gone by the wayside, so I will be on my way. Someone will run you around a list of what I need in a few. See that those groceries are delivered early tonight."

"Will do, Mo."

He then turned to Solange. "Very nice meeting you, pretty lady, stop by anytime."

"Thank you, Pap, I will."

Refocusing her gaze, she continued. "Oh, and Mozetta?"

"You don't get the last word this time, bitch." Mo said nothing else. Through the automated doors she simply turned and exited the supermarket. She made her way out to her car and began to look through her purse for her keys. Finding them, she decided to head straight home—a sense of urgency had arisen. Putting the key into the ignition, she realized she'd be here awhile longer. The car was dead— it would not start. *Christ Jesus can't you help me out just once!* In frustration, Mo rested her head against the steering wheel. *I'm gonna beat her down ... if it's the last thing I do, I'm gonna beat her ass down ...*

✳✳✳

Pierre had readied the room for the ceremony. In days past, when neighborhood stores abounded, owner families would reside on the second floor of the building. Boliviee's had such a dwelling, and both Mo and Pierre did indeed live above the restaurant. Only members of the Secret Circle would attend this meeting, for the magic that was to be performed tonight was some of the most powerful known throughout the world of occult. The spells were sacred and not for the faint of heart. If performed incorrectly or worse yet, managed to fall into the wrong hands, disastrous consequences could result. This magic opened a spiritual doorway that could inadvertently provide dimensional passage for spirits better left on alternate, higher planes of existence. To allow them to enter a lower plane, such as the human one, would give them godlike status. They would be most powerful and visionary of both future and past occurrences. Throw evil in on top of that and you have a force from Hell with which to be reckoned.

"Arletha, where in the world is Mo?"

"I don't know. I call her cell and keep getting a recording that her mailbox is full and she's not accepting any calls."

"That sure is strange. She told me she was gonna pass by Pap's and pick up a few things for the restaurant. She's been gone well over an hour."

"Maybe we should go look for her."

"Pierre, we don't have time. We have to perform this ritual before sunset or we might let a whole lot of evil out of Pandora's box."

"Yeah, you right. Let's call role."

"There ain't but six of us here. You see everybody."

"Mo always calls role." Pierre cleared his throat and moved a legal pad to arm's length.

"Get yo' glasses, man. You are blind as a bat."

"Hmmph. We'll see … Arletha Jackson."

"Here. I'm standin' right in front of you. "

"Verdiasee McFarland."

"Here."

"Thelma and Edith Blankenship."

Simultaneously, they answered, "here."

"Coretta Jones."

"I'm here, Pierre, better late than never!"

"Retta, you ain't never been on time for nothin'! Why would you expect me to think different now?"

"Don't give me no sass out of that big mouth, Mr. Conerly. Let's get on with things."

"Arlee and Verdee done set up the table with the Star of David candle configuration. Roman numerals XVIII–XXII mark the pages in the *Book of Spells*. I took the liberty of copying this page for everyone so we could all recite the incantation together. Verdee, light the candles."

Verdiasee struck a wooden match and began to light the candle arrangement. There were six candles set about in a six point star configuration. The candles sat in votive cups made from cobalt glass; the glass was so richly blue, that the candle flame was barely visible through the ribbed container. After she'd finished lighting the six candles, she poured a thick layer of salt around the candle setup. "There, that should do it. If somethin' that don't belong comes moseying by, it can't pass the salt circle."

"Turn off the air. We don't want nothin' disturbin' that circle."

Pierre raised the thermostat.

"Everybody join hands and close yo' eyes once the spell begins. Open them just long enough to read yo' part and then close them again."

Pierre looked at Arletha. "Arlee, you sure you know what you're doin'?"

"Mo usually does this, but we're running out of options. I've assisted on this ritual a few times … it'll be OK." *I hope it'll be OK.*

Arletha continued. "There are six of us here; therefore all six of us have to recite the entire incantation. I'll go first and then the person on my left will follow. There will be no time lapse between recitations or the spell will fail. The energy level will increase with each repetition. Do not—I repeat—do not break the circle. If you do, you will leave a hole in the veil. The size of that hole depends on how many recitations have been completed … so you see, it could be devastating. This ain't play, folks, this is for real." Swallowing hard, she continued. "Damn, I wish Mo would get herself back here!"

"You and me both," added Coretta.

"I will say the first incantation in French to insure the spell is done right. The rest of you may say the spell in English; it does not really matter which language you use. Once the sixth recitation is complete, open your eyes and you will see where the evil force shall be returned to. Remember, you're just a spectator, so you cannot alter or change anything. They can't hear you there or see you." *I hope …*

"I have a couple questions."

"Go 'head, Retta."

"What exactly are we tryin' to do here? Mo was kinda' vague. Who are we tryin' to send back to Hell?"

"A real, bad demon—her name is Solange."

"What kind of demon has a name like that? I ain't never heard of such … at least Mama never mentioned nothin' like that." Coretta paused a moment in thought. "Solange…?" She stopped again. "Arlee, are you sure?"

"Retta, I have no idea why yo' mama did not school you on this one. Solange is one of the worst. She's scary 'cause she's virtually omniscient."

"And what does that mean?"

"Almost all knowing and all powerful."

"And so you think five old women and one Voodoo spell can handle that? Maybe we better rethink this. I'm not sure any of this is right."

Pierre loudly cleared his throat.

Momentarily, Coretta turned toward him. "Sorry, Mr. Conerly, you too. Didn't mean to leave you out." Looking expectantly, she once again focused her gaze upon Arletha.

Arletha answered. "You got a better idea?"

"Yeah, let's wait for Mo."

"Retta, our window is closin' as we stand here flappin' our jaws. We are out of time. It's either now, or not at all."

"And why is that, because you say so?"

"No, not because I say so, but more like if anything happens to one of us, there really is no other circle knowledgeable enough to handle her. Look around, Coretta. We are already down by one. No one knows where Mo is, and she'd never be late for something as important as this. Now, take one more out and the power of this circle is totally shut down. She'll have effectively eliminated yet another enemy." Resting her hand on her hip, Arletha took a deep breath and exhaled. "You got that or do I need to elaborate further?"

"OK … OK then … you have made your point." Looking away from Arletha's penetrating stare, Coretta focused her gaze toward the four other women. "Go ahead. I ain't got nothin' else to say."

"Good. So with Mrs. Jones now in agreement with rest of us, we should join our hands."

Forming a circle, everyone clasped hands. Asking the Holy Spirit to surround them with his white light, they began the ritual with a prayer. Protecting them from evil spirits lurking close by, the light would serve as a gauntlet.

To further insure their safety, the six of them then recited a decade of the rosary. Finally, using holy water, Arletha made the sign of the cross on her forehead. "Dear Lord, cleanse my thoughts and make me a vessel worthy of your power. Allow your pilgrim to serve as a capable instrument in returning this vile demon to Hell."

All preliminary prayers had been offered. Before closing her eyes, Arletha grasped the hands of those beside her. Using smooth, fluent French, she began the first recitation.

***

"Cool gallery. I'm glad we came here."

Before beginning, Ariel took the obligatory sip of her white wine. "Me too."

Crossing the room, they made their way toward the James Coignard exhibit. As they did so, Tim stopped just short of her favorite painting. "I still don't see ten thousand dollars worth of brushed nickel, glass and contemporary artwork here. You're really planning on buying this?"

"I guess to each his own. I love it. I've wanted this piece for years; it's an original, signed work of art. James Coignard actually created this. It's no reproduction."

"Glad it rings your bell in such a big way. At that price it had better continue ringing it for awhile."

"It's an investment. Who knows? It may be worth a smooth fortune one day."

"Well, let's hope it's at least worth a small fortune now, because that's what they're charging for it." Looking about the exhibition, he then waved his empty bottle toward her. "I need another beer."

"The bar's in the front of the gallery."

Eventually managing to slide alongside the bartender, Tim side-stepped the crowd.

"What can I get for ya?"

"Is the beer cold?"

"Yes sir."

"Then I'll have a glass of red wine."

The bartender opened his mouth to answer and then smiled. "Makes sense to me …" He poured a glass of dark, red wine into a glass. Handing it to Tim, he said, "Here you go."

"Thanks, buddy." Tim shoved two one dollar bills into the tip jar.

Looking toward the easel in the front window, he turned to Ariel. "Is that the poltergeist pic?"

"It is. That's *La Paresseuse* by Erté. The previous owner of this gallery had some unusual connection to it. Things don't fare well if it's removed from the window."

"Let's test it out."

"Are you crazy? You'll get us thrown out of here! That artwork is worth thousands. Don't touch it!"

Tim lifted the serigraph from the easel. "There … see? No ghosts."

"Put it down, Tim. You're just asking for trouble. I'm not bringing you to another one of these if you're planning to make fools of us in front of the art community."

Before he could answer, an odd sensation followed. Tim felt an infiltration begin uptake at the very tips of his fingers. He looked at Ariel. As the feeling progressed, oddly enough his thoughts retreated to childhood days of taking a bath. The sensation of unforgiving, ice cold water infiltrating his rich, warm bath came to mind. Like unwelcome fingers of discomfort, the cold water neutralized the soapy, nurturing effect of his bathwater. Intrusive, unwelcome cold water had a lonely effect; he thought it amazing how such an incipient interloper could ruin such a pleasant experience.

The scenario then changed. He envisioned a pitcher of cold water. A mere splash of brown rust from the tap would ruin the whole drinking experience. He watched how the fiery orange intruder gracefully expanded and bounded toward the bottom of the decanter. Soon, it would discolor the entire lot. The volume of cool, fresh liquid would be forever contaminated; it would be ruined.

"Suddenly, I'm a little chilled."

"Put the painting down, Tim. It's your imagination. There's nothing cool, anywhere. I'm about to melt."

Tim returned *La Parasseuse* to the easel. "I think this wine is messing with my head."

"Have you eaten?"

"I could eat."

"I spotted some buffalo wings on the hors d'oeuvre table. Let's have some. I haven't eaten supper. Maybe a little heat from that sauce will warm you."

Tim downed the last sip of his wine.

"I thought it was messing with your head. Is that what you want it to do?"

"Yeah … alcohol makes you more vulnerable."

"What?"

What the hell … why the fuck did I say that?

"Tim, what did you drink before we got here? Are you drunk already?"

"No … just had a beer before this glass of wine. Maybe they don't mix too well."

"You need to eat."

"Let's do it."

Arm in arm, they headed for the hors d'oeuvre table.

CHAPTER FOURTEEN

Thelma Blankenship recited the last repetition of the incantation. As the stanza concluded, all six of them opened their eyes to see the ink-like darkness begin to lift. A crystalline shaft of golden light cut a swath through the center of the room. The shaft burst into a starburst explosion; suddenly, all six of them found themselves in a large, dark warehouse structure.

The room was immense, but empty. In the back of it was a small staircase; complete with railing and spindles, the bank of stairs led up to a balcony.

"What in the hell is this? Where are we?"

Pierre turned toward Thelma. "You just said it. We're in Hell."

"This don't look like Hell to me."

Verdiasee turned toward her and whispered, "How in God's name would you know what Hell is supposed to look like, Thelma?"

"Both of ya'll shut yo' faces up. This is Hell. This is where we must bring the demon back to."

Edith looked at Thelma. "I never thought of Hell as a warehouse … learn somethin' new every day."

Pierre began again. "Edith, this is strictly a depiction. We don't know what it represents; all we know is that her ass is about to be here, any minute."

"Then how in the holy name of sweet Jesus do we get out of here?"

Shrugging his shoulders in resignation, he replied, "I really don't know."

Suddenly, there was a furious banging at the warehouse door. "Open the door and get out! Get out of that warehouse right now! I'm not playin' around. Every one of you has to leave immediately!"

Pierre turned to Arletha. "If I didn't know better, I'd say that sounds like Mo."

"How in Heaven's name would she be here?"

"I don't think Heaven has nothin' to do with this. Mo! Is that you behind that door? How did you get in here?"

"Close the incantation and get out of there! Pierre, you all have to leave now. If you don't, I can't save you! Get out of there, and hurry!"

They all looked at each other. A feeling of doom began to infiltrate the atmosphere.

Verdiasee began. "I feel evil comin'."

"Mo! How do we get out?"

Banging furiously on the door once more, Mozetta yelled, "The Apostle's Creed ... Say the Apostle's Creed! The spell will dissipate!"

Pierre looked at the women around him. "All together now:"

I believe in God, the Father Almighty, the maker of heaven and earth, and in Jesus Christ, His only son our Lord:

As they recited the prayer, the atmosphere around them grew thin. The warehouse began to dissipate, and their consciousness initiated a return to normal surroundings. As if held under water for too long, all of them began gasping for breath. Amid the coughing and desperate lunges for air stood Mozetta. Hands on both hips, disgustedly, she looked about the room.

She then began. "Well, well, well ..."

Still breathing heavily, the six of them cast expectant looks upon her.

"You all really put on quite a show."

With a hand over her heart, Thelma walked over to Mozetta. Her chest heaving, she asked, "What do you mean? We did what we could. You were nowhere to be found."

"I was in the parking lot of Pap's Supermarket. I had to walk home. My car would not start and I very well know who was behind that."

"Who?"

"Thelma, what were you in line for when God was handin' out common sense?"

She bristled. "I have had enough happen to me today, Ms. Conerly, and I don't need nothin' else flyin' up out of yo' face at me."

"Why did you people not wait for me?"

Arletha stepped forward. "Blame it on me. The window was closing and I wanted to have the spell in place before sundown."

"OK, I will blame you. How many candles are lit?"

"Six, Mozetta. Look at the Star of David … there's one for each of us."

"And how many of you here?"

"Six, Mozetta."

"How many recitations?"

"This is getting ridiculous …"

Mozetta's face suddenly went purple. "HOW MANY!"

Through gritted teeth, Arletha began. She spoke slowly, distinctly and deliberately. "Don't you scream at me again."

"Arlee, you better tell me how many recitations were chanted here tonight or I will drag yo' ass out in the street by yo' extensions and beat the perm out of yo' nappy head. I do not plan to ask you a second time."

"Six recitations, Mozetta … SIX RECITATIONS, BITCH! And now that you have yo' information, me and my nappy-ass extensions are ready for the street. Let's go!"

The two women were now nose to nose. Neither of them blinking, Pierre knew a fight was inevitable.

"Break it up or I'll beat both of yo' damn asses." Pierre grabbed Mozetta by the arm and threw her toward the sofa. As he did this, so not as to be the target of her projected path, the other ladies scattered.

Mozetta landed on the floor face up. Unfazed, she pulled herself back to a standing position. "Six candles … six recitations … and six people. Did any of you think of the perfect number? Did any of you happen to remember the imperfect number? Did any of you remember the seventh candle of the Holy Spirit? Do any of you stupid asses remember who represents 666? Look in the bible and it will tell you in plain English! Do you people know what you've just done and who you've conjured up? DO YOU!"

No one answered. "Ladies and Gentleman, God's number is seven. If you want his help, you must have seven for the ritual, and seven lit candles in the Star of David. Guess who's coming to dinner? No, it ain't Sidney Poitier, you sons-of-bitches; you've all invited Lucifer over for supper. You opened a damn doorway and said, 'Come on in!' This is his season, Ladies, and you've just issued an open invitation!"

"What about the salt circle? Shouldn't that protect us?"

"OK, go 'head and look at the salt circle. Tell me what you see."

The six of them then realized there was no salt around the Star of David

Arletha turned to Mozetta. "Oh God ..."

"No, you better think again. He didn't do that. Did you really think a box of table salt would handle this? Yes, when it rains, it pours, but it's no match for the Devil. Did anyone happen to remember the blessed salt from the Sea of Galilee? Hmmm?"

Arletha hung her head. "I'm so sorry ... I didn't know."

"You gonna be sorry ... you just don't know how sorry, yet. I ain't got no sympathy for you people ... I ain't got no forgiveness, neither. You knew better. If you did not, you should have. This should not have happened. No excuses."

"What do we do now?"

"What do we do? Oh so now you see fit to ask? Well, Edith, since now you seem to value my opinion, I'll tell you. We do nothing."

"What?"

"We do nothing. We do nothing because we now have no idea what all we're up against. If it's any consolation, this is small potatoes for Satan. He has lots bigger fish to fry. He'll send someone to handle this mess; we'll just have to wait and see who it is. Until then, we wait."

Sheepishly, Edith replied, "Oh ... I see."

"Party's over. Get out. Everyone get yo' asses out of my house. I'll send word about the next circle meeting. And Arlee, Verdee and the rest of you, just so you know, I will be running things from here on out. You've made a huge mess of things and I will be the one to straighten it out. Understand?"

All answered almost in unison. "We do, Mo." They all began to randomly apologize.

"GET OUT! ALL OF YOU!"

Mozetta slammed the door behind them. She then turned to Pierre. "And yo' ass will be sleeping on the couch tonight. Do you understand?"

"We did the best we could, Mo. Wasn't no bad intentions in any of it."

"Well yo' stupid best wasn't good enough. Goodnight, Pierre, and sleep tight. I may have to get drunk to do the same."

"Stay sober, Mo. I'm not sure what tonight will hold."

Mozetta did not answer him. She knew he was right. This was one night she needed all her wits about her, for she had no idea what was lurking in either world beyond her door.

✳ ✳ ✳

"I need another drink."

"I'm about ready to go, Tim."

"Where's the bar?"

Ariel gave him a puzzled look. "Where it's been all night … right there by the window."

"Let's go."

The bartender smiled at him. "Another glass of merlot?"

"Whiskey. If fact, give me the bottle."

The smile faded from his face. "Sorry, Sir, no can do. We're only supposed to be serving beer and wine, but I can fix you a drink. I believe the gallery owner stashed a couple of fifths under my table."

Reaching into his pocket, Tim pulled out his wallet. Opening it, he removed a fifty dollar bill.

"Here. Give me the fucking bottle."

"Tim, what's gotten into you?"

"What's with the Tim shit? The name's Tom."

Ariel stood nonplussed. After a moment she began again. "I think you've had enough for tonight. This mixing of alcohols is not good for you. I think it's time we leave."

"The bottle."

The bartender took the fifty from him and handed him the bottle. "Don't tell anyone. I could lose my job."

"I don't give a shit about your fucking job. I just want to get drunk."

"Sounds to me like you're already there, let's go." Walking ahead of him, Ariel made her way toward the door.

As they left the gallery, Tim tucked the bottle under his arm. Heading up Royal Street toward Canal, she looked at him. "I'm not impressed. I'm not impressed at all with your behavior tonight."

Tim grabbed her by the throat and shoved her into an alleyway. "If you don't want to die right here and now, you best shut your fucking face. Now we're going back to my apartment and I'm gonna fuck you. Then I'm gonna get drunk and fuck you again. After I'm done, I'm gonna fall asleep. When I awaken, you're gonna suck my dick until I cum in your fucking mouth. After that you can get the fuck out of my life forever. If you don't, I'll slit your fucking throat. You got that, bitch? Is that plain English enough for you?"

Ariel didn't move. This assault took her by surprise. Tim had always been a friend, and the two of them had never shared a cross word. This person was someone she'd never met; he was absolutely someone that she did not know. Her thoughts returning to the present she realized, *I'm in real trouble here.* Taking a deep, ragged breath, she knew she needed to answer him. As she made the attempt, her voice wavered. "Wh- Wh- Whatever you say, Tim." *He's a psychopath. The man's is deranged ... He's dangerous and violent ...*

At point blank range, he screamed in her face. "The name is Tom! TOM! Why the fuck do you keep calling me Tim?"

A deep, thick quiet washed over her. Regaining composure, slowly, she turned her eyes toward him. Taking a deep breath, she began again. "Whatever you say, Tom."

"Let's go. Lead the way, whore."

Break away as soon as you reach a crowd. Scream, yell and attract attention however you can ... call 911 as soon as you reach a large number of people. With people around you should be safe ... you should escape ... pray to God that you do escape ...

CHAPTER FIFTEEN

How does one describe a soul? How does one describe a demon? Both are intangible, yet both exist. One is beloved, and the other despised.

We must work valiantly to save that which we cannot see? That is not always the case, for I have, indeed, seen a soul. The very essence of a living being traversed time and space to deliver a message to me. I was too literal to comprehend the magnitude of the situation. If I had been open to suggestion, and if I'd been available to God's envoy, I'd have understood the urgent message. A life would have been saved, and a terrible demon would have remained imprisoned forever.

I must live with the failure. I must embrace it and incorporate its essence into my being. I must understand that good intentions are not enough; one must listen and obey God's commands in order to enable good to triumph over evil. I have not done that, and my actions have brought about dreadful, irreversible consequences. This weighs heavily on my soul. May God's mercy one day lighten the burden of dismal failure ...

"Damn, this shit is deep. Toward the end, this priest did not have a good life. I kinda feel sorry for the old geezer."

"Vince ... Who are you talking to?"

"Myself. Call me crazy. As per Mo's orders, I'm reading this pitiful book Shell gave me."

"The stalker book?"

"Yeah, the stalker book."

"Ole Daria got you hooked, huh?"

"Well, the book has me hooked … asshole. I caught that, by the way."

"Hey, don't blame Doug if you got a way that drives these chicks crazy."

"Yeah, right … whatever …"

Vince read a bit further. "Hey, listen to this."

Much like a dandelion blown into the wind, the evil has been unleashed. Having no boundaries, she is free to travel among the ages. This freedom comes with a price, however, for nothing in God's kingdom is invincible but the Lord himself. How do we discover the Achilles heel of pure evil? We must pray. In order to combat a spirit that has amassed fortitudes of supernatural ability, we must incessantly pray.

There exists an icon which will allow man even footing with this demon. Even Solange has no realization that others may attain supernatural equality, if on this window the energy signature is correctly applied.

A viable match for Solange? Hard to believe, but with much study, acquired knowledge and proper training, she can be challenged. To do so without all of the afore-mentioned means damnation until judgment day. I shudder to think of confronting—without proper armamentarium—an entity so powerful.

The next chapter offers a list of requirements as well as methods of preparation for challenge. Woe is he who does not follow them to the letter!

"You go, Daria!"

"Doug, I'm gonna beat your fat, lazy ass if you don't shut the hell up!"

"My, you're touchy!"

"You know you're trying to piss me off. If you want me out of here, you need to help me figure out how to get out of this mess."

"You're sure Solange is after you? I mean, we haven't heard anything from her."

"OK, then listen to this:"

Hiding from this demon is fruitless. She is virtually omniscient. If by some chance she doesn't have a sixth sense as to the location of her prey, she'll retaliate for the lack of knowledge by killing everyone close to the intended victim's heart. Her methods are brutal as well as barbaric; the violence associated with her killings tends to weaken the resistance of the victim. Countless times Solange has destroyed a surrendered victim by first eliminating those most emotionally close to him. Sometimes, the bereaved victim actually welcomes death.

"Oh man… Vince, do you realize what this passage is saying? Maybe that's why Mo's been urging you to go back to the Big Easy. Are you about to get all your friends offed?"

"I dunno. Damn … I don't know what to do, Adair."

"Sleep on it, Man."

"Hmmph. Like there'll be any sleep tonight. I'm all wired."

"Want a sleeping pill?"

"You got some?"

"Yeah, I got four or five. I'll go get 'em"

Leaving the room, Doug returned a few moments later.

"Here, take a couple Ambien."

"Where'd you get these?"

"Remember that girl I fucked the other night?"

"No, Doug, 'cause it's a different fuck every night."

"Well, I stole 'em out of her purse, so they should be good. They ain't old or anything …"

"Thanks, man, I could use a good night's sleep."

Vince took the sleeping pills. "Nighty-night, Adair. Now get out of my room. I'm tired."

"Sheesh … that's the thanks I get? Sleep tight, Vince. We'll figure this Solange shit out in the morning."

"In the morning, Adair."

✳✳✳

Imagine after having nearly frozen to death, sitting by the fireplace. Better yet, imagine after almost dying of thirst, there are gallons of cool water at your fingertips. One would not simply sip the water bit by bit, but while gulping down volumes of the life-saving liquid, would virtually aspirate.

Now, imagine a heroin withdrawal without medical intervention. The body is screaming relentlessly for the addictive substance it has come to rely upon for subsistence. The entire survival mechanism is in jeopardy of collapse because of a curt, abrupt imbalance. Pain, anxiety, and longing are but a few words to describe this nightmare.

The aforementioned scenarios pale in comparison to the need of life-force replenishment. Every fiber of a being's makeup is in agony and must be satisfied, or the being is subjected to a hellish torment. The individuals learn over the years to intercede before the debt reaches a critical level. For when this occurs, one will replenish it at any cost. If the lack is too great, and too much is taken, the individual then creates one of his own. Because of his negligence, he robs another of his mortality. Thus perpetuates the cycle once again.

"Help me, Vince!"

Vince opened his eyes. *At that moment, he swore he heard the clatter of a streetcar outside. What was that? There are no streetcars in Key West ...* He rubbed his face in disbelief. As he arose from the bed, he made his way to the top of the stairway. It was steep, but, racing away from him toward a lower blackness, had a beautiful, graceful curve. *I don't know where I am.* His attention was diverted. He heard a moan. It was the same voice that had cried for help—it was a voice that he recognized but could not recall.

"Vince, help me!"

He ran to the window. Pulling the heavy draperies aside, he looked outward. In an attempt to process his surroundings, for a moment, he stood frozen. *St. Charles Avenue? It couldn't be ...* Turning toward the doorway, he returned to the stairwell. *Where was the freakin' light switch?* The passage was so black—too black to make his way down it. He had to try; he had to somehow get out of there. His right hand brushing the wall in order to maintain his bearings, Vince began to inch his way down the stairwell. *The voice ... where is it coming from?*

"Where are you?"

There was no answer.

"I'm here! Talk to me! I can't hear you! I don't know this place!"

"It's too late …"

"What? Why? Where are you? For God's sake where are you?"

The impact was cold and abrupt. He'd hit some frozen impediment. He began to fall backward toward the stairway. *I'm gonna be hurt* was all that came to mind as the stairs came rushing toward him.

Soaking wet, Vince opened his eyes. He wiped his hands across them. "What the f…" He looked around his bed. The sheets were soaking wet. With an empty pan in hand, Doug was standing in front of him.

"Dude! That was some nightmare. I couldn't get you out of it."

Vince wiped his face again. "Thanks, man … I think. You couldn't have thought of some other way? My bed is soaked."

"Vince, you freaked me out. You were screaming in your sleep. Who were you looking for?"

"I don't know, but it was so real. I know the voice, too. I can't place it, but … that was some scary shit."

Doug looked toward the clock on the wall. "Well, it's 4:00 a.m. You could stay up."

"I ain't goin' back to bed. For one thing, it's cold and wet. For another, I ain't goin' back to bed."

"Wanna go to the Waffle House? We can grab some coffee."

"Sounds good, I need to get out of here. Doug, let's get the boat out."

"Got any money for gas?"

"I got a few bucks. I might have enough in case we get in trouble."

"I got a five."

"Let's skip coffee and head to the boat. I'm spooked. I need a change of scenery. That was a mean fucking nightmare."

"Cool. I'll get my stuff."

Vince knew nothing would really change after a day at sea, but somehow being disconnected from the mainland—even for a short time—gave him a feeling of escape. *Some bad shit went down last night … I can feel it. I don't know what happened, but it's not good. It's not good at all.*

✳✳✳

The room was immense. Painted cream—off white would be a more accurate description—the light color served as a backdrop for elaborate antique furniture. Ornate and darkly stained, the four poster bed sat opposite a large bank of windows. Providing a never ending frame to an ever changing canvas, heavy raw silk drapes adorned the glass panels. The room faced St. Charles Avenue; a person sitting in the richly upholstered window seat would have a ringside view of daily happenings on the famous boulevard.

She awoke around six a.m. Her mouth was dry—too dry. Instinctively, she ran her hand down the front of her belly. Much like a cover of dried perspiration, it was gritty. Her pubic hair was matted with semen, and there was dried blood on her inner thigh.

Immediately, she sat up in bed. Looking about the room, she realized she was in unfamiliar surroundings. *Am I dreaming? Where am I?*

Wearing only a hooded navy blue robe, he entered the room.

Trying to process the scenario, she said nothing.

"Good Morning, Sunshine!"

Either I'm having a nightmare, or I've died and gone to Hell. "You better start explaining fast." She then grabbed her cell phone. "I'm about to call the police!"

"That will make matters much more complicated."

"I'm calling 911."

"I won't stop you, but I assure you it will be the biggest mistake of your life."

"You bastard! You drugged me and then you raped me!"

"Yes, Delia, I did both of those."

"Kiss your career goodbye, asshole. I'm gonna have your perverted, criminal face splashed all over the *Times Picayune!*"

"No, you won't."

"You're demented. You are crazy!"

He began to walk toward her.

"Do not come near me! I may not be as strong as you but I can cause you severe bodily harm. I'll die trying, anyway ... you, you ... sick bastard!" She pulled the covers further toward her neck. Covering it, she then brought her knees up in front of her.

"You need me."

You may not make it out of this alive. He's psychotic. Play along until you find an opportunity to escape ...

"How, Joubert? How could I possibly need you? You have criminally violated me. What do I need from you? Are you planning to kill me or something? Am I being held hostage?"

"No, you're free to leave, Delia, any time you want. From this point forward, though, I do not think that you'll want to."

"Ever heard of the Morning After Pill?"

"Yes, I've heard of it."

"Because if your warped, delusional mind thinks we've conceived a child, you're crazy. I'll abort whatever you've shot up in me!"

"No need to be crude, Delia. Even if you wanted to, you can no longer have children."

"What?" *This gets more bizarre by the moment. The man is insane ...*

"Unless you plan to kill me, I'm leaving, Joubert. I'm going to the police to report a rape. If you want to murder me, now is the time to give it your best shot. Unless you have a gun under that robe, I can assure you it won't be a pleasant fight."

"I don't plan to kill you, Delia. I've already done that."

Nonplussed, she paused for a moment. "What am I missing here? Are you a serial killer? Is this your sick cat and mouse game before the murder?"

"The deed is done."

"Well then, apparently you're not very good at it. I still seem to be very much alive."

"Seem is the key word. Appearances can truly be deceiving."

"I can see how having to have sex with you for eternity would definitely fall under the category of never-ending damnation. I don't, however, feel inclined to believe at this point that will happen."

"It will not. You can no longer serve my needs."

"What? You drug and rape me, and then you have the audacity to dump me? You dump me when I've never acknowledged you in the first place? You French men are off the charts! An ego is one thing, but a criminally insane ego is just about more than I can handle. Not only do I want to cut your dick off and stuff it in your mouth, but while you bleed to death, I want to slap your stupid face. You've violated and assaulted me and I still feel insulted! I must be just as crazy as you are!"

Wrapping it around her toga style, she tore the sheet from the bed.

"Careful, Delia, those are silk sheets. They cost a fortune."

For a moment, she stood still. *Right now, I cannot think of a painful enough way to murder him. Please, God, let this be the worst nightmare of my life. I'm ready to awaken.*

She said nothing else and began to walk toward the bedroom door.

"Is it really worth the pain and agony, Delia?"

As he said this, she then paused. Slowly, she began to turn around.

"Have you heard of an animal that's gone feral?"

"Joubert, even criminally disturbed, you're an idiot!"

"Do you really want to acknowledge that you're now a monster?"

Turning back around, she proceeded to leave.

"Hear the last bit, Delia. Before you decide that you'll destroy me forever, hear this one last bit. It's vital to your quality of subsistence."

This time she merely turned her head. "You got one minute."

"It's true I've been taken with you for some time. Had you been more willing, we could have been together longer. Oh, the outcome would have eventually been the same, but you've heard of savoring the moments?"

"Thirty seconds."

"You made me wait too long. I couldn't stop; there was not enough life force left to wait for another one. You see, Delia, at the hands of Solange Deshotel, I, too, died long ago."

She froze. "Whom did you just say?"

"Solange Deshotel. She's the one that severed the silver chakra and destroyed my mortality."

"You said Solange?" *The police aren't trying to kill me, Mel. That Solange bitch has some business with me.*

"You know her?"

"I think we have a friend in common."

"Not possible. Solange has no friends. She's not human; she's an escaped demon from Hell."

"That was a figure of speech, Joubert. For whatever reason, she's after my friend."

"Vincent Jacola … it all makes sense now. He suddenly disappears … the murder on his front porch …"

"You better keep your damn mouth shut. I haven't told you anything."

"I will not have to divulge a word. Solange knows of Vincent's whereabouts. He's only making it worse by hiding from her. If he had any sense about him, he'd surround himself with her adversaries."

The Voo-Crew

"The what?"

"Wait a minute. I didn't say anything. You can hear my thoughts?"

"Depending on your sympathetic output, I can sometimes hear thoughts. If the fear level is high, the mind is easy to read."

"Oh God …"

"Maybe the Voo-Crew has enough magic to shield him—at least temporarily—from Solange. But that situation, my darling, no longer concerns you and me."

"I'm not your darling and there is no you and me."

"You're right. Those days are gone."

"You keep saying that. So, after you sexually abuse women against their will, Joubert, they're no longer desirable to you? Are you a chauvinist on top of all of your other sick, sadistic characteristics?"

"You are now like me."

"Oh, I'm nothing like you. Never have been and never will be."

"Until the remaining life force dribbles away, for a short time human emotions remain with you. The need to survive will circumvent any residual humanity that lingers. If you let your level of life force diminish to critical levels, you'll become feral. As I said before, you'll become a monster. If you do not stay with me and let me teach you how to manage this situation, you'll know nothing else but destroying lives and creating others like yourself. In its wake, your existence will leave an ever increasing swath of destruction. There are many out there with this affliction. Without understanding, if you ebb too far away from humanity, it will no longer matter. More visceral urges will surface and you'll be governed only by survival instincts. You'll take no matter what the cost and no matter what the outcome. Destructive, rogue, and barbaric will be the only words to describe you as you spiral away from civility. Do you want this? Do you want the life of a supernatural animal?"

"Oh, you mean like a Hell Hound?"

"Not far from it, Delia. The choice is yours."

"Fuck you, Joubert. I don't believe any of your crazy shit, although I must say for an insane person, you're fairly imaginative. Enjoy jail, and hope you have a tight asshole. They like that in there—so I've heard."

With that she made her way down the stairwell. Somehow suspecting this outcome, Thierry had been kind enough to set her keys, purse and overcoat by the door. Even though he'd been brought over years before, he still managed a vestige of human empathy. He did not relish the thought of her going feral … he wished the outcome would be different.

CHAPTER SIXTEEN

This was far from her first visit to New Orleans, although this time the reason for the sojourn was much different. Gentilly was not an area with which she was familiar. A bit congested, the suburb was not an easy maneuver for locals. Throw age and tourist on top of that, and the situation became even less appealing. This was not vacation, however; this was a much dreaded event she'd been anticipating for years.

As she turned right on Dreux Avenue, she began the search for Boliviee's Restaurant. The streets were horrible. She had to drive slowly as parts of them were a virtual obstacle course. The hurricane had greatly contributed to this, although they were in much need of repair before the storm. Halfway down the street, she spotted the sign. A sigh of relief washed over her, for at least part of the journey would soon be past. Attempting to make her way inside, she found the door to be locked. Loudly, she knocked on the center glass pane.

From the back of the restaurant, Mozetta heard the incessant rapping on the door. *I guess these damn idiots can't get it through their thick heads that we do not open that door until eleven.* She walked a bit further. *Same thing every blessed day!* Squinting to see who—at such an early hour—was standing in front of her establishment, she approached the front of the restaurant. She then froze. Attempting to swallow the lump in her throat, she subsequently continued her trek toward the opening. Pulling her keys from her pocket, she unlocked the entryway. Opening the door, she began.

"Well OK, then. I guess you did receive my message."

"I did receive it. I can't say I was happy to, but I certainly got it."

"I'm Mozetta Conerly. Most of my friends call me Mo; I guess you can, too. No reason to waste anymore time, we may as well start off as friends."

"I'm Roberta Staten, Mo. It's nice to finally put a name with the face. You weren't expecting me, so how did you know who I was?"

"Couple ways … In my position, you make it yo' business to know who yo' allies are. Also, the internet is a powerful thing. Bein' a doctor, yo' picture is all over it."

"Retired doctor, I don't practice anymore."

"Well, Dr. Roberta, the neighborly thing to do would be to invite you in and fix you a cup of New Orleans coffee."

"I'd love that."

"I will warn you, though, it's mighty strong!"

"At this point, that may be just what I need. I'm a nervous wreck driving around here."

"Oh, well then by all means, baby, make sure you are off the road at five o'clock!"

"By then I hope to be on a plane headed for Conway."

"You fly into Conway?"

"No, we fly into Little Rock. Conway's only about thirty minutes from there."

Mo set a cup of steaming, freshly brewed CDM coffee in front of her. "Want cream?"

"Yes, please."

"This stuff makes a great Café au lait."

Roberta smiled. "I have what you asked for."

"I cannot thank you enough."

Roberta turned and reached into her purse. From it she removed a worn, black leather box. "Here you go."

Mozetta opened it. Inside, encased in clear Lucite, was a gold coin. It was a 1907 twenty dollar gold piece. "Yes, this certainly is it. The energy signature is almost overwhelming. I can only imagine what that Ark of the Covenant would throw off."

"I don't detect any energy, Mo. To me it just feels like a coin."

"And that's exactly what it should feel like to you, baby. You don't want none of this; you really don't. This is a tall mountain to climb." She looked up from the coin at Roberta. "Believe me when I tell you this."

"I believe you, Mo."

"Pierre!"

"What is it woman? What you yellin' all down the hall at me for?"

"We have company. Get in the kitchen and fix us some beignets and callas. There may be some grillades and grits left over from brunch. Fix those, too."

"And then after all of that I can join you ladies for breakfast? Seems only proper since I'm doin' all the cookin'."

"We'll see." She turned to Roberta. "Give me yo' coffee mug, baby, you need a refill."

***

"Imagine me coming to someone's rescue. Now that's a new one."

"Baby, you look good enough to eat. Let's fuck."

"While somewhat amusing, it wouldn't do you much good."

"What's up with you? I was having a good time with that chick from the gallery."

"Your good time would have killed her in a few moments."

"Damn ... I know I'm good, but ... Hell, I don't think I'm that good." He thought for a moment. "On the other hand, maybe I am ..." He smiled after he'd said this.

"Before your ego becomes as psychopathic as the rest of you, no, that's not it."

"Aww, come on now ... You've been on the other end of my talents."

"Apparently, it has become necessary to explain your new existence, Tom. You see, you didn't accidentally escape eternal damnation. A portal was opened solely because those Voodoo idiots performed that pathetic ritual with six instead of their perfect number of seven. For reasons that I am now beginning to question, I allowed your re-entry onto this plane of being."

Taking a few steps away, she again turned to face him. "To your misfortune, however, you've managed to inhabit a weak, vacuous individual. You're not the same man you were in your other lifetime, and adjustments have to be made."

Holding his arms toward her, he merely replied, "So adjust me."

"Because you have usurped most of her life force, this woman is near death. That's why you feel so good."

"Oh really? Well, if this is the result, I'm gonna usurp every piece of ass I can find."

"No, you imbecile, you will not."

"Hey, baby, what's eating at you?"

"Over a period of time, this woman's life force will recharge. You will let her recover, and we'll use her. She now knows too much. Therefore, we cannot let her leave."

"Got me my own sex slave ..."

"If you don't grow a brain, I will not see fit to save you from your-self—once again. We'll let this woman recover. We'll nurse her back to health and find a way to camouflage this mess you've created. I'll have to think on how to mitigate this. In the meantime, while your life force is high, maybe you'd better go sew some wild oats. In that way you won't unnecessarily destroy another human being. That creates real problems in an environment I very much need control of. I have plenty of lives that I intend to destroy to accomplish my goals, but this parenthetical garbage just gets in the way."

"Whatever you just said, baby. I'm headed for the bar. We need to call her a doc or something?"

"No, I'll tend to her needs. I think I can spiritually mould her to fit my objectives. Now go, but stay out of trouble. Also, try not to forget that your given name is Tim. That should not be hard for even the likes of you to remember."

"Ouch, baby ... you keep throwing those daggers."

"I have work to do. Heed my words." Turning away from him, she walked toward her bedroom.

With a crooked smile, he watched her leave. "I just can't get enough of my little auburn-haired hottie!"

After he'd said this, she turned back toward him, but continued to her room. Saying nothing, she entered it and closed the door.

***

"Do you think history will repeat itself?"

"I do not plan to let that happen. For one thing, Roberta, things are different now. The playing ground is not the same. We are dealin' with real lives, not just a time imprint."

"I hardly think my father was merely an imprint in time."

"He was not. But the alteration of his destiny did not come from a straight timeline. It was skewed off course. Solange warped that small branch of history, and now we're living with the fallout. You have lived yo' entire life with the fallout."

"Rupert Staten was a good man. He was a good father ... in fact, he was a great father. I do have regrets, though. I've always wondered how my life would have been different. I guess if that path worked out, I'd have never had my brother James."

"Given the path thrown at you, you followed yo' chosen destiny, baby. Looks like you did a real good job with it, too. Not all of us are dealt the same deck of cards, honey. We just have to make do with what we are given."

"Why would God let this happen?"

"God had nothin' to do with this. It came straight from Hell. And now you know, beyond a shadow of a doubt, that it exists."

"I surely do." Roberta brushed the grey platinum hair from her face. "I surely do ..."

"Now, I have the means to put her away for good."

"That coin?"

"Along with some combined mag ..." Mozetta stopped mid-sentence. "Never you mind about the particulars, just take my word that this bitch is about to be shaggin' her ass back to Hell."

"Scary to know that things like this really do exist."

"Ever heard that knowledge is power?"

"I have."

"Now I have everything I need to level the playing field. I just need to make sure I know how to play."

"When will you do this?"

"When will I do what?"

"Level the playing field."

"In due time, baby, in due time … Old Mo's about to give Solange somethin' to talk about. Let's just hope she likes hot weather … her next Hell will not be so picturesque."

"I don't really care what happens to her."

"Good. Me neither."

Mo knew she'd have to use some of her oldest magic to gain mastery knowledge of the energy piece. Her tactics would be flawless—they had to be. Would it be enough? The outcome would answer that question. The outcome would determine if perfect was good enough.

CHAPTER SEVENTEEN

Nowhere in history has it been written that this evil will prevail, for if it were the truth, no means to destroy it would exist. What must happen to the immortals if the dreaded one ceases to exist? Will they surrender their prevailing presence to the forces which created them, or to a merciful God who might grant their tortured existences respite? Are they deserving of Heaven? Should one, who is demonized against his will, be forced to endure eternal damnation? Surely a forgiving, all powerful God would see fit to intervene ...

"Surely."

"What?"

"This book, it's some heavy shit, man."

"Hey, you had me drag the boat out so you could get away. Why the hell did you bring it with you?"

"Can't quit reading it."

"That good, huh?"

"No ... for this book, good is not the word to use."

"Captivating?"

"Adair, when have you ever used a word like captivating? I didn't know it was in your pea-brained vocabulary."

"You asshole ... I know lots of words. I know lots of phrases, too. You are such a smart ass, you piece of shit!"

Vince smirked. He then laughed a little to himself.

"Why don't you put that book down and let's do some snorkeling. While we're out here, we may as well have some fun."

"OK." He began to arise, when the cell phone in his coat pocket began vibrating. "Think I should answer this?"

"Dude, I think you would have left your phone at home if you didn't plan to answer it. See who it is."

Vince pulled the device from his coat. "It's Race."

"See there? Can't be all bad. See what the Dr. Race wants."

Vince put the phone to his ear. "Psycho man! 'Sup?"

"Vince … Hey."

"Man, it's good to hear your voice. What's goin' on?"

"Just calling you to check on things. I'm calling to check on you. You know, man … stuff like that."

Covering the mouthpiece, Vince dropped the cell to his lap. *Stuff like that?* He waited a moment and returned the device to his ear.

"Well, I'm glad you're calling me and stuff like that …"

A deadpan silence followed.

"Race … you there?"

"Yeah man, I'm here."

More silence.

"Everything OK on your end?"

"Uh, yeah … everything's cool. I was just calling to see when you may be coming home."

"Don't know. Don't know if I'm coming back, Race."

"I … uh … have a message for you from your tarot card reader."

"What?"

"Remember Tim?"

"What? Race … who are you talking about?'

He heard Race swallow thickly. "Not too long ago, he did a reading for you."

"That dude in the Quarter? Luna Azul?"

"Yeah, him …" Race again swallowed hard.

Vince took a deep, heavy breath. "Race, I don't remember giving that guy any of my personal information. He only knew my name."

"You better get your ass back to town and face the music, asshole or you're gonna get a whole lot more killed. You want blood on your hands to save your own ass? Stay gone, then."

In an attempt to process what he'd just said, Vince stared straight ahead at Doug.

Doug whispered, "What?"

Vince ran his hand through his hair. "This isn't Race. Why would he say something like that to me?"

"It is me, Vince. I had to say it … That was the message."

"Don't call me again, Race! If you're trying to mess with my head, don't you call my ass again!" Vince dropped the device to the floor of the boat and began to stomp it with his tennis shoe. He then picked up the phone and threw it overboard. "FUCK YOU! FUCK ALL OF YOU!"

Vince sat back down and put his face in his hands. Beginning to sob, he then began crying so hard that he fell off of the seat and onto the floor of the boat.

Frozen in a mixture of fear and amazement, Doug stood speechless. After a moment, he swallowed and approached him. "Vince … man, this is bad. You're cracking up." Doug grabbed a beer and pulled the tab from it. "Here … drink this. What do we do here, man? Right now I don't know what the hell to say or do …"

From the beer can Vince took a long, breathless drink. After he'd swallowed, without pausing he poured another large drink down his throat. He then released the can from his lips and drew a gasp. "Get the snorkel shit and let's go."

"Doug arose and began to gather the gear. Neither of them said much after that; they simply readied themselves for the dive. Holding his mask, Vince jumped overboard into the sea. The warm sea water cascaded around him like a salty, tranquil gust of wind. Here, at least he had peace. The undersea beauty would divert some anxiety for awhile.

"Good boy, Dr. Vidrine. You did a real, fine job."

In front of his telephone, Race sat bound in a chair. His hands were tied behind him, and his feet had been fastened to the front legs. "Glad I could oblige."

"Hopefully, our friend of the tarot will do as you say."

"I guess time will tell."

Tom smiled at him. "Thanks, man." He then pulled a knife from his jacket and plunged it deep into the chest cavity. He let out a slight grunt while he heaved the blade upward. As the fibers were released from their bonds, bone and tissue popped. In an attempt to insure the effectiveness of the incision, before he removed it, Tom gritted his teeth and gave the blade a slight twist.

As the central nervous system is not immediately able to process a massive injury, Race felt only the initial sharp sting. Before he'd realized the magnitude of the situation, he had well begun to bleed out. A calmed ensued as an event horizon appeared in front of him. Framed at the bottom by a thick rim of lemon yellow sunlight, the sky was steel grey. The sunlight then met and dispersed over a sea of grey whose color matched that of the sky. As twilight took over the atmosphere, the light began to dim. Recognizing inevitability, in anticipation of the pending darkness, Race closed his eyes.

✳✳✳

"Good afternoon. I thought you'd never awaken."

Slowly she opened her eyes. Rubbing her forehead, she attempted to pull herself to a seated position. "Where am I? Is this the parlor apartment? I'm in Tim's apartment?" Suddenly she arose. "Oh God … I have to get out of here. He'll kill me!" Climbing out of bed, she began to flail about for her clothing. "I can't … I'm too weak." Returning to the bed, she sat down.

"Ariel, you must rest. You're not well. You almost died last night."

"I remember. Tim tried to kill me."

"You're actually not too far off."

Ariel turned toward her. "Who are you, anyway?"

"I am Solange Deshotel."

"Whom did you say?"

"Solange Deshotel."

"That's impossible."

"I assure you I am who I say."

"She exists only in legend. Solange Deshotel was presumed dead in the 1930's. There was a fire in the French Quarter; after that, she was never again seen alive."

"I can assure you there's much more to the story than that. I noticed that you used the word presumed."

"After that fire, around that time, anyway, she was never found. She simply disappeared from sight."

"Here I am."

"Yes, here you are. Almost eighty years after your disappearance, still young and beautiful ... Somehow, I find that hard to swallow." She sat up a little straighter and turned toward her. "Assuming, by some strange coincidence, that you are telling the truth, why are you here?"

"This story is very complex."

"Too complex ... In fact, bizarre is a better word. This whole thing is bizarre. Did someone slip something into my drink?"

"If it were only that simple."

Ariel took a deep breath and exhaled. "Well, you're certainly as beautiful as legend has it."

"Thank you."

"So, I'll ask again. Why are you here?"

"Ariel, you've created quite a problem."

"A problem? I haven't created anything. I trusted a savage maniac and he raped me!"

"That is not what happened, Ariel."

"That means you're either covering for him or calling me a liar. The only problem, Solange—or whoever you are— is that I was there. I damn well know I was attacked. The man tried to kill me. It was as if he were trying to screw me to death. I felt my life ebbing away; he must have been strangling me or something ..."

"You people who dabble in the occult have no idea what a danger you represent. With your limited knowledge, you open spiritual doorways and allow whatever may be passing by to enter this dimension. It's like spiritual Russian roulette, Ariel, and the consequences can be grave. In your case, had I not been there to save you, they would have been."

"What? You're blaming me?"

"By some means, your little tarot practices have opened haphazardous portals in the veil. You've allowed a dangerous demon to escape. Didn't you notice, from one moment to the next, a marked difference in Tim's behavior?"

Her thoughts returned to the gallery. "I did, Solange. Suddenly, he became this violent, disgusting person. I thought it was the alcohol …"

"Chemicals further debilitate the spiritual barrier. If a person is weak, alcohol will increase vulnerability. Your friend is apparently weak and distracted, or he would not so have easily been overtaken by this demon. Your involving him without proper training in the fringes of the occult have lead to a demise of his spiritual existence."

"Demise … Tim's is gone?"

"Unfortunately, yes."

"Oh, God … where is he?"

"We will not know that until Death comes for us as well."

Staring ahead, Ariel said nothing.

"And now we must protect you from this demon, Ariel. I can do that, if you will allow it."

"How? How can you protect me?"

"I'm powerful enough to govern this entity. I can control to some extent his actions. You must leave him here in this place. In that way we'll have him confined to a space. We'll know where he is."

"He can't read tarot anymore, Solange. He's crazy. He'll kill someone."

"Don't be a fool. Of course not, we must isolate him from society, Ariel. What did you not understand when I said the word 'demon'?"

"I … I was … I can't think. This is all so overwhelming."

"Then let me take care of this. Stay away from the apartment. Run your business Ariel, but steer clear of Tim. I'll see to your protection."

"How can I ever repay your for this? You've literally saved my life from God knows what?"

"Rest assured God knows exactly what. Let's summon a cab and get you home. You must rest, Ariel. You have much recuperation ahead of you."

"You're right, I feel horrible. Solange, you'll stay in touch about this? I'm really afraid."

"Not to worry, I'll be in touch soon. Do not worry about this matter; I have a plan."

"Thank God, Solange. I don't know what I'd do if I had to go this alone."

I wouldn't thank God, Ariel … He may actually be a little offended by that, for he had nothing to do with it. His little Voo-crew did all the work this time.

* * *

Over time, memories become thick. At times they appear grainy and brown with age. They grow dense as well as opaque. Like too much if a good thing, too many memories can be overwhelming. Much like a penny, she remembered the copper hair. Very straight, and not yet thick, it shone like fine, flaming silk. She then looked about the flat. *Dirty, cramped and small … I well remember the smell.* She walked toward the back of the apartment. He was drunk, high or however he'd managed to alter his state of mind; soon his shadow would grace her doorway.

She looked away. With disgust, she again took a look at the flat. Anger began to consume her.

"Mmm-hmm … looks like back in the day, you had a real, hard time."

Surprised at the intrusion, she turned to face her. "So now you're able to invade memories? I find the encroachment a bit insulting."

"Most normal folks would just say nosey."

"I have a hard time relating to that genre."

"I'll translate for you one mo' time: You think you are better than most of us common people."

"As you wish … why are you here, Mozetta? I find it most disconcerting that you would delve into my past—especially since I did not anticipate this impromptu visit."

"You sure I'm here? Maybe I'm just on yo' mind these days …"

"No, I'm not sure." *She saw him make his way out of his room toward her bedroom.*

Mozetta turned to face her. "Incest is a terrible thing, ain't it, baby?"

"Don't worry ... I made him pay. He's still paying."

"And so are you."

"Therapeutic advice from an apparition? I think not. At least present yourself as something modestly appropriate."

"Them's some lofty words from something that's presently hiding in the past."

"Not hiding."

"Then what?"

"Listen for the scream ... no one came. No one ever came ..."

"And they never will, baby."

"He suffers from every scream that was uttered from those innocent lips."

"I guess at some point in yo' life that descriptive fit. Been a long time, though."

"It was not lost by choice, but was avenged so."

"So I heard. You still avengin', but it don't seem to heal the wound now, does it, baby?"

"They're part of me now ... part of who I am. They made me. They molded me, and now I need them."

"Such awful fodder to draw from."

"I'm not used to prose approaching literarily intelligent uttered from those lips."

"Not my lips, baby, remember?"

"Of course ... I hate the sated afterglow in those black-brown eyes. That was my first destructive ambition. Time and time again, their penetrative allusions ignited murderous ambitions."

"You still have those."

"Can you hear the tears? The muffled sobs?"

"I can. I can hear them."

"Had I been older, I would have ripped his heart from his chest just as he enjoyed his orgasmic release."

"He'd have killed you before that, Solange."

"He may have."

"You should leave now."

"You're right, Mozetta, as the past can't do a damn thing to help you."

"And memories are nothing more than cerebral ghosts."

"I never told you that. How did you remember?"

"The only ally one has, baby, is the present. Remember that?"

"Oh, I remember. The question is, Mozetta, will you?"

"I sure hope so, Solange."

"It would bode well for you to remember that soon ... very soon."

"Hell's not too far away, honey, maybe you better remember that, too. It's just a few steps out yo' back door ..."

Her hands clenched into fists. "You'll find out soon enough, Mozetta. Then we'll see who's offering sage advice."

✳ ✳ ✳

She heard the familiar buzzer. Loud and pungent, she pulled the plug on her dishwater and made her way toward the back porch of the restaurant. She began her descent down the steps and smiled as she looked to her right. A post hurricane poinsettia she'd planted in the back yard was flourishing. Only a potted plant when she'd bought it, the Christmas flower had now grown well past the eaves of the house. Working feverishly, Pierre was edging the fence row on the driveway side of the yard. She walked toward him. "I sure hope my poinsettia blooms this year. Look how big it is. It is a sight to behold!"

"Mmm-hmm."

"You know, you could have put the clothes in the dryer. You walked right past them. You saw they were through. I guess I'm supposed to do everything around here?"

"I ain't studying no clothes."

"We'll see what you are studyin' when you ain't got no clean underpants."

"Woman, did you come out here just to bitch or what?"

"I want to make sure you don't chop down my Four O'clocks like you did last year."

"I ain't studying no Four O'clock's, neither. We gonna have snakes in this back yard if we don't keep this fence row clean. Lord knows our neighbors don't do shit."

"Pierre, I'm tellin' you not to chop those down. You will have Hell to pay if you do."

"You know all about that, don't you? You done been there."

"Now you got a damn mouth on you, don't you?"

"Shut yo' face for a minute. Did you hear a door slam out front?"

Mo listened intently. "I think I did, and somebody's ringin' the bell. I'll go see."

"Wait up. I'll go with you."

Mo and Pierre made their way through the restaurant. As she approached the front door, she grabbed the heavy ring of keys from the sideboard. She opened the door to find three uniformed officers standing in front of her. Several more were milling around Vince's house across the street.

"Well, I do say. What in heaven's name did we do to warrant three cop cars?"

"Morning, Ma'am, I'm Officer Dennis Courtman, and these are my partners, Kenny Frost and David Messina."

"What can I do for you gentleman? We ain't open, yet, but I can fix you some coffee."

"We'd like to talk with you two for a few minutes if you don't mind."

"About what?"

"May we come in?"

Mo stood aside and allowed them to enter. "Have a seat, fellas, and I'll put the coffee pot on."

"That's not necessary."

"Yes it is. I need some."

The three of them looked at each other and then sat at the table closest to the door. Pierre sat with them. "What's this all about? What are all of those cars doing over there?"

Mo hollered from the kitchen. "Wait a minute! Don't say nothin' until I get back. I'm almost done."

She then made her way back to the dining room. "OK, now what is this all about?"

"We have to find your neighbor, Mrs. ..."

"Oh, you'll have to forgive me. We did not introduce ourselves, did we? I am Mozetta Conerly and this is my husband Pierre. What do you need with Vince?"

"Do you know of the whereabouts of Vincent Jacola?"

"Why do you want to know?"

"There has been another murder, Mrs. Conerly."

"Lord have mercy Jesus ..."

Pierre turned to face Officer Courtman. "Who was it this time?"

Mo shook her head. *This time ... there's been so many murders we have to find out the latest ...*

"Sources tell me it was a close friend of Mr. Jacola's—a psychiatrist by the name of Dr. Race Vidrine."

Mo's face immediately paled. "Saint Agnes in heaven, help us all ..." Her eyes immediately became liquid. "I think I am going to faint. Tell me you did not say who I think you just said."

"Did you know Dr. Vidrine?"

"He came in here all the time with Vince. He loved my stuffed bell peppers." Mo arose. "You will have to excuse me for a moment, Officers, I need a tissue." In an increasingly unsuccessful attempt to stifle impending sobs, she quickly left the room.

Pierre leaned in closer to Officer Courtman. "How did they kill him? And where did they do it?"

"He was bound to a chair in Mr. Jacola's living room. Apparently, a large knife had been driven into the chest cavity. There's a good chance the blade may have pierced his heart, and he died instantly. Whoever did this, knew how to make it quick and lethal."

Pierre shook his head 'no.' "That's terrible."

Shortly thereafter, with tissue in hand, Mozetta returned from the back of the restaurant. "So what does this have to do with Vince? He ain't even here?"

"I was just telling your husband that Dr. Vidrine was murdered in Mr. Jacola's living room."

"What?! Ain't nobody got a key to that house but me, and there wasn't nary a light on in that house last night. I would have seen it … You can be sure of that!"

"There wasn't a light on, Officer. We did not see anybody. How long has Race been dead?"

"A few hours as well as we can determine."

Pierre continued. "So … I'm a little confused here. How did you discover him? Ain't nobody gonna report him missing in a few hours … and how did you know to look at Vince's place?"

"That's the eerie part. We received a phone call reporting the incident."

"From whom?"

"They didn't give a name, Mr. Conerly."

"And you did not trace the call?"

"Yes sir, we did. We traced the call back to Dr. Vidrine's cell phone, which we found lying in the front yard by Mr. Jacola's steps."

A cold chill ran down Pierre's spine. "So he was out there this very morning?"

"It seems that way."

"And nobody saw him?"

"No one saw the perpetrator."

"That phone call … was it a man or a woman?"

"A man's voice made the call."

After he'd said this, Mo and Pierre looked at each other.

Officer Courtman saw the exchange of glances. "Am I missing something here?"

Mo answered. "No, no … it's just that someone was murdered right across the street, and the killer was using the phone in the front yard. While we slept, he gave you all the details. Now how would that make you feel, Officer?"

"I can ask for extra patrol around here."

"That sounds real good."

"And Mr. Jacola … you have his whereabouts?"

"I don't know exactly where he is, Officer. I would tell you if I did."

"So you know 'about' where he is, Mrs. Conerly? It's important that we know. There have now been two murders at that house, so knowledge of his whereabouts is imperative. We must protect him as well as others; I suspect we may have a serial killer on our hands. I need to know how Mr. Jacola fits into all of this."

"No need to suspect, baby; the puzzle is falling all together. You got yo'self a serial killer." *And you got mo' trouble than you can handle, Officer. You gonna have to let Mo' rein this one in for you, or you may find yo' self on the wrong end of a knife, too …*

✳ ✳ ✳

Such vivid dreams. She'd never had those before … what was happening to her? So thirsty, but water did not seem to quench. Her throat was parched. She could barely sit. Was she dying? Perhaps … but according to Joubert, that was no longer an option.

"Hey you—you OK?" Wearing nothing more than a tee shirt, Delia's boyfriend, Ray, returned to the bedroom.

"I'm not sure."

"Not meaning to jump on your bandwagon, Mel, but I'm beginning to feel your pain. This morning I woke up feeling kind of prodromal myself."

"Felt good having your arms around me all night."

"Me too, baby, although we didn't sleep much last night, did we?"

"I need a hug."

"Comin' your way Ms. Melancon."

Ray shed the tee shirt and returned to bed.

"I'm cold."

"Me too. Let's see if we can warm each other." Ray snuggled up close and spooned himself against her. "Feel like going to the Quarter today? Thought we might get a reading."

"A what?"

"Get our cards read. I have a friend there who reads the tarot."

"Who?"

"A guy by the name of Tim Johnson. He works at a paranormal parlor on Royal."

"I'm not sure if I feel like doing that or not."

"We may need to spend the day in bed."

"I could see that."

"May have to spend all night here, too."

Delia pulled herself away from him and laboriously made her way to the bathroom.

"Where are you going?"

"To get dressed."

"Come back to bed. We don't have to do that today."

"No, it may help to get moving. Let's go do the card thing. Why do we want to do the card thing, anyway? I think I missed that."

"I usually get a monthly reading to get a fix on what direction fate plans to steer me."

"You're serious, Ray …"

"Yeah … I'm serious." His voice trailed off for a moment. Seeing her expression of disbelief, he began again. "Hey, I'm just saying that it works for me, but we don't have to do it. We can stay right here."

"No, no, no … wouldn't want to deprive you of your fated directions. These days I could use a few directions myself."

"The tarot won't give you any directions, Mel, it'll just make you aware of what possibilities are headed your way. In that way, you may not miss an opportunity."

"You're a weirdo, Ray. I love you, but you're a very strange man."

"Thanks much, Melvin."

"And I don't ever want you to leave."

Running his hands through his hair, he half chuckled after she'd said this. "Well … since you so lovingly threw that out there, I'll see what I can do."

"You do that. In the mean time, I think I'll run a bath."

"And I plan to embark upon a hunt for some aspirin. You want some?"

"Doesn't seem to help."

"How about a Bloody Mary?"

"I would literally hurl."

"Oh, OK … Maybe just a bath, then?"

"We'll start with that. Give me about a half hour and I'll be ready … ready as I'm going to be, anyway."

"Going commando," he chuckled as he put on his blue jeans. "And take your time. Soon as I brush and floss, I'm ready, too." Running his arms through the sleeves, he again put on his tee shirt.

Ready, too, but feel like shit. Maybe a day in bed would not be so bad after all …

∗∗∗

"I think I'm freakin' sunburned."

"You're in the Keys, remember? You're below the tip of Florida. I told you to spray some of that sunscreen on before we left the house."

"I figured it didn't matter since we were spending our time underwater."

"That's what you get for figuring, dumbass. Here, use some of this benzocaine spray on your shoulders."

As he began to step from his bike, he stopped for a moment. "Man, that was a weird call from Race."

"Let's don't bring that shit up again, Vince. I can only handle so much weird, and these days you're pushing the limit. One can only stay so stoned …"

Vince walked toward the house. *I need to check in with Mel. Maybe she can get my last paycheck forwarded to Shelley, if that Joubert asshole doesn't figure out some way to stiff me.*

"I don't have a phone …"

"You think? Should you maybe have thought of that before you stomped the shit out of it and ripped it to shreds? The way you annihilated that son of a bitch, there really wasn't much reason to throw it overboard."

"I was freaked out."

"Putting it mildly …"

"Man, I need a phone. You got an old one?"

"Dude, you threw sim card and all into the deep blue sea."

"What am I gonna do?"

"Get a roll of quarters, I guess."

"Suck it, Adair."

"I got a disposable, Vince, but you'll have to load it up with minutes. I ain't doing that for you. I didn't take your middle-aged fat ass
to raise."

"And I'm fixing to beat your middle-aged fat ass into next week if
you don't shut it. Where do I get minutes?"

"Go to Wally-world. They'll load it up."

"OK."

"I about to grab a shower."

"Cool … hey one more question."

"What?"

"Got some funds for the minutes?"

✳✳✳

Three rings before she answered. "¿Hola?"

"Umm, hello? How you doin'?"

"I'm OK. Who may I ask is calling?"

"I need to speak to Shelley Levy. Is she there?"

"This is Mrs. Levy."

"Mrs. Levy, my name is Mozetta Conerly. I need to get in touch
with yo' brother, Vincent."

"Why are you calling me? He has a phone."

"Well, I have some news that's rather urgent. That's why I'm calling you."

"And how did you get my number?"

"Mrs. Levy, I am from New Orleans, and yo' brother lives across
the street from me. He's my neighbor, and, well, I've kind of adopted
him, too."

"Is this Mo?"

"Yes, it is. You've heard of me?"

"Heard of you? I can't have a conversation with my brother without
'Mo said this, or Mo said to do that.' I finally had to ask him who is
this 'Mo person?' He thinks a lot of you, Ms. Conerly."

"I think a lot of him too, baby, and you, too, can call me Mo. I wish I was callin' under happy circumstances, but I am not. I really need to get in touch with him."

"Have you tried his cell?"

"It goes straight to voice mail. Let's just hope he paid the bill."

"You do know my brother, don't you?"

"Mrs. Levy,"

"And you call me Shelley, OK?"

"Thank you, baby. Shelley, some terrible things have happened around here since Vince left. It's of the utmost importance that I get in touch with him immediately. Do you know anybody else in Key West that I could call?"

"Well, I could give you the number of the bar at which he works … and I might could get hold of his roommate's number from someone who works there. What happened, Mo? What is so wrong?"

"Murder, baby, and now the cops are lookin' for him. They may have taken him in for questioning already."

"Vince didn't kill anyone."

"I know that, honey, but two of his dear friends have been brutally murdered at his house."

"Oh, my God! Mo, we had a murder here, too."

"I already know that, Shelley. Get me a number, or these might not be the last ones."

"Do you think my brother is in danger?"

"No, baby, I do not."

"That's a relief …"

"Well, it shouldn't be."

"What do you mean by that?"

"The way this situation is unfolding, honey, I think you may be next."

CHAPTER EIGHTEEN

"Here it is."

"I'm starting to sweat. It's so hot already."

"Lots of concrete in the Quarter."

"Luna Azul … the Blue Moon Paranormal Parlor? Sounds like something right out of a B movie on the Sci-Fi channel."

"Around here they call it LAPPs. And what's wrong with Blue Moon? Kinda catchy if you ask me."

"Remind me not to ask." As she began to step through the threshold, Delia looked around. As bright as she could remember, the sun seemed to be reflecting off of virtually everything. "My eyes hurt. They're becoming really photosensitive these days."

"Well get inside, silly. Where are your shades?"

"I have a pair in my car. Forget it, though, let's just get read. I want to get this over with."

"Don't sound so excited."

As they made their way inside, Ray walked toward a large, frosted glass window. To the right of the window was a sign that read, *Please ring for service.* Assuming they meant the bell sitting on a ledge beneath it, Ray slapped the bell two quick times. After a moment, revealing a tall, slender woman standing behind it, the glass window began to slide sideways.

Smiling at the two of them, she began. "Hi, I'm Ariel. May I help you?"

Stepping forward toward the opening, he answered her. "We'd like to see Tim Johnson for a reading."

Upon hearing this, the woman shifted uncomfortably. "I'm sorry, that won't be possible."

Turning toward Delia, Ray simply uttered, "Oh …"

"Is there someone else who might help you?"

"Well, I don't know. I sort of know Tim; he's a friend."

"He's on sabbatical. I'd be glad to suggest another reader for you. We have several experts in the field."

Stepping forward, Delia leaned into the opening as well. "A card reader on sabbatical? What kind of sabbatical is that? Do you even know what that means?"

Obviously insulted, Ariel bristled. "I'm sorry you find my choice of words distasteful. Perhaps you will find this more appropriate: Tim's not available and won't be doing any readings in the foreseeable future. If you deem the notion of an alternate reader unsuitable, I'm afraid that I will not be able to help you."

"Now, now, Arrie … don't send away business. We'll never make it turnin' down good money."

As she turned to face the disembodied voice, Ariel felt the color drain from her face.

With a cross between a smile and a sneer, Tim began to descend the stairway.

"Hey man, how's it goin'?"

"Well, we're about to find out, now, aren't we?"

"This is my friend, Delia Melancon, thought we might get a couple of readings."

Stopping his decline, he began to study both of them.

"That is, if you have time or whatever …" A little uncomfortable with the scrutiny, Ray shifted positions in front of the stairwell.

"I'll do your reading," he then turned his attention toward Delia, "but her cards have already been read."

Feeling her face become hot, she answered him. "Well, you're already batting zero. I've never had a reading."

He smirked again. "You don't need one."

"Why? Is it because you already know everything about me? Or is it that you know I can spot a fake. Maybe it's because you're able to surmise that I don't really want one. Body language can be pretty damn indicative, huh Tim?"

Laughing aloud, he continued. "All good theories, Dee, but unfortunately for you, we only do readings for those who have a future. You and me … we don't need 'em. Our path is already mapped out."

In total disbelief she stood transfixed. "First of all, we're not friends. From the looks of things thus far, it's safe to assume that we never will be. So it's Delia, Tim, no one calls me 'Dee.' Secondly, how would you know anything about my path? I've never met you before in my life!" Closing her eyes, she took a deep breath and exhaled. After a moment of silence, she began again. "Let's go, Ray. I don't need this."

Tim then took another step forward. "I just told you that. Don't you want to see how long this one will sustain you? He's about out of juice."

As Ray heard him say this, a furrow crossed his brow. "What do you mean by that? Are you trying to piss us off?"

"No … what did you say your name was?"

"Ray."

"No, Ray, quite the contrary. I'm trying to help your lady friend out, here. In fact, to show my good faith, I'll waive the reading fee."

Ariel turned toward him. "What? You just said …"

Tim interrupted her. "Fuck that. The reading's free if you want it, Ray. Come on back." Walking around the front desk, he opened the door for them.

Reluctantly, Delia followed Ray through the doorway.

"Y'all have a seat. Let's deal some cards."

"Have them choose three crystals, first, Tim."

"Oh, yeah, that." Tim went to an armoire and pulled from it a rattan box. He then threw a handful of stones onto the table. "Grab some rocks."

Staring at the quartz crystals, Ray asked, "Why?"

Tim shrugged. "Hell if I know …"

Ariel stepped forward. "Because crystals vibrate with natural energy." She then looked directly at Delia. "And they're useful for chakra cleansing …"

"You know, a few days ago, I'd never heard that word. Now it seems to dominate every conversation."

Cutting his eyes toward her, Tim's sneer reemerged. "So maybe you should listen and pay attention."

"Ray, I'm out of here."

"Wait up, babe; I'll go with you. We don't need this shit."

Lunging around the table, Tim made his way to the doorway. "No, no, baby doll, not just yet. I have a card all picked out for your sweetheart. Here, big man, here's your reading." Tim handed him a card.

As Tim held the card out to him, Ray looked first at Delia, and then at Ariel. "We're leaving. Get out of our way before we call the cops."

Pulling a revolver from his back pocket, Tim pointed it at both of them. "You ain't callin' shit. I'll blow your fucking head off before the operator gets, 'Your number, please,' out of her fucking mouth."

Delia and Ray met each other's glance. "Maybe a hundred years ago … are you really planning to kill us? Or are we part of some Candid Camera movie plot?"

"No, to whatever the hell that is. I just want you to look at the fucking card and get your reading."

"And if we do that, you'll let us leave?"

"Sure."

Tim again extended his hand.

Delia reached for the card. "Not you, you stupid bitch! The card is for him."

Taking the card from him, Ray looked at it for a moment and then began. "The Hanged Man." He looked back at Tim. "OK, so I'm a whimsical idiot. I get it." He then took a small step sideways toward Delia. "So … can we leave now?"

"Don't you want the reading?" Tom raised the gun once again.

Swallowing hard, Ray answered him. "Yes, by all means, give us the reading."

"As timeless as this moment of clarity may seem, my friend, very soon you must right yourself. But when you do, things will be different—much different. Like the rest of us, you'll have to act by what you've learned. You and your little doll here both have that lesson to learn. You see, my new found friends, much like the hanged man, your new, unique positions have you dangling between the spiritual world and the mundane one." He returned the revolver to his back pocket. "Quite a trick to juxtapose yourselves between both ..." He then began to laugh.

"Is that all?"

"Isn't that enough?" Tom began to laugh more loudly. "You stupid motherfucker ... isn't that enough?" As he finished the statement, his pitch had risen to that of yelling.

"Can we go now?"

"By all means, get the hell out of here. You have all you need to know, Ray, but don't say I didn't warn you. And Delia, don't bother with the cops. We both know they can't help us." After he'd said this, he burst into laughter once again."

Delia whispered to Ray, "He's crazy. We have to get out of here or we're dead."

"You are, doll, you've been that way for awhile now." Trying to stifle his outburst, he attempted to clear his throat. "Arrie, show our guests out."

Ariel opened the French door onto the Royal Street sidewalk. "I'm really sorry about this; I think he's had some kind of breakdown."

Quickly making his way onto the street, Ray turned toward her. "Breakdown? He pulled a gun on us for Christ's sake! He's dangerous. He needs to be behind bars ... or at least padded walls!"

"Are you calling the police?"

Ray answered, "Hell yeah!"

Delia interrupted. "No. Just leave us be and we'll never bother you again."

Tim then shoved Ariel through the doorway onto the sidewalk. "Good call, Delia. We un-deads have to stick together, huh babe?"

In an attempt to get away from him, Delia and Ray began to run up the street. "When we get to Canal, call 911!"

"No. Just get us home, Ray. Don't call anyone."

"What?!?"

"Just do as I say. Don't argue. When we reach home, I'll give you more details."

Human emotions remain with you for a short time until the remaining life force dribbles away. The need to survive will circumvent any residual humanity that lingers. If you let your level of life force diminish to critical levels, you'll become feral.

∗ ∗ ∗

He dialed the number. Two rings, three rings and then, "¿Buenos?"

"Hola, Tomas."

"Whassup, Vince?"

"Shell around?"

"Yeah, she's here. I just saw her walk through a minute ago. Hang on. Where are you, anyway?"

"The bar, I gotta work this evening."

"Here she comes. You feeling OK?"

"I'm feeling good, thanks."

"Te extraño, mi hermano. Dios te bendiga."

Shit, now I know I'm screwed. I miss you, my brother. God bless you? Maybe he's dying …

"Vince?"

His thoughts came back to the present. "Hey, sweetie, how are you?"

"I can't believe you've called."

"I … uh … lost my phone, and now have another one. I wanted to give you the number."

"So ironic … your neighbors from New Orleans just called awhile ago."

"Mo and Pierre?"

"Well, actually just Mozetta."

"Why on earth did Mo call you? What's up?"

"Vince, I have some disturbing news."

"Oh Jesus … Just what I need. Do I really need to know this or can I just give you this number and hang up. I've had about all I can handle today, Shell. This day was off to an early start." *Much too early …*

"Well, that being said, I'll just ask that you call Mozetta as soon as possible. She's been trying to get in touch with you."

"I'll call her. You want this number?"

"Do you have texting ability on that phone?"

"I think so."

"If you'll do that, I'll program it into my cell. That way, I won't have to try and remember where I've written it down. And Vince, your friend Mozetta said something really strange—almost disturbing—to me."

"Imagine that."

"I don't think she meant any harm. In fact, I think she was trying to warn me."

"Warn you of what?"

"She told me she felt that I, too, was in danger."

What the f ...

"I did not quite know how to respond to that."

"Why you, Shell? Why are you in danger?"

"Based on Eric's murder, she thinks I may have been the intended victim."

Before he replied, Vince paused a long moment. He then lit a cigarette. Taking a drag, he exhaled and began. "So ... you think Eric's murderer can't distinguish a kid from a middle aged woman? I think we can both do better than that."

"I'm just telling you what she told me."

"I'll call her, Shelley. Mo's not one to blow smoke up someone's ass, so maybe you'd better be careful."

"Hang on, Vince, I hear the doorbell."

Vince took another drag. *She'll kill everyone and everything that matters to you.* He then looked past the French doors of the bar. Mo came to mind. *Now I know that wasn't no accident— you meetin' her in my restaurant.* Walking toward the doorway, as if in midsentence he suddenly stopped. *I wonder if my sister really is in danger. What if I'm about to get her ass killed? What the hell do I do now?*

"Vince? Are you still there?"

"Yeah, Shell, I'm here."

"Daria Landry just dropped by."

"What in God's freakin' name does she want now? Tell her I'm reading that horrible book."

Shelly lowered her voice to a whisper. "I don't know what she wants. She insisted I see her today and said it was extremely important."

"Where's Tomas?"

"I haven't seen him for a minute."

"Shell, check and see if his car is still there."

"Hang on, I'll have a look. I can see it through the garage window."

After she did so, she returned the device to her ear. "Nope, he must have left. Kind of strange that he didn't say goodbye or where he was headed..."

"Call him and tell him to get his ass home. I don't want you there with that weirdo."

"She's harmless, Vince. Let me see what she wants. Don't forget to text the number, OK?"

"Call me after Psycho-Dario leaves. And quit hanging around her—she has issues."

"Vince, listen to yourself. The master of 'life with issues' is criticizing a slightly Bohemian but otherwise harmless individual."

"OK then, maybe it takes one to know one. Is that a good enough reason for you?"

A defeated sigh followed the comment. "I love you, sweetie. Do not forget to call Mozetta."

"Love you too, Shell. I may drive up in a day or so."

"You're always welcome, honey."

✳✳✳

"Good afternoon, ladies and ... gentleman."

Pierre acknowledged the greeting. "I guess I should take a step back and say thank you."

"No, you just need to sit there and close yo' face. I'm sure you're all wondering why I've called an emergency meeting this afternoon."

Verdiasee raised her right hand. "I sure do. Did you have to drag us out on a Saturday afternoon? I have washing to do."

"You ain't gonna be washin' much of nothin' if we don't get a handle on this situation."

Mo redirected her attention toward the rest of the group. "We are gonna try this again—with me at the helm. We have to get this Solange entity out of our lives, once and for all. Things are getting out of hand fast, and I mean real fast."

Coretta then raised her hand. "I'm not sure if I'm up to another round so soon, Mo. You better count me out of this one."

"I ain't countin' you out of nothin'! You made a commitment when you became a part of this circle and you will fulfill it, Retta. You got that?"

With a disgusted look, she answered, "I guess so."

"Don't bother to guess, baby. We have a quorum here, and that is all we have. We need every warm body in this room to complete our mission."

Arletha Jackson stood up. "Who died and made you God, by the way?"

"Go ahead an push yo' luck, bitch. I told you last time that I will sweep the streets with you. What part did you not understand?"

"The part about how you fixin' to get us all killed. That's what I do not exactly understand."

"Well, I guess you could let that red-headed hell hound do it for me? Would you rather that?"

"What I'd rather is for all this shit to go away. That's what I'd rather. This is gettin' too complicated."

Mo put a hand on her hip and began to roll her neck as she said, "Then by all means, let me call our dear friend Solange and see if we can reschedule. Would that better suit you, Mrs. Jackson? I'm not sure how amenable a demon is to change, but we can give it a try. Never hurts to try now, does it, Arlie?"

"I'm sick of yo' fat face."

"You better have a look in the mirror, sista, 'cause I ain't the fat one. And you want to know what I'm sick of? I'm sick of yo' big fat mouth, Arletha Jackson, and you better shut it real soon or we will be doing this ritual with yo' big ass in a stretcher. You hear me? Did you hear every word I just said?"

"Oh I heard every damn word. Everyone did. We all have to listen to the almighty Mozetta."

"Pierre, shut her ass up before I lose my temper. I'm telling you it ain't gonna be good …"

"Ladies, ladies, order, please!"

As she sat down, Arletha mumbled something. She then focused her attention past the window to her left.

"Looks like you got company, Mo."

"I ain't expecting nobody. Pierre, handle that and tell them we're closed."

In anticipation of a knock, Pierre went to the front door of the restaurant.

As he opened it, he found himself standing in front of a tall, attractive blonde. "The restaurant is closed."

After he'd said this, she smiled. "I'm not here for the restaurant, Sir, it is important that I speak to a Mrs. Mozetta Conerly."

"Mrs. Conerly is not available, and will not be for quite some time. Any message?"

"It's really important that I see her."

"I said she was not available. I will, however, be happy to relay a message."

"This concerns Madame Solange Deshotel. Could you tell her that? I must speak with her about Solange as soon as humanly possible."

"I'm sorry, but I didn't catch yo' name."

"Ariel Cullotta."

"And how by chance do you, Ms. Cullotta, know about Solange Deshotel? Better than that, why would you need to discuss her with Mo?"

"Who?"

"Let me start again. Why do you need to discuss Solange Deshotel with my wife, Mozetta Conerly? What do you think that you know that is so urgent?"

"It's personal."

"Ain't too personal for me, Miss, I'm married to her. Anything you have to say to Mozetta can run by me. You got that?"

"Please, Mr. Conerly, I must see her at her earliest convenience."

"Well it ain't convenient right now, baby." Wondering who was so insistent to speak to her at the front door, Mo had made her way toward Pierre.

"Oh, Mrs. Conerly, I assume."

"OK ..."

"You are Mrs. Conerly?"

"Get on with it, baby. What do you want?"

"I need to speak to Mozetta Conerly about Solange Deshotel. It's urgent."

"Why so urgent."

"I have information which could affect a lot of lives. It's not good news, I'm afraid."

"And how convenient that you chose this moment to deliver yo' bad news ... Ain't that somethin'?"

"You must hear me out."

"I 'must' not do anything. The fact is that I don't have to listen to a word you say."

"Please, Mrs. Conerly."

"Move, Pierre." Mozetta stepped around him onto the front steps of the restaurant.

"Now say what you have to say, and make it quick. I have a whole room full of people in there waiting on me, and they're not the patient sort."

"Mrs. Conerly, I'm the proprietor of the Luna Azul Paranormal Parlor in the Quarter."

"LAPPS? You own LAPPS?"

"That's right. You've heard of it?"

"Everybody in this circle has heard of LAPPS."

"Apparently, Solange Deshotel is friends with one of my employees."

"She ain't got no friends. That's not how she operates."

Ariel took a step forward and leaned in toward Mozetta. "I'm telling you this woman means to do great harm. She has some kind of association with my employee and it's not a good one. You must listen to me."

"Baby girl, you need to get out of my face, and I suggest you do it right now. You don't know me like that."

Obviously embarrassed by the comment, Ariel took a step backward. Her face scarlet, she began again. "I didn't mean to be forward, Mrs. Conerly."

"Honey, when you come from my walk of life, you tend to be cautious when people get all up in yo' business. You may want to remember that for future reference. Some folks got their personal space."

"This woman is trouble."

Crossing her arms, Mo leaned against the wrought iron railing of the steps. "Imagine that … why don't you tell me somethin' I don't already know?"

"Please, I need help."

"You need help? How so? And just what do you expect me to do to help you?"

"I need this man out of my apartment. Her cohort is dangerous. I'm afraid he's going to kill me. I think he raped me the other night; Solange saved my life."

"Well now I know you are either crazy, stupid or a lyin' fool. Solange don't save nobody. Solange Deshotel is all about destruction and greed. And how do you think it sounds for you to tell me this man may have raped you, but still works for you?" She uncrossed her arms and turned toward the house. Looking back at Ariel and Pierre, she began again. "Get the hell out of here and call the police. If you don't, I will, but it will be to haul yo' ass off of these premises. I told you I was busy and don't have time for such asinine goings on. Pierre, get her out of here."

Pierre turned toward her. "You got to go."

"Tom Banks has made his way to us."

Mozetta froze. Slowly, she turned around. "Who did you just say made his way?"

"You heard me."

"How do you know about Tom Banks?"

"I'm telling you, Mrs. Conerly, I know what I'm talking about. You need to listen to me."

Mozetta turned toward Pierre. "Perhaps the rest of the group needs to hear this as well. Come on in baby, and I'll fix you a cup of coffee. We may need to hear what you have to say after all."

✳✳✳

"Since we don't have all day, I'll simplify the introductions. Now what did you say yo' name was?"

"Ariel ... Ariel Cullotta."

"Ok. Everybody, this is Ariel Cullotta. Ariel, this is everybody."

Everyone cautiously nodded their hellos.

"Now that we're done with the formalities, what do you know about Tom Banks? And how do you know about Tom Banks?"

"Solange told me about him. She said you rescued him from Hell."

As Ariel said those words, a chill ran up her spine. *That damned Circle of Six. Well, obviously the mystery is over. We know who was sent.*

"Well, that's a mighty huge feat if you ask me. I wonder how we managed to do that?"

"Mrs. Conerly, I was there when he took over my friend's body."

"Say what?"

"We were at a Gallery open house the other night and I could almost see the evil infiltrating him. It didn't happen all at once. Bit by bit, it just kind of crept into him until he became this ... this monster. I'm telling you he was the kindest, most docile man until ..."

"Until what?"

"Until he began to change. Even his eyes were different ... they were empty and devoid of emotion. They were dead— at least they looked dead." Ariel took a deep breath and brushed her hair from her face. Swallowing hard, she began again. "That's the best way I can describe them. No soul. No remorse in them."

"You may have the remorse part right, baby, but there is certainly a soul. In fact, that's about all you saw." Mo turned to face her. "Not every soul is a good soul."

"I don't understand what happened to my friend. Where is he?"

"I do not know. We may never know. I'm not sure we can still help him."

"How can something just willingly take over a person's being? That doesn't make any sense."

"Ariel, when that man tried to rape you, did you just willingly welcome him into yo' arms'?"

"Of course not! Why would you say something like that to me?"

"So if a demon plans to take over yo' body, do you get the emcee to yell, 'Come on down'?"

Simply staring at her, Ariel said nothing.

"Didn't think so. Thieves rob, murderers kill and demons possess. Just like thieves look for an open window, so do demons. This man did not have his house filled with God, so another tenant moved in. Does that make sense to you? Do you understand?"

"I understand perfectly, Mrs. Conerly, but the point could have been just as easily conveyed without the condescension."

Still looking at her, Mo closed her eyes as she said this. "Maybe that's just my way …"

Ariel swallowed again. "I don't know what to do. That's why I'm here. I don't know what to …" Her eyes filled with tears. "Everyone says this Solange is so horrible, but she's actually been so nice to me."

"Then why don't you ask her for advice?"

"First of all, she hasn't been around lately. And second, all she tells me to do is to go on with my normal life and leave Tim upstairs. That's crazy. I'm terrified. I can't live with someone who's not only assaulted me, but threatened to murder me, Mrs. Conerly. It's almost too inane to talk about."

"Then call the police, Ariel. Why have you not done that?"

"Solange asked me not to."

"Oh, I see. And that makes perfect sense, too." Shaking her head 'no', she refocused her gaze toward her. "Yo' elevator doesn't quite make it up to the top floor, does it baby?"

"I guess that mean comment was just 'your way,' too."

"I just call it like I see it. Now did she ask you or instruct you not to call the cops?"

"Maybe persuaded might be a better word. At the time it made sense. Some of it still does; the police will not believe that Tim is possessed. They'll think I'm the crazy one."

"And that's why you came to us?"

"Yes."

"I would like to know how you managed to get my name."

"Daria Landry."

"Did I hear who I thought you just said?"

"Yes ma'am."

Lord have mercy someone could drive a dump truck through that girl's mouth! "Daria, as much as she'd like to be, is not an insider in our group. You may be better off not listening to her." *And one day soon, I plan to shut her ass up!*

"She's an odd one, isn't she?"

"That's bein' real nice about it, baby."

"You still haven't told me if you can help me."

"I'm not sure that I can, yet." Mozetta stopped for a moment, as she'd noticed Ariel suddenly seemed unsteady. "You OK?"

"I just need a bit of fresh air." Ariel walked over toward the window.

Mozetta grabbed a chair for her. She then unlocked the window and threw it open. "Here, honey, have a seat. You look like you are about to pass out."

"I'll be OK." Ariel rested her head in her hands.

"Sit for a moment. I'll get you some sweet tea. Yo' blood sugar might be low. Stress can cause that, you know."

"Thank you."

Arletha stood up. "Well, this has been a real nice show, but if Nurse Mo' is done here, I got things to do."

"Sit yo' ass down, Arlie," Mo said as she reentered the room. "We ain't even started yet. This was an interruption."

"A long one at that."

"You think I should have just let her flop out? She was about to hit the floor."

"I really don't care. I really don't care about any of this. I'm ready to go."

"Ariel, I ain't bein' rude, honey, but you have to leave now. We have business to attend to. You feelin' better?"

Ariel handed her the glass. "I am. I just became lightheaded for a moment. That fresh air helped."

Arletha shifted in her seat. "Hmmph. Ain't never heard that about New Orleans air."

"Sorry I couldn't have been more help, baby. Maybe things will work out. If you think you're in that much danger, I suggest you stay away from LAPPS. You got a place to go?"

Managing a weak smile, she answered. "I do, thank you. Thank you all and I'm sorry for taking your time."

Most of the women returned the smile. Arletha just looked at her and began to fan herself with a magazine.

Ariel then turned to leave. "Goodbye, Mrs. Conerly."

"Mmm-hmm, take care." Closing the door behind her, Mo returned to the group. "OK, Arlie, it is show time."

"It's about time."

"We'll see. Rhetta, walk around the room and close the drapes." As Coretta arose, she continued. "I will now give instructions. Let us hope for a successful result." *And let's hope it will not be our last result …*

✳✳✳

"Arlie, finish setting up the Star of David candle configuration, and this time do not forget the center candle for the white light of the Holy Spirit. I will turn to page XVIII in the Book of Spells." Retrieving a stack of papers from the tabletop, she handed them to Edith Blankenship. "And Edith, please hand everyone a copy. Verdie, light the candles."

Verdiasee struck a wooden match and lit the candle arrangement once more. Coretta poured the layer of salt around the candle setup.

Mozetta went to the sideboard and took from it a vial. "We don't need to use too much of this; we just need to make sure the circle is unbroken. Evil spirits cannot penetrate this."

Edith watched her pour the circle. "We forgot that last time, but I don't think we'd have found it if we were lookin' for it."

"Pierre knew where it was. Wasn't no excuse in forgettin' the sacred salt from the Sea of Galilee."

"Easy for you to say since you weren't here."

"Shut it, Arlie. Pierre, raise the thermostat."

Pierre walked over to the thermostat and turned the switch to the off position.

"OK, everybody … join hands and close yo' eyes. Remember: once the spell begins, open them just long enough to read yo' part and then close them again."

"We will read the entire incantation in French."

Coretta opened her eyes and looked at Mozetta. "I thought that was optional."

"We doin' it my way this time. No options … French, Retta."

"Well, I'm a little rusty."

"Well oil yo' face and get it right. We ain't got no room for mistakes. And now, I will begin …"

✳✳✳

"This phone sucks."

"By all means, pardon me. I'll see if I'm due for an upgrade. Especially since it was free, asshole."

"Shut it. I'm trying to call my neighbor."

"In New Orleans?"

"Adair, do you realize how stupid you sound sometimes? Of course New Orleans, I'm callin' Mo."

"For what?"

"Apparently some bad shit went down with that Race phone call. I'm scared, Adair. I ain't done nothin' to nobody and I'm scared for my life. What the fuck?!"

"Call her."

"I've tried. It goes straight to voice mail."

"Call Race."

"I tried. His goes to voice mail, too. Something's seriously wrong, Doug."

"It must be. You've never called me Doug before. Vince, level with me. What have you done?"

"Nothing, I swear. I've told you everything."

"Well, it does not add up."

"That's why I gotta talk to Mo, ASAP."

"Dude, you may have to break down and go to the police."

"What are they gonna do?"

"Maybe give you the facts?"

"Adair, they'll think I have something to do with this."

"OK, then hang out here and go crazy. Watch everyone drop like flies and keep wondering why. I don't know what else to tell you."

"You can tell me how to get Mo to answer her damn phone."

"No, buddy, actually, I can't help you with that, either."

"Where is she? She always picks up."

"You know anybody else to call?"

"I've called Race, Mozetta, and even Mel. I can't get in touch with anyone."

"Get a shower and we'll head up to Miami."

"For what?"

"What do you mean, for what? To find your sister, dickface."

"She's not lost, Adair, she just doesn't answer her phone, either."

"Look, we ain't got nothin' to do, and you're goin' crazy around here, so let's hit the road. At least we'll be doing something."

"OK, for some stupid reason, it makes sense. Actually, it makes no sense—which worries me, because it seems logical."

"Shut the fuck up."

Vince laughed. It was the first time he'd actually smiled in a while. "I'm grabbing a shower. When I get done, you need to get one. You stink like shit."

"Because of all the stupid shit that's been coming out of your pie hole …"

"I'll be ready in ten."

Vince made his way to the shower. Much too thick, the air seemed heavy. Taking a deep breath, he stopped for a moment. Looking ahead at an imaginary target, he exhaled. *I'm about to step in front of a freakin' locomotive … I can feel it. I just hope to God the impact isn't any worse than the anticipation …*

***

"I don't get it. Why don't you want to call the police? That guy is deranged—he's going to kill someone!"

"No he's not."

"What?! He pulled a gun on us for Christ's sake!"

"Just so you know, I really hate that expression. The man pulled a gun on us for intimidation purposes, Ray. God doesn't murder people."

"You're as crazy as he is! You can't stand here now and tell me you weren't scared out of your wits."

"Yeah, I was, but I caught on to his hidden meanings and veiled references."

"Delia, what on earth happened between there and here? That guy's a lunatic. He's crazy and you're saying he was conveying hidden messages to us?"

"To me, not to you."

"Well, enlighten me, because I'm dying to know."

"That's pretty much the case."

Standing speechless, Ray said nothing else.

Delia turned from him and headed toward the bedroom. "Follow me if you really want to know."

Looking around the room, he exhaled. After a moment he shrugged his shoulders in defeat. "OK … whatever …" He then began to walk toward the bedroom as well.

You'll understand a lot more about Tim after tonight, Ray. Too bad it's knowledge that neither of us asked for. We'll have an eternity to ponder it, though. Maybe we'll understand 'why' by then.

***

Mozetta had begun the ritual in a manner that allowed the incantation to proceed in the usual order. With Thelma Blankenship once again concluding the ritual, all of them recited the spell in French. As each stanza was spoken, the room became progressively darker. With each passing verse, the candles in the Star of David configuration increased in brilliance. Finally, as the conclusion arrived, much like beacons at sea, they were stellar in their optical illuminations.

Mozetta began. "We can open our eyes, now."

As the seven began to do so, the ambient temperature began to plummet. The room was so dark, that the burning candles were the only thing visible around them. "Don't move. Somethin's not right."

Suddenly, as if riding on a wave of torrential proportions, a blistering hot wind enveloped them. The magnitude of the gust was unnatural; many of the women lost their balance.

"Don't move!" Mo shouted again.

Leaving them in total darkness, the candles were subsequently extinguished.

"Oh my God!" Arletha exclaimed. "This is not right, Mo, this ain't right at all!"

The wind increased in intensity. The table containing the configuration was then toppled.

"The salt circle, Mo … it's gone! It's been blown away! How could that be?"

Mo looked behind her. Illuminated some kind of way, the window beneath which Ariel was sitting stood open. The drapes adorning it billowed furiously in the hot breeze. Mo swallowed hard. She closed her eyes and began again. "Jesus in Heaven help us … she's done tricked us. The room wasn't sealed, ladies; the window is open. She somehow must have sneaked around and opened it during the ritual."

Thema looked up. "And what does that mean, Mo?"

"It means we're at the mercy of Hell now, Ladies, as our circle of protection dissipated with the wind."

Arletha put both hands on her hips. "Since you was so all up in it, what do you have to say now, Yo' Highness, Mozetta'?"

"Nothin' except may the Lord have mercy on our souls, 'cause we're gonna need it, Arlie!"

The wind began to recede. As it did so, the inky black darkness began to lift. Suddenly, once again the starburst appeared.

"Where's the window?"

Mo looked toward the wall. "I do not know. It has disappeared." She began to look at her surroundings and walked about a bit. She then turned to the others. "We're in that warehouse."

Edith stepped toward her. "I recognize this. It's the same place as before. Hell is a warehouse, Mo."

"It's only a perception, Edith. Remember, ladies, this is not real."

Verdiasee turned toward Mozetta. "Close the incantation, Mo! Close it now and get us out of here!"

"Can't do it, it'll trap us here forever."

"Then let's all say the Apostle's Creed. That worked last time!"

"And that won't help, 'cause there ain't nobody on the other side. We're all here, this time …"

"Then what do we do?"

Mozetta turned toward all of them. Her face solemn, she quietly answered, "We wait for Solange."

CHAPTER NINETEEN

The Overseas Highway gives way to some of the most spectacular scenery on earth. Towering over miles of rich, vibrant, turquoise-infused ocean, long span bridges link the lower Keys together. Some of the most magnificent sunsets on earth can be viewed in the lower Keys of Florida. Trailing away from the tip of the state, this small dribble of land gives rise to a unique ecosystem of animals and plants long sequestered from the rest of the world.

As a brash, foreign ringtone began to emanate frantically from his pants pocket, Vince's train of thought was broken.

"Damn. What did you download here? Music from Hell?"

Turning toward him, Doug addressed the comment. "Once again, I'll remind you about beggars being choosers. Either answer it or push the 'F-YOU' button."

The remark brought forth a laugh. "Do they really call it that?"

"Answer it!"

"OK, OK!" He then pushed the button which housed the illuminated green phone. "This is Vince."

"¡Cuñato!"

Brother-in-law?! All of a sudden I'm family? "Hey, Tomas … kind of ironic that you called …"

"Why is that?"

"We're headed your way."

"Thank God."

Thank God? "OK, that's it. What's up? You're never this nice to me. Are you dying and don't want to go to Hell?"

"Cut the crap, Vince. I got a situation here."

"What now?"

"Have you heard from your sister? I can't seem to find her. She won't answer her cell, either."

Shifting in his seat, he continued. "That's strange … I talked to her earlier and told her to call you."

"Really?"

"Yep, I did. That Daria Landry chick was over there." Pausing, he unscrewed the cap of his water bottle. Taking a long drink, he exhaled. "You know, Tomas, that woman creeps me out. I can't put my finger on why, but she does. I told Shelley it might be a good idea to call and ask that you turn around."

"I heard none of that; she never called me. All I got was a text message with your new number. To make matters worse, there's all kind of weird shit on my kitchen table."

"Weird shit? Like what?"

"Candles and salt."

"Maybe they made some Margaritas?"

"Zip it, Vince. This wasn't no party. Tenemos una problema y yo sospecho el situación es muy mal."

"Stop jumping to conclusions Tomas and bring it back to English. I always know you're panicking when you dive off into that shit. Don't create a problem and a horrible situation. They come by themselves without our inventing them."

"I'm telling you something's bad wrong, cuñato. How far are you from me?"

"Depending on traffic, about an hour forty-five. We can't speed; you know how they patrol this son of a bitch."

"Get here as soon as you can. You have to help me figure out what to do."

"If something is up, Tomas, the police won't touch it for forty-eight hours."

"I ain't waiting no forty-eight hours, cuñato. I'm gonna get this straight tonight."

"OK, OK, we'll do it. I'll say it again, don't panic, man, just keep trying to call her. I'll do the same. I'll see you in a few."

"OK, my brother. Nos vemos."

"Nos vemos, Tomas. Hasta pronto."

Before he began, Doug waited for Vince to put his cellular device away.

"'Sup?"

"Don't know, but it doesn't sound good. Tomas can't find Shelly … And I get the feeling we're bonding here."

"She's probably at the grocery store or something. What's wrong with that?"

"What's wrong with that is I told her to call Tomas and tell him to get his ass home. I don't trust that Daria Landry. I got a bad feeling about her. And unless Shelley got locked in the store freezer, she ought to answer her cell phone—if indeed she is at the grocery store."

"Maybe we need to drop by Daria's before heading to your sister's."

"Or maybe when we get to Miami, if we can't get hold of my sister, we need to pick up Tomas and pay Daria a little visit. Then we can decide if we need to call the police."

"Shit …"

"Yeah, I know. The fucking plot thickens."

"And I don't like your story, man. I was just down here in the Keys minding my own business."

"Shut your face, Adair. You're supposed to be my friend."

"I don't remember reciting 'till death do us part', Vince. I don't like you like that. I'd rather remain in one piece, and that's becoming increasingly questionable these days."

"Especially in the next hour if you don't put a lid on it … Just try to drive with your mouth closed. That way, I won't have to endure anymore of your shit."

"How about I throw your ass out and go home? That would accomplish the same thing."

"OK, you win. You win, you win, you mother-fucking win! Just drive, Adair."

"Such language …"

"I'm gonna shoot your ass if you don't leave me alone."

"Alright, buddy, don't shoot. Let's try and chill out. You'll laugh about this when we get to Shelly's."

"Good, I hope so. In the mean time, quit aggravating me."

"It's my job."

"Then you're fired, asshole."

✳✳✳

She loved uptown New Orleans. The architecture there was like no other. Delia had always imagined that one day she would marry and spend the rest of her life in the Lower Garden District. She'd raise her family in one of those beautiful double-gallery style homes.

How ironic that her destructive nemesis lived in just such a house. The very being that destroyed her reality was living her fantasy existence.

The Joubert residence was nothing short of magnificent. Situated one house off of St. Charles, one could peer through the window and watch the street cars of the Avenue clatter past.

With the galleries tastefully painted a contrasting white, the exterior of the home was light cream. Ornate moldings, architectural trim and carvings decorated the soffit of the structure, while an elaborate entablature served as the perfect pedestal backdrop for the demilune capital. All in all, the structure personified the definition of good taste.

Almost trancelike she stood staring at the house.

You bastard ... you murderous bastard!

He was right, and as he'd predicted, she'd taken her first one. Just like her, poor Ray has no idea what has befallen him. He'll learn soon enough, though. In order to help guide Ray, she must first learn from Joubert. Hopefully, he won't make the same mistake as she. Had she listened to her perpetrator, she may not have taken a life; it is possible to maintain immortal existence by taking just a bit of life force from each individual. True, this turns one into a sexual whore—not by free will of course, but out of necessity. In her situation, however, a promiscuous survival is morally justified over the taking—or more accurately described as an obliteration of mortality. If not depleted too severely, the life force will somewhat regenerate.

A moment after she'd rung the doorbell, he appeared. After opening the tall, heavy door, he stepped aside.

"I knew you'd come."

"Imagine that."

"You've taken your first one, haven't you?"

"Yeah, I have. I have murdered my first one, Thierry. You've taken a perfectly normal girl and turned her into a monster. If I could kill you right now, I would do it. I'd put a gun to your head and blow it off."

"Your boyfriend?"

Delia smiled. The smile vaguely resembled one of pleasant bewilderment, but if examined closely enough, resentment and malice defined the edges. "How'd ya know?"

"You called me Thierry. You've never done that before."

"Well, Thierry, the playing field is kinda level now, isn't it? No more need for formalities. Also, since you've taken any semblance of life independence away from me, the need for civility has reared its ugly head."

He smiled. "So now we're friends?"

"If there is a way to destroy you and send you packing straight to Hell, I'll find it. In the mean time, I have to rely on you as a mentor of sorts. Boggles the mind, doesn't it? It's just amazing how far we are from Brigtsen's."

"I apologize for that, Delia. I'd gotten too far."

"Doesn't matter now … two more down and a world full of brimming life to go …"

He chuckled. "We do have an ample supply of spiritual nutriment, don't we?"

She stepped forward. "Thierry, I'm gonna find a way to undo this. I realize I'm dead and don't mind moving on. That being said, I want you to know I didn't sign up to be a dark world parasite. I won't go through eternity destroying innocent lives."

"You no longer have a choice. If you're careful as well as judicious, Delia, you can minimize this. Sooner or later, though, you'll have to imbibe a total life force to sustain yourself."

As he finished the sentence, she became aware of an injury to the palms of her hands. Inadvertently, she'd clinched her fists so hard that she had drawn blood.

Thierry's eyes fell to the injury. "You may want to be careful. Injuries like that require more precious energy to heal. You'll be taking much sooner if you don't watch out."

"Acting as if you actually care makes me so want to cut your guts out. Keep your jaded compassion away from me; it sickens me. I want to vomit. I came here to learn, so I need you to talk. I need you to teach me as I now have someone I must help avoid a feral existence."

"Go get him, Delia. I'll teach you both. I'll help you; it's the least I could do."

Listen to what you just said. It's the least you could do? You will realize this regret for the rest of your existence, Joubert. You brought over the wrong person this time. Just you wait and see …

✶✶✶

Sunday, May 8, 1932

"We're downtown in some city. The sign says Second Street. Looks like a movie set or somethin'. Old cars, building styles …"

"Pierre, get yo' face back in here. Are you crazy? You have no idea what's out there!"

"Just lookin' so we can get a handle on the situation, Mo."

Thelma crept past Pierre. "Well I do say." She turned to face the others. "This can't be. I recognize this place, and it still looks exactly the same."

Mo stepped forward. "You do?"

"My mother used to bring me here as a little girl. I had an aunt who lived here. People, if I didn't know better, I'd say we're in Memphis, Tennessee."

Coretta then took a step forward. "What on earth? How did we get all the way to Memphis?"

Mo turned to face them. "We ain't on earth, and we ain't in Memphis, neither. I have told you both that this is a depiction; it ain't real."

After she'd said this, Thelma gently pushed the door shut. She then turned toward the rest of them. "Well, the depiction sho' looks like Memphis."

Lost a moment in thought, Pierre began. "Thelma, how old are you, anyway. This looks like a long time ago. You couldn't have been around back then."

"You forget I'll make eighty-six this year."

"For real?"

"Mmm-hmm. Lord knows I got all the aches and pains to prove it."

Putting her hand on her hip once again, Arletha assumed her customary stance. "Well, I guess we weren't all dealt the same deck of cards. I'll never make it to eighty six and I sure won't be in yo' kind of shape if I happen to."

Thelma smiled. "You never know, Arlie ..."

Suddenly, they were startled by a presence behind them. At the top of a stairway stood a woman. Dressed in ordinary, modern day clothing, the woman paused a moment before she began her descent.

Squinting as she watched the woman move closer to them, Mozetta realized the person walking toward her looked familiar. Racking her brain in an attempt to remember where before she'd seen her, Mo studied her features. The woman had shoulder length brown hair, brown eyes and fair skin. Her face had a familiar fullness about the cheek area that she already knew so well; at some point in time their paths must have crossed. She was ordinary, though, and there was nothing particularly striking about her. Strangely enough, something about the way she carried herself brought with it an air of intense familiarity.

Mo took one small step toward the stairway. "Stop right there. If you value your existence, don't move any closer to us. I'm only going to ask you this one time and I suggest you give me yo' best answer. You are standin' in front of a pretty powerful crew here, lady, and believe me, looks can be deceiving. Who are you?"

As Mo accosted her, the lady stopped where she stood. Her lip began to quiver. "I ... I'm Shelley Levy, and I have no idea how I got here."

"Who did you say you were?"

"You don't know me. I'm from Miami, Florida. My name is Shelley Levy and this has to be some sort of dream … or nightmare."

"Well it ain't no dream, baby, that's for sure. Now whether or not it's a nightmare? Well, that's debatable. And I think you're wrong, Shelley Levy, I may just know you. In fact, not too terribly long ago, I may have talked to you. Now I know why you look so familiar. You're Vince's sister, aren't you?"

Shelley stood stunned. "Who are you? How do you know my brother? This is crazy … I think I'm going to faint."

"Get down those damn stairs before you do. Hurry up!"

"You told me not to move. You threatened me if I moved; I'm not going anywhere."

"That was then before I knew who—or what—you were. Come down here baby, you're among friends."

Gingerly, she began her descent.

"Don't fall and for God's sake don't pass out!"

Shelley finished the stairs and made her way to the group. "Who are you people? What am I doing here?"

"Well, we're a group from New Orleans who has a specific purpose for being here. The real question is why you are here?"

"I think an acquaintance of mine has drugged me or something and I'm not able to awaken. This makes no sense. The last thing I remember was Daria reciting some sort of protective spell in French and the room went dark. And then there was this bright starburst of light …"

"Baby girl I know the next name fixin' to fly out of yo' face is not Daria Landry? You better tell me right fast that's not what it is."

"You know her, too? What did you say your name was again?"

"I didn't. It's Mozetta Conerly, and this is my husband Pierre."

"Mo?!? Vince's Mo? Are you serious?"

"As a heart attack. If I could get my hands on Daria right now, I think I'd rip her face off. That damn girl causes our group more grief than you know. Ever watch old shows on television?"

"Sometimes … I mean I have before, why?"

"Step a little closer, baby and let me fill you in on this." In an attempt to close a bit of the distance, Mo also took a step toward her. "You see, Shelley, Daria Landry has been branded sort of the 'Aunt Clara' of the Voodoo world. She knows just enough to literally wreak havoc wherever she goes—and always manages to do so."

Making sure there was sufficient eye contact between them, she continued. "There is no tellin' how many people she's inadvertently exiled to other dimensions, and the powers that be always look to our group to try and straighten her messes out. I've warned that fool a dozen times to stay out of our business, but for some reason—one that I cannot begin to understand—she thinks she's one of us. I am sure, once again, that she was tryin' to help."

"She's also the one that gave me that book to give to Vince."

"Now that was not necessarily a bad thing. But this— sending you into the depths of Hell—was not a good thing, baby. You ain't prepared for it, and neither are we. We represent the perfect number of seven, and how in the world we're gonna fight this demon with eight of us is beyond me."

"What?"

"Solange, baby. You and I are in Solange's territory. This is her eternal punishment—her own version of Hell."

"I have to be unconscious. I've been drugged. Maybe before I die, my husband will find me in time…"

"I doubt that. You ain't there no more, and even if he could find you, there ain't a damn thing he could to do help you, Shelley."

"So what do I do, Mo? Wait to die?"

Mo looked down at the floor. "Maybe … maybe so. Unfortunately for you, the only one who has a chance of salvaging yo' soul is Daria. Now ain't that a fine how do you do? The clumsiest paranormal on earth is responsible for yo' rescue."

Shelley began to cry.

"Now, now, don't cry, baby. You got seven of us here to try and help you, and at least for now, you're one of us. Stick close to us, for the worst is yet to come."

"How could it possibly get any worse? I'm in freaking limbo …"

"How could it get worse? You ain't in limbo, baby; that's purgatory and that is God's country. At the risk of repeating myself, I'm gonna tell you this one more time: it gets worse, Shelley Levy, because Daria Landry has done sent yo' ass to Hell. That's how it gets worse."

CHAPTER TWENTY

"I say before we head over to your sister's house we pay Ms. Landry a visit."

"GPS says to turn here."

"She must live in this cul-de-sac."

"Looks like a pretty normal place to me. No ghosts, goblins or scary figures peering at us from the upstairs window."

"Maybe that's because there is no upstairs window, you idiot?"

"Vince, do we just park in her driveway?"

"You got a garage door opener?"

"It's been a long four hours, Vince. I don't need a smartass. "

"Well, I just had a brainstorm. Why don't you park out front and then we'll simply knock on the front door, Adair?"

"Because we'll block the other driveways, dickhead, so I'm parking in her driveway."

"Looks to me like you could have saved yourself a lot of breath on that one."

"If you don't shut up, you're gonna quit breathing. Now knock on the freakin' door and quit giving me a hard time."

Revealing a woman who may be described as Bohemian at best, the door slowly opened. In front of him was a girl with long brown hair. Adorned with a large, golden, peace sign necklace, she was wearing a multi-colored, floor length handkerchief hem dress. A braided leather headband encircled her forehead, and her feet were clad in sandals.

Taken aback, Vince paused for a moment. "Daria?"

"Yes ... Do I know you?"

"Well, I can honestly say your acting leaves a lot to be desired."

"I'm sorry?"

"You know damn well who I am."

Daria put her hand to her chest. Spreading her fingers in a fanlike manner, she began again. "I'm sorry again, but I honestly have no idea what you're talking about. I don't mean to be rude, sir, but I'm extremely busy right now." She began to close the door.

Blocking the closure, Vince stepped into the doorway.

"Where's my sister, Daria?"

"Your sister?"

"Daria, I can tell you right now this isn't going well. It's about to get a whole lot worse if you don't tell me where the fuck my sister is. You got that?"

"I'm about to call the police."

"You do that. You go right ahead and call them, because your ass is about to be the prime suspect in a missing person's case. I'll bet there's enough substantial evidence in there to get the ball rolling. Here, let me call them." Vince began to dial 911 on his cell.

"Wait! Don't do that. I have an explanation."

"Oh you do, do you? Well, I can't wait to hear it. Where's my sister, Daria?"

"I've made some tea. Would you gentlemen like to join me?"

"Oh, sure! As luck would have it, I happen to have crumpets in the car. Tea would be marvelous!"

Pushing her aside as he did so, Vince walked into the house. Looking around as he walked into the room, he noticed the kitchen table in total disarray. "You had a freakin' hurricane in your kitchen, or what? Why is all that shit blown down over there?"

"Oh … please pardon the mess."

"Mind if I come in?"

Both of them turned around to see Adair standing in the doorway. "It's kinda warm out there."

"Oh by all means, please come in."

Vince turned toward her once more. "This ain't no social visit, Daria. Fourth time's the charm. Before I call the cops, where is my sister?"

"Vince, I …"

"Oh, so now you know my name?"

Her shoulders slumped in defeat. "I knew who you were all along. I was hoping I could buy some time to fix this."

"Fix what?"

"Well, Vince …" She hesitated for a moment.

Waiting expectantly for an answer, he finally replied. "Daria, spit it the fuck out, and I mean now. I'm out of patience."

"Vince, I think I've inadvertently sent her away."

"OK, where'd you send her, and why won't she answer her cell?"

"She can't answer it."

Clenching his fists, his face turned scarlet. In a futile attempt to maintain his composure, he took a deep breath. "Daria, what have you done?"

Doug took a step forward. "Easy, man, let's back it down a step. You ain't gonna accomplish nothin' by beating her ass."

Daria swallowed hard. "You'd actually hit me?"

"That and lots more, so you best be finishing your story."

"Vince, I'm kind of an extended member of this group from back home. We have ways that you may not understand of dealing with forces that are … well, for a loss of better terminology, beyond your comprehension."

"How comforting."

"For whatever reason, one such force seems to be after you."

"Solange."

"Yes, Solange. Solange is famous for killing everything around her intended target, first. It's one of her favorite ways to inflict extreme pain and suffering upon her victim."

"And you think Shelley's life was in danger because of Solange's fixation on me?"

"Perhaps."

"So … without consideration that she has a family—a son and a husband—you sent her away? That leads me to the conclusion that you're either dumb as shit, or well … dumb as shit."

"Thank you. I was only trying to help. I was trying to save your sister's life."

"And just how did you accomplish that, Daria?"

"I used a guardian spell and enlisted the protection of the Circle of the Sacred Seven."

"Which means nothing to me."

"Of course it wouldn't. The leader of the Circle of the Sacred Seven is a powerful individual who can help protect Shelley from Solange's demonic influence. Mozetta has been known to stand face to face with her many times."

Lord, oh Lord! All we need is Daria Landry to get up into all this mess. His thoughts momentarily diverted, Vince's attention returned to the present conversation. "You and Mo are pretty tight, huh?"

"Very tight, we're like soul mates."

"Mmm-hmm ... and back to my sister. You're saying she just left here after the spell?"

"I'm not sure. Things got kind of hairy; the room became very dark and this incredible wind came out of nowhere. As you can see, everything was knocked over and blown around. The last thing I remember was this brilliant starburst—a tremendous flash of lightning—and then all was silent again. It took a moment to catch my breath, and I asked Shelley if she were alright. She didn't answer."

"Why not?"

"She must have left. I looked for here everywhere and have yet to find her."

"So she left without saying goodbye or anything?"

"Yes, and I'm not sure that she would have been able to."

Doug stepped forward. "You must have really scared the hell out of her."

"Or you're fucking lying."

"I'm not lying, Vince. Everything I've told you is the truth."

"Daria, how'd you get her over here, anyway? I was on the phone with her when you arrived."

"I explained to her just how grave your situation was and the means I had available to help you. I also explained to her that she also played a vital role in completion of the protection spell. The more energy one enlists initiating the spell, the more powerful its protective influence will be."

"And she believed that shit and came over to your house?"

"Crudely put, but adequately descriptive, yes, that is what transpired."

"You're story is about as airtight as a piece of Swiss cheese, Daria. I'm headed to my sister's house and she better be there."

"I'll go with you. I want to find her as much as you do."

"Yeah, you do that. You come with us because if you've harmed so much as a hair on her head, I'm gonna rip your fucking scalp off and cram it up your ass. You got that?"

As he finished the statement, Doug stepped in between them. "Shut it, Vince! Get hold of yourself."

"Don't tell me what to do, Adair. Something's wrong here and she's at the bottom of it."

"I've told you all that I know. I could try and do a reversal incantation …"

"Get in the car, Daria. You're explaining this to Tomas. You're gonna tell him everything you've told me."

"I'll take my own car."

"You better get in that damn car before I stuff you in it. I'm not kidding."

Walking toward the door, Daria swallowed hard. She meant well, but had managed to buy herself some trouble this time. Hopefully, before the wrath of Vincent Jacola rained down upon her, she'd be able to straighten it out. Somewhere deep inside, however, she felt it was already too late.

✳✳✳

"They're all gone."

"Of course, Ariel, what would you expect?"

"Solange, I have no idea. I'm not really even sure what has transpired here. I simply did what you asked and opened that window. Beyond that, I'm clueless."

"That may actually be a good thing. If they make it back at all, which I doubt will come to pass, it will not be for some time. You have some breathing room to look around and find an item that I would much like to again have in my possession. It's not that I need it, of course, but it is something I'd rather keep out of the grasp of certain individuals."

"What is it?"

"I'm almost one hundred percent certain Mozetta has a gold coin in her possession that could prove to be a nuisance for me. If you could look around and find it, it would be appreciated."

"Is it money? Jewelry? Or what?"

"It's a 1907 twenty dollar gold piece. The piece has a tremendous energy signal that I doubt you'll recognize. In the wrong hands, however, it may prove quite powerful."

"You have no idea where it may be?"

"None. Take some time and have a look around here. You may run across it. If by chance you do, bring it to me immediately."

"OK … feels kind of strange rummaging through these people's home. You're sure I won't get caught for trespassing or stealing? Robbery carries a pretty serious charge around these parts, Solange."

"I assure you that you will not be discovered searching this house. You have my word on that."

"A new adventure every day … well, I guess there's no time like the present to get started."

As she finished the sentence, she looked around the room and contemplated where to begin. Suddenly conscious of the fact that she was now alone, she became aware that she had not even realized Solange's departure. *I swear that woman materializes out of nowhere and then fades like some kind of Houdini. She literally disappears into thin air!* Feeling a pang of conscience, for a moment she contemplated what she'd done. *Surely those old ladies would be OK … surely she'd caused them no harm.* Ariel then took a tissue and wiped the perspiration from her forehead. *It's gotten warm in here. Looks like I need to turn the thermostat down before I start this search.* She then made her way toward the hallway. Lowering the thermostat, she decided to begin her search in the kitchen. As she started to walk in that direction, with a loud, sudden thump the lights went out. *Oh great … a transformer must have blown ... exactly what I need while milling around a strange house.* Having no windows, the hallway was dark. Using her left hand as a guide, Ariel leaned against the wall. She made her way out of the hallway and up toward the kitchen area.

Perhaps it was the color that caught her eye, or maybe it was the movement. At the same time she saw this, the realization that the house was unbearably hot took shape. The air filling with smoke, she attempted to process what was happening. *The house is on fire ...* Becoming thick, breathing was now difficult.

How to get out?

Ariel stumbled to the other side of the structure. Her movements were now awkward and clumsy as oxygen levels were greatly depleted. She spied a vent near the floor. In hopes of gaining precious oxygen, she knelt down by it and drew deeply . While almost prostrate on the floor, and so intent on drawing a breath, she did not hear the raspy, forlorn resignation of the rafters as their charred members came crashing toward her. It was OK, though, she'd decided that sleep would be the best medicine. At this moment, an altered state of consciousness would be the best modality of escape.

The shrill whine of the fire engines was welcome, but too late as the structure was completely engulfed. She was safe, though, for she'd risen high above the restaurant. As the topography exponentially diminished, barely could she see the bustle of activity in the neighborhood. She was good, and everything would be fine. Hopefully she had not caused harm to Mozetta and the others, and she would be forgiven for her recent actions. Boundless love and forgiveness were her only hope for salvation; she must ask and pray that it is now not too late.

CHAPTER TWENTY-ONE

By now, things had gotten pretty bad. My sister was missing, I couldn't get in touch with anyone back home, and a neighbor had called with the news that Boliviee's had burned to the ground. In hopes that she was OK, frantically, I dialed Mo's cell. I did not have the luxury of reassurance on that one, however, for she never answered. Where was Race? Where was Shelley and where was Mel? I have not done a damn thing to anyone, and, like a house of cards, my whole life was collapsing around me. I don't understand this. Why me? I'm a nothing … a nobody.

Vince paced back and forth across the room.

My Aunt Frances always said, 'prior planning pays.' I have to do some 'prior planning' on this one. First order of business is to find my sister. I'll break this news to Tomas and hope he doesn't break Daria's freaking head. Right now, all I need is his Latin temper to get out of hand. Then, on to the police … they should be able to help. They should be able to sift through this hocus pocus bullshit of Daria's and help me find what she's done with her.

I have to get in touch with Mel and find out what has happened to Boliviee's. My only hope and prayer is that Mo was not in that restaurant when it burned.

If 'prior planning' really pays, after this I should be freakin' rich!

✳✳✳

"My little 'auburn hottie' is lookin' good!"

"Tom, when did you start using descriptives like 'auburn hottie'?"

"Dunno. It just came to me. Maybe it goes with the territory?"

"Perhaps … Let's hope that's a plausible explanation."

"Come here. I wanna get my sex thing on!"

"While vaguely intriguing, you may want to remember your new station in this existence. You'd waste a lot of valuable life force on that useless expedition and not accomplish a thing."

"What do you mean, not accomplish a thing? We used to rock together."

"I'm extremely pleased that I managed to evade tendencies to use current slang when making the transition, however, I'm quite annoyed that you were not so successful. Do you think it may be possible to use a modicum of proper English as well as grammar, or did that imbecile you managed to overtake lack even a scrap of civilized behavior?"

"I just want your body right now."

"Then all of the information after the conjunction in my previous statement answers my seemingly rhetorical question."

"Is that a yes, or a no?"

"While you're contemplating a response to hopeful fulfillment of your basic needs, I have more important matters to attend to."

"Like what? What could be more important than me getting in your pants, Solange?"

"One last piece of this puzzle."

"I don't get it."

"You don't?"

"Have no idea what the hell you're referring to."

"Once again, I'll have to spell it out for you."

"Don't make it sound so bad, baby. We work good together!"

"I've managed to get rid of Mozetta Conerly and her ridiculous cohorts. We've taken care of that Ariel loophole, and also any parenthetical material adrift in that godforsaken Miami, Florida."

"You don't like Miami?"

"Which is absolutely irrelevant to this conversation. Pay attention, Tom. The last piece of this pesky puzzle to which we must tend is Vincent Jacola."

"That fat dude?"

"It has to be leftover personality imprints. You'd have never appeared this stupid before … a little crude, maybe, but not airhead stupid."

"Thanks for the compliment, baby. How would you describe him?"

"I'm not at all interested in a physical description, Tom. I just want him eliminated. In that way, the last loose end of this pathetic scenario will be tended."

"Ok, how do you want me to kill him?"

"It really makes no difference how you do away with him, just don't get caught. Don't be sloppy and don't leave a trail."

"I never do."

"I won't bother to dissect that last statement and explain to you how ignorant you sound. Just do as I say. We don't want any confusion. Need I remind you of Heloise Pullman?"

"I will say this one more time. She was wearing a fucking apron with the name Ruby on it. I didn't know the woman, Solange. You'd have drawn the same conclusion."

"Now, instead of some present day slang slinging idiot, you're sounding like the man I once knew."

"Where is fat dude?"

"I spoke too soon."

"As if again asking the question, Tom raised his eyebrows."

"Presently, I detected his energy signature in Miami."

"So you want me to go to the shithole to do your dirty work …"

"If you like, you can have that. I won't argue."

"OK. I'll look him up. Got some info on him?"

"I have everything you need."

Tom arose and walked over to the armoire. Opening it, he then grabbed his leather bag. "Get your affairs in order, fat boy, D-Day is fast approaching."

✳✳✳

Briefly, Coretta walked out of the warehouse and into the street. "Well I do say …"

Mozetta grabbed at the back of her dress. "Get yo' ass back in here! You were around back then and well remember what it was like. Do you really think you need to go cavorting about in the streets of some strange rural town?"

"You said it wasn't real."

"I said it was a depiction, and probably an accurate one at that. You can for sure get yo' butt killed here, Retta, bank on that."

"So what do we do? Sit in here and starve to death?"

"Retta, you ever watched that movie about that young girl who realized she wasn't in Kansas anymore?"

"Mo, there ain't a child in this country that ain't seen that movie. What I'm tryin' to figure out now is what that has to do with anything?"

"You remember that beautiful good witch that always came through when things were really bad?"

"Yeah, I remember her."

"Well, it's kind of like that for us. Even though we're in a bad way, the good Lord is always peekin' over our shoulders. Why do you think Shelley is here?"

Arletha stepped forward. "Because Daria Landry is stupid, that's why."

Shelley chuckled. "Glad to know I'm stupid mistake."

"Ain't nothin' against you, honey, but all of us well know about that bumblin' nuisance. Look what she's gone and done to you. You don't even know where the hell you are right now—no pun intended."

Mozetta continued. "But this may be a diamond in the rough. Shelley can help us, Arlie. What Solange did not count on was this." Mozetta pulled the gold coin from her pocket. "This is our ticket to freedom and also our leveling the playing field. I bet Solange has been racking her brain trying to find this coin. This, ladies and gentlemen this is our ticket home."

"Sounds good to me."

Mozetta began to pull bobby pins from her hair. "Shelley, you and I are about the same size. Now I'm gonna look ridiculous in that short skirt, but I ain't goin' nowhere, anyway." Handing her the bobby pins, she began again. "Pull yo hair back and pin it up."

Shelley took the pins. "OK …"

"This plain, white dress should not stand out too much. I tend to wear my dresses mid-calf, baby. Momma said I never did have pretty legs."

Pierre stepped forward. "I don't know about that. Yo' momma got on my nerves, sometimes. I think my baby's got some hot lookin' legs."

Mo smiled. "And just what do you want?"

Pierre answered with nothing more than a wink.

"Anyway, Shelley, I'm gonna need some supplies to get us out of here. The sooner we escape, the safer we will be. You're gonna have to find a store, get the supplies and not be conspicuous about it. You think you can do that?"

"No, I don't."

"Well, you're gonna have to."

"And just what am I going to buy these supplies with?"

Edith stepped forward. "I just happen to have some money in my pocket. Here, baby, here's forty-three dollars."

"Umm, Mrs. Edith, have you by any chance checked the date on that money? It's pretty much play money in this date and time."

Her mouth slightly open, Edith stood nonplussed.

"Shelley, were you listenin' to me a few minutes ago?" She then held up the coin. "Have you checked the date on this one, baby? Seems to me it says, 1907."

Shelley stood silent.

"Now, it may attract a little attention, but here it is definitely legal tender. Twenty dollars should well buy the few supplies that I'll need."

Thelma interrupted. "What about the protective circle? We have no Sea of Galilee salt?"

Putting her hand on her hip, she began. "Thelma, we're in Hell. We're a little post-protection, don't you think?"

"Well now you know, I had not thought of it that way."

"It's OK, baby. I appreciate the good intentions."

Shedding her dress, Mo handed it to her. "Put this on, and let me borrow yo' clothes. I'm gonna' make you out a list of exactly what I need. Get back here as soon as you can and let's get ourselves out of this place."

"Don't we want to bring Solange back here?"

"At this moment, she has us over a barrel, Shelley. We are extremely vulnerable. We need to get home to our resources before we tackle that. One thing at a time, honey, and for now, it is self-preservation."

"This dress fits pretty well."

"Take off them stilettos. Anybody got some flats on?"

"What size do you wear?"

Shelley turned to answer Arletha. "I wear an eight."

"These don't have much heel, but I wear a ten."

Walking over to Shelley, Thelma began. "Try these, sweetheart. I wear an eight. These are 'old lady shoes,' but hopefully they'll do for a little while."

"Black patent leather shoes with a white cotton dress … I guess apparently having no taste really makes no difference …"

Mo began again. "It's all we have, Shelley. My momma wore clothes made out of flour sacks. Wasn't no fashion wars back then. You wore what you could get. It ain't gonna matter here. Folks were poor and times were hard."

"You don't look too back in a short skirt, Mo."

"You're just delirious, baby. Here, take this list and be on yo' way. Hurry back and don't talk to no one if you don't have to. This is a small town, and folks are gonna be nosey."

"What do I say if someone asks me?"

"Just tell them you're passin' through. Tell 'em yo' folks were briefly in Memphis years ago and always loved this place. Tell 'em they went on and on about how beautiful it was, and you just had to see what they raved about. Then tell them yo' folks were right and that this is just as beautiful as they described it. Watch yo' language, honey, and try not to use any slang. Speak proper and use the words they use. Above all, make no more conversation than you have to. Tell 'em that coin was yo' mama's and she wanted you to spend it here because that's where she got it. That will explain using such old currency."

"Wow … that's a lot of information."

"Just do the best you can, Shelley. If you mess up, hopefully I can get us out of here in time!"

"Zip me up, Mo. Zip me up and wish me luck."

"Oh my stars and garters …."

"What's wrong now?"

"I'm not sure zippers were invented yet. Back then dresses had buttons."

Coretta interrupted. "Some of the real uppity clothes had them. I remember seeing that in a magazine."

"Mainstream clothing, Rhetta, do any of us look uppity?"

"Well all we can do is hope that no one notices, huh? None of us here have a dress with buttons."

"Yeah, you right, and maybe it'll be OK. At any rate, we might as well get this over with, so good luck, baby. God be with you."

"I sure hope so …"

"Remember that movie, honey, and that he's always right around the corner lookin' after you. He ain't gonna leave you in this place; you do not belong here." *And I'm gonna put who does belong here in this place real soon. Enjoy yo' vacation from Hell, Solange, 'cause yo' break from the heat is fast comin' to a close … real fast!*

✳✳✳

Shelley eased through the door of the warehouse. A warm, humid gust of wind assured her she was close to a river. *Wherever I am, I'm downtown.* She began to walk up the street. Minding their business, scads of people were bustling about. *How would I go about asking someone where I am without appearing to be a nutcase?*

She walked several blocks before happening upon a hotel.

The Peabody … I've heard of this place. Something about hotel ducks in the lobby? Suddenly, it occurred to her. *Memphis, Tennessee … I'm in some time-warped Memphis, Tennessee.* Pausing for a moment in front of the hotel door, in hopes of the clerk steering her toward a pharmacy, she decided to enter.

As she opened the brass laden hotel doors, the first thing to catch her attention was a rich, highly polished floor of marble. Her mouth dropped in amazement. *Oh my God, this place is incredible!*

Her eyes them followed the room. Obviously, no detail had been left untended. Elaborately carved stained wooden beams partitioned the ceilings, finally giving rise to wall-mounted marble columns. Intricate hand painted moldings framed these partitions, making every ceiling square a literal work of art.

So beautiful, and so thick with European influence...

Vizcaya then came to mind. *Mr. Deering would have loved this place.*

She took a left and made her way across a vast, expansive lobby. As she did so, she passed the famous, elaborate fountain to which the Peabody ducks called home. *And I thought we had lush architecture in Miami ...*

Her sojourn across this vast expanse terminated at the reservations desk. As she approached, a man standing behind it ceased writing.

His eyes traveling the length of her person, he managed to have a good look at her before he began. "Good afternoon, and welcome to the Peabody."

Nervously smoothing the back her hair, Shelly managed a reply. "Wh ... Why ..." Swallowing hard, she took a deep breath. "Why, thank you."

"Do you have a reservation?"

"No, I do not. Actually, I just need some directions. See, um, I'm not from here and really need to find a pharmacy."

"Are you ill?"

"No ... no, I'm not ill. I just need some ..."

In anticipation of her completed statement, the clerk's eyebrows remained raised.

"I just need various sundries in order to complete a project."

Taking a deep breath, she attempted once more. "I'm sorry. What I meant to say was in order to complete a project, I'll need various and sundry items."

His brow furrowed. "You did."

"I'm sorry?"

"You just said that."

"Right. I … I did just say that. So … if you'll just point me in the direction of the pharmacy, I'll be on my way and out of yours."

"Ma'am, you're not from here, are you?"

"I think we've already established that."

"I can't quite put my finger on your accent. Where are you from, actually?"

And I'm having a hard time discerning either why you care or what business it is of yours …

"Originally from Louisiana, but I've lived in Miami for many years, now."

"So far from home."

You really have no idea how far. "So, so you think you may have those directions?"

"I don't mean to pry, but if you do not need prescriptions filled, at the intersection of Union and Front, there is a Piggly Wiggly grocery store. It's just a few blocks from here. Tell you what, in a few minutes I'll be on break and could accompany you there. In some small way, some help from a local may indeed be beneficial."

You're kidding. She tried her best not to roll her eyes. "Oh, that's not necessary but thank you."

"Well, feel free to return if you do not find your way."

"You've been most kind."

"My pleasure." He returned his attention to his desk and again began writing.

Shelley turned and made her way toward the front of the hotel. As she passed through the main doorway, she paused. "I wonder which way is front street … right, or left?"

"Left."

Abruptly, she turned to face the voice. Smiling and standing in front of her was the hotel clerk.

"My heavens! You startled me!"

"Forgive me, as it was the furthest from my intentions."

"You're British?"

"Originally from Gloucester, but I've been in the states some thirty years, now."

"Well, thank you so much, and I'll … just … I'll just head to the supermarket now."

"I thought you needed to go to Piggly Wiggly?"

"That's where I'm headed."

"No, you mentioned some other market."

Damn …

As he stood there speechless, she took a deep breath and attempted to begin again. "It's just some slang I picked up from my kids. I meant the grocery store."

"Oh … I see. Say, would you be offended if I walked over there with you? I have a bit of shopping to do myself."

"Oh, OK. I guess that would be OK." *Like I need some 1930's hotel guy hitting on me right now."*

"You know this is one of the first self serve grocery stores around."

"Really? How interesting."

"Yes, it was built—let's see if I remember right—I think around fifteen or sixteen."

"As in 1900?!"

He smiled. "None other."

"So that would be about …" Shelley hesitated.

"Sixteen years ago."

"Right! Sixteen years ago because this is 1932, right?"

"Ah, a mathematician …" He laughed aloud. "I'm Albert, by the way, Albert Janway."

"Encantado. I'm Shelley Levy."

"I'm sorry?"

"Oh, forgive me, it's a habit. That's Spanish for pleased to meet you, Sir."

"Call me Bert."

"OK … sure, Bert."

"Here, let me open the door for you. Could I possibly help you find anything? This is a different concept of a store, you know."

"I see that. Well, Bert, here is my list. If you think you may be able to quickly put your hands on some of this stuff, I'm all about asking for help."

Albert perused the list. "Hmm … shouldn't be too complicated. Let's start here in the back of the store. Grab a basket and I'll help you assemble the items."

"I thought you had shopping to do as well?"

"Oh, not to worry, I'll wedge my tiny little grocery list in between these items. We won't waste a moment. Now follow me and I'll have you set up in no time."

Just so you mean groceries Bert … I don't need any set up other than what's on that paper …

✳✳✳

"I think that's about all." Bert placed the basket onto the wooden counter in front of the cash register. "A rather curious, but ingenuous concept this store is. Who'd have ever thought of a self-serve grocery store?"

Shifting uncomfortably in front of the clerk, she began. "Yeah, Bert … that really is something. I mean it's swell and all …"

Bert chuckled. "Think you have enough candles and salt? Looks like someone may be making ice cream by moonlight."

"How on earth did you know?"

"I have a second sense about these things. I assume you have a strapping fellow to turn the crank?"

"An older gentleman, but yes … strapping …" *whatever in Heaven's name that means …*

The clerk turned to Shelley with the total. As she paid him, Bert's eyed widened.

"Are you absolutely sure?"

"About what?"

"Using that coin. Are you absolutely sure you want to use that gold dollar? It looks rather old."

"Not so old. It's a 1907 twenty dollar gold piece. Besides, it's all the money that I have."

"I see …"

"Well, Bert, it's been a pleasure getting acquainted, but I really must run."

"I understand." He began to say something and then paused. After a moment he began again. "Do you think you might wait for me just a moment outside of the store?"

"Uh, well … I'm not sure that I …"

"No ulterior motive, Shelley, I assure you. I won't take more than a few seconds of your time. If you'll just give me a couple of minutes …"

"I don't understand."

"I know I'm a stranger Shelley, but give me sixty seconds."

A 'no' began to form on her lips.

"Thirty seconds … just one moment is all that I ask."

"OK, Bert, I'll wait a minute or two on you outside of the store. Nothing more … and if this is some kind of trick, I swear I'll scream."

"Nothing like that, I assure you. I'll follow shortly."

Shelley walked from the counter and made her way through the wooden door. The screen door in front of it slammed in echo of her departure. As she held the paper bag with her right arm, she began to count the seconds on her watch. Less than a minute later, Bert exited the store as well.

"Here you go."

"What? What is this?"

"Your twenty dollar gold piece."

"How did you get it? Did you pay for my things?"

"Never mind that, Shelley, I just couldn't let you part with this valuable coin. Not in some neighborhood grocery market."

"Bert … seriously? You don't even know me. I'm a stranger that simply asked for directions. Now you've taken your entire lunch hour to go shopping for candles and salt and then paid for them. What am I missing here? Is this some 1932 pickup tactic? You cannot be that nice."

"If you wish, Shelley, you're entitled to your point of view. I guess I can understand the grounds for suspicion."

"And now we finish as the injured victim? I don't think so. I'm just not buying it."

"No, you're not. I just bought it."

"Bert, I had money and asked you for nothing. I don't mean to be rude, but …"

Bert interrupted. "Well, you are rude. You're extremely rude. With that, I'll make my departure. Sorry to have inconvenienced you."

Shelley stood silent. She could not believe she was now feeling guilty for confronting the advances of a stranger, who thirty three years before she was born, had hit on her. How to comprehend?

"Bert, please stop. I'm sorry. It's just that in Miami, we don't have this kind of southern hospitality. If you say you had no ulterior motive, then I stand corrected. Please accept my apology and sincere thanks for everything you've done to help. Again, I'm sorry."

"No hay problema."

"What did you just say?"

"I, too, speak a little Spanish. I have but a few minutes more if you'd like help carrying your things. If not, I must return to the hotel."

"No, no, I'm fine. Thank you again, and it really was nice meeting you."

"I feel the same." Bert pulled a pencil and a slip of paper from his pocket. He then began to write. "Here is the hotel telephone number and my home number as well. If you have any further problems, don't hesitate to call and I'll do what I can."

"You are too nice. If this is indeed genuine, you are too kind for your own good, Bert Janway."

"Ah, you remembered my name."

"Why wouldn't I?"

"I didn't' think I'd made an impression on you."

"You made an impression. I'm just trying to digest exactly what impression you've left with me. Buena suerte, Bert. I hope all goes well for you, and thank you for buying my things. "

"It was nothing. Until next time, Shelley."

Shelley hesitated. Taking a breath, she opened her mouth to speak and then stopped. She then looked into his eyes with a smile of resignation. "OK, yes, Bert … until next time." With that, she turned and began to walk toward the warehouse.

*** *

"Hey doll."

"How sweet, in a condescending male chauvinist sort of way ... What can I do for you, Sir?"

"I need a plane ticket."

"Well, we're in the business. Where would you like to go?"

"Miami."

"No problem. We have direct flights from New Orleans with a couple of major carriers. When would you like to leave?"

"As soon as possible."

"As soon as possible ... are you thinking today?"

"If you have one, I'll leave right now."

"Let me see what I can find here for you."

"I have a six P.M. flight leaving from Louis Armstrong International."

"Book it, baby."

She smiled. "My name is Theresa Davidson. It's not doll and it's certainly not baby. I'll need your name if I'm to issue a ticket. Do you have a driver's license?"

"Nope, Theresa ... Davidson, I have no license."

"I.D. card?"

"No ... well, maybe. I may have a license. I'll just have to look through my stuff."

"You mean you don't know?"

"Seems like I just made that pretty clear, Theresa ... Davidson."

"Well, since we've apparently become acquainted, I'll need your name, too, if I'm to issue a ticket."

"Tom Banks."

Staring at him for a moment after he'd said this, she began again. "Have booked with us before, Mr. Banks? The name doesn't ring a bell, but the face is awfully familiar."

He smiled. "I get that a lot."

Returning the smile, her eyes once again focused on her paperwork. "OK, Mr. Banks, I'll need an address."

Crap ... "No ma'am, that's not right. I just had a big ole brain fart. The name's Tim. Er ... Tim, Tim ..."

"I'm afraid you cannot use an alias, Sir. Because of the threat of terrorism, security has become really tight. I'm sure you understand."

"Johnson, that's it! The name is Tim Johnson."

"I'll need your real name, Sir."

"That's it."

"Which name, Tim? Are you Tom Banks or Tim Johnson?"

"Both, actually. You see, Theresa, I was Tom Banks in a different place and a different time. That was then. I'm Tim Johnson, now."

Wouldn't I love to throw up my hands and start over? "Well, good for you, Tim Johnson. I'll need to verify your information with your license. That is, as soon as you find it. We'll have to get it in the system pretty quick, Tim, if you're to leave at six tonight. Also, I'll need a credit card."

"I don't have one."

"Electronic check?"

"Nope, all I got is cash."

"I'm afraid that will not work. We must have a paper trail, Tim."

"How about you create one? Can I use your card? I'll give you the cash."

"I'm afraid that's impossible."

"A thousand bucks?"

"Surely you're not serious."

"As a heart attack."

"Well, don't have that. I can only process one humongous hurdle at a time."

"Will you do it?"

"You are serious."

"Need more?"

"No ... no, that's quite generous of you."

"Here's your money. How much for the ticket?"

"Umm ... Five hundred sixty two dollars and thirty three cents will get you down there. It's a bit expensive since you're buying your ticket the day of departure. I did get you a last minute discount, however. That saved you almost three hundred dollars."

Tim then handed her the ticket money.

"Let's get your address and personal info into the system and we'll print the ticket. Oh, and you've have to have that I.D. in order to board the plane."

"Works for me."

"There … OK, that should do it. You're all set."

"OK, Theresa Davidson, looks like I'm Florida bound."

"And here is your ticket."

Tim took the ticket from her. "We didn't even discuss return, Theresa Davidson."

"You never said round trip."

"That's right, I didn't."

"Do you want a return flight? I can get a round trip reissue. The transaction has not posted yet."

"Do I want a return flight? You tell me."

She shifted uncomfortably in her chair. "I'm afraid you'll have to make that decision on your own, Tim."

"I'll get back with you, Theresa Davidson."

"It would be cost effective to book it now, Tim."

"Well, now, I hate to appear wasteful and inefficient, Theresa Davidson, but I'm just not sure when I'll need a ride back. I'll reiterate that I'll get back with you. Got it?"

"Got it, Tim, you just call me anytime. Will there be anything else?"

"I sure hope so."

Theresa blushed. "I'm referring to your travel needs."

"I'm not."

Turning from him, she reached into her purse. Earlier this morning, as she settled herself in for work, she'd hung it on the back of her chair.

"Here you are, Tim. This is my business card. It has my cell number on the front. Just give me a call when you need a ride."

"I'm gonna do that, when I need a ride." He arose. "It'd be nice to have someone to ride with me."

She blushed again. "I'm sure you'll be fine."

"Long as you're sure, Teresa Davidson, hold that thought."

"I'll do my best."

"We'll see."

As he finished the statement, Tim smiled. He then turned from her and left the room.

As he left the room, her eyes followed him. *Need a ride, Tim? That makes two of us. I may just need a ride, too.*

✴✴✴

"Well lookey what we have here … a cop car in the driveway."

"Do you think Tomas called the police?"

"Looks that way."

Daria strained her neck to see the vehicle. "Why did they call the police? I haven't done anything wrong?"

"Before you burn it, do you smoke a little of that patchouli?"

"Very funny."

Vince turned to face her. "My sister is missing. You were the last one to see her. No one—including you—seems to know where she is. Now who would you call?"

"Well you could at least give me a chance to straighten all of this out."

Vince looked at Doug. "You're kidding."

Doug returned the glance. "Maybe she puts it in her brownies, too."

"I do not put patchouli in my brownies, thank you very much. I'll also have you understand that I know what I'm doing."

"Sounds good, we'll let you explain that to Tomas and the police."

"I have nothing to hide. I'll be glad to tell them whatever I know."

All three of them got out of the car. Vince led the trio toward the front door. With Daria in the middle, Doug followed. Vince knocked twice on the door.

Tomas answered. "Cuñato, venga."

Vince turned to the rest. "Ya'll come in." He then focused his attention on Tomas. "¿La Polícia esta aqui?"

Holding out his hand, Tomas looked toward the living room. "They're here."

"Good. Maybe they can shed some light on my sister."

Vince, Doug and Daria entered the house. After doing so, Vince began. "Buenas Tardes, agentes. Aqui esta su sospechoso."

Both officers turned toward him. "I think you'd better leave the police work to us, Sir. We'll determine who is a suspect, if indeed there is any reason for suspicion."

Tomas turned and approached the group. "This is the woman who last saw my wife?"

Vince replied, "The one and only."

"Mr. Levy, if you have a few moments, I can explain."

"Oh, I have all the time in the world."

Officer Oriega interrupted. "Since you summoned us here, Mr. Levy, why don't I be the one to ask the questions?"

"Of course, Officer, I meant no harm."

"I'm Officer Derek Oriega and this is my partner, Manuel Lopez." All nodded their hellos.

"For how long has your wife been missing, Mr. Levy?"

"As well as I can remember, since just before noon."

"Today?"

"Yes Sir."

"So what makes you think she's gone missing? That was only a few hours ago."

"Well, first of all, I can't reach her on her cell. Secondly, at this moment, no one seems to know where she is. None of us know and that's not like my wife. She always checks in—we talk several times a day."

"Where does this woman come into the picture?"

Daria began. "I called Shelley and asked her to come over. I thought I could help her?"

"Help her? How?"

"Using a protective spell to surround her with the white light of the Holy Spirit."

In an attempt to stifle a smirk, Officer Lopez cleared his throat.

"So … Miss …?"

"Daria … My name is Daria Landry, Officer."

Officer Lopez took note of the name. Holding a pad in his left hand, he began writing furiously.

"And did it work?"

Vincent stepped forward. "Um, Officer Oriega, you're kidding, right?"

"No, not kidding, I want to hear of the result."

She continued. "Well, things did not go exactly right."

"How so?"

"Well, with a protective spell, I summoned the bright light, and it did envelope her. But as it did so, she sort of … disappeared."

"How does someone 'sort of' disappear?"

"She disappeared."

"And has not been heard from since?"

"No."

"Did you frighten her, Miss Landry?"

"I don't know."

"Did she turn and run from your house?"

"I don't think so. You see, Officer, the door was still closed. I had also engaged the dead-bolt lock. It hadn't been disturbed."

"So what you're telling me is that she basically dematerialized. After this spell, Miss Landry, Mrs. Levy just evaporated?"

"In a manner of speaking, yes, she did. She's somewhere, Officer, we just have to find where."

"And how do you propose we do this?"

"Well, if I could have a few moments alone, I could perform a recovery spell and reverse the consequences. It's that simple."

"And why have you not yet done that?"

"These men won't leave me alone long enough to do it. They drug me over here against my will."

"Oh, I see. Are you saying they kidnapped you?"

"Yes, something like that."

Vince interrupted. "You lying bitch! You know what you did. Don't try to play the victim. I'm not scared of you or these cops. I'll find my sister with or without them, and if something's happened to her, you're gonna pay. You hear me?"

Officer Oriega stepped in front of him. "I suggest you shut your mouth, Sir, you're already in enough trouble."

"Me?! I haven't done shit!"

"You've brought this woman here against her will. That's kidnapping. I could take you in right now." He then turned to Daria. "Do you want to press charges?"

Looking toward Doug and Vincent, she answered him. "No, I guess not. If you gentlemen could give me a ride home and ask these men to stay away from me, I'll consider the matter closed."

"Matter closed?! Daria, where's my sister?" Tomas took a step toward Vincent.

"Mr. ... I'm sorry, what is your name, Sir?"

"Vincent Jacola."

"Mr. Jacola, forty-eight hours from the time she has been reported missing, we'll file a missing person's report."

"Then, we'll never find her! By then her trail will be ice cold!"

"Leave the police work to us, Mr. Jacola. Believe it or not, we know what we're doing. In more than ninety percent of these cases, it's all a big misunderstanding. The person was never really missing at all."

Tomas interjected. "I know my wife, Officer. Hay algo mal."

"I truly hope there is nothing wrong, Señor Levy. In hopes that an Officer sees her in the area, we'll put an alert bulletin out for her. At the appropriate time, we'll file a missing person's report. That's all we can do."

Vince again turned toward the officers. "Boy, I feel better. I feel really safe, too, knowing that you guys will eventually get around to looking for her. Hope you've got a great forensics department."

"I think we've discussed all that needs to be discussed, Mr. Jacola. I understand your frustration, but need to warn you that one day that mouth of yours may just land you in jail. Most of our force is not as patient with hotheads as I am."

"Unbelievable ..."

Doug shook Vince's arm. "Shut it, man. Now is not the time for three hots and a cot."

Vince opened his mouth to reply.

Tomas interrupted. "Cállate."

"Don't tell me to shut up, Tomas."

"Do it. We need time to think."

Addressing them once again, Officer Oriega took a step toward the door. "We're leaving now, Mr. Levy. I'll call in this report from your driveway. If you hear of anything, don't hesitate to call. We're on this, I assure you."

"Yeah, right."

Tomas stepped in front of Vincent. "Gracias, Officer. I'll await your call as well. If Shelley does not return, we'll file the missing person's report."

"We'll be ready."

Tomas looked at him once again. "Find my wife, Officer, please."

"We'll do our best, Mr. Levy."

"No, you and I are getting our asses in that street Tomas, that's how we're gonna find her." He then turned to Daria. "And I'm not through with you, either."

"Is that a threat? Right here in front of the police, is that a threat?"

"Take it however you want to."

"Officer, I'd like to file a restraining order."

"Perhaps that would be wise, Miss Landry." He then stepped toward Vince. "Don't give me an excuse to throw you in jail, Sir, because unlike Miss Landry, I'm not afraid of you. You, on the other hand, should not feel the same toward me."

"Is that a threat, Officer?"

Tomas grabbed Vince by the shirtsleeve. "Get your ass to the back of the house, Vince. Shut your face and get out of here."

"Wise choice."

"Thank you, Officers."

"We'll be in touch this evening, Mr. Levy."

With that, accompanying Daria, both officers turned and left the Levy residence.

✳✳✳

Shelley set the two paper bags in front of the warehouse door. She then proceeded to knock upon it. "Mo? Pierre? It's me, Shelley."

Slowly, the heavy warehouse door began to open. "Get in here, girl. Pierre, help her with those bags."

Pierre grabbed the bags. "Thanks. Wow … what an experience!"

Shelley had seven pairs of eyes staring at her. Mo began. "Do tell."

"This is 1932."

"I'm not surprised. I knew we were far from home."

"And I managed to get everything you had on the list."

"Good work, Shelley. This'll go a long way in getting us back to New Orleans."

"I have something else, too." Shelley handed Mo the coin.

"Oh, I know that you did not steal all of this. Girl, you better tell me that I'm right."

"Of course I didn't steal it. I bought it just as you instructed me to."

"With what? Yo' good looks?"

"Kind of … I met this man … a gentleman, actually, who for some strange reason became smitten with me."

"Mmm-hmm …"

"No, really … I stopped at this grandiose hotel to ask directions, and he was the front desk clerk. He ended up escorting me to the store, and then in order to give this coin back to me, went back and paid for all these things."

"That wasn't no accident."

"Yes it was."

"OK, then, what did this man look like?"

"Well, Mozetta, he was nothing spectacular, if that's what you're getting at. He was about 5'9" with medium brown hair. Kind of had a receding hairline … blue eyes and straight white teeth. He had a medium build and was rather fair-skinned. Is that good enough?"

"You really looked him over, didn't you?"

"You know as well as I do that when a strange man approaches, a woman tends to do that."

"Mmm-hmm … so did he walk you back here?"

"No, no … I left him at the grocery store. He only had a few minutes left on his lunch hour, so I told him not to bother."

"Well, that was awfully kind of you—and him, too. Sounds like you two got real chummy, and in such a short time?"

"I thought the same thing, Mo. For the life of me, I could not figure out why he was being so nice to me. I finally just attributed it to southern hospitality."

"Honey, that was not it. You ain't even close on that one."

"Then what?"

"I'm not sure, as I haven't yet pieced it all together. However, I do think that there must be somebody up there lookin' out for us."

After saying this, she let her gaze fall to the floor. *There has to be … it's too coincidental.* Her train of thought then broken, she returned to the crowd. "That coin was returned for a reason. It is meant to aid our safe passage home."

"You think?"

Mo's patented look of conviction resurfaced. "I don't think, I know. What was this man's name, anyway?"

"Albert Janway."

Mo turned toward her husband. "Pierre, you ever heard of any Janways?"

"I do not believe that I have."

"Where do you suppose is his link in all of this?"

"Now you know, I really don't know."

"Arlie, Edith, Thelma?"

All shook their heads, 'no.'

"Well, regardless of the answer to that question, I can assure you that we have not seen the last of Mr. Janway."

Arlie stepped forward. "Is that bad or good?"

"At this point, I really don't know that, either."

"Then by all means we do not need him hangin' around here. We're already in enough trouble. What if he's some of Solange's people?"

"He could be, although Solange ain't usually that subtle. Whether it be a warning or just plain murder, she tends to get right to the point."

Edith turned to face the other women. "I heard that. Mo just said a mouthful."

Arlie answered her. "Well, I still don't think we need his ass around here. We do not know what that man is up to."

Shelly walked over to Arletha. Gently patting her arm, she began. "I don't plan to bring him around here, nor do I plan to see him again. He was just a nice stranger, Arletha, that's all."

Mo interrupted. "No it ain't. I just told you that was not it. Were you listening? Because I really don't think so."

"Mo, I'm just saying that I don't plan to …"

Mo interrupted again. "I heard you the first time. You don't have to plan nothin', Shelley. You will learn in situations such as these, a lot might just be planned for you."

"I hope you're wrong on that one, Mrs. Conerly. I don't need any more help."

"Mmm-hmm … we'll see."

You may just need plenty of help, Shelley, and you may just find that out real soon …

✳✳✳

"Keep in touch, Adair."

"How long are you staying in Miami?"

"Until we find my sister, I'm hanging out here with Tomas."

"Hopefully she'll come home tonight and all of this will be just a bunch of shit."

"Yeah, I hope you're right. You better get going; you're gonna be driving mostly at night."

"I don't care. I like to travel at night."

"That Overseas Highway is dark as a bitch, Doug. You sure you don't want to stay here until morning?"

"No, man, but thanks, I have to work tomorrow. How are you getting back to Key West, anyway? You want me to come back for you?"

"I don't know yet. I'll get back with you as soon as I find something out."

"It'll be cool, man. She's OK."

"I hope you're right. Now get your ass on that road."

"Call me when you know something."

"Yeah, as soon as I hear. Later, Adair, and thanks again."

"No prob, old buddy."

As he began to back out of the driveway, Vincent walked toward the house. Stopping just short of the doorway, he turned back around and watched his friend drive away.

✳✳✳

Ixora … one thing she loved about Miami was the lush planting of Ixora. Maui Orange was her favorite color, as the bright, burnt orange flower clusters made the plant irresistible. In the city, they were actually used as hedges. Since frost was uncertain in New Orleans, their outdoor survival was unpredictable, but here they flourished year round.

Planted in concrete pots, several orange Ixora lined the perimeter of her patio. Daria always made a point to water them first thing in the morning, and if the day had been extremely hot, she gave them a small drink before bedtime. Perhaps that was the reason she'd forgotten to lock the sliding glass door?

Making her way inside, she fumbled for the key to the deadbolt lock. She had also forgotten, in case she returned after nightfall, to leave the front porch illuminated. Nevertheless, she managed to find the key in the dark.

Upon entering, a deep breath was followed by a long, exaggerated exhalation. *Oh my God, what a huge mess!* Walking over to the breakfast table, in spite of the broken glass, she managed to upright it. Recalling what had transpired, she looked at the space again. *There has to be a way to fix this.* Retrieving the broom from the corner, she began to sweep the breakfast room floor. A long sigh followed as she swept glass into the dust pan. *Wait a minute …* Standing upright, she realized she still had eighteen candles in the garage storeroom. A glance toward the corner of the room then revealed an overturned box of salt. *Looks like I still have everything I need.* After a quick toss over her left shoulder, she returned the rest of it to the table. *I could try and straighten out this mess right now.* She pulled a lighter from her shoulder bag and placed it on the table. *But it's only just me. Cardinal rule of incantations states never to perform a spiritual ritual alone. The results could be disastrous, and there is no one to help you.* "Well, what could be more disastrous than this?" Walking toward the garage, she made her way to the storage room. Suddenly, she froze. *No sacred salt from the Sea of Galilee.* She walked a few steps more. *Worth the risk? If that girl is trapped in some horrible place, it's well worth the risk. After all, I put her there.* "My safety is really not the issue here."

Upon her return to the breakfast room, she up righted the other three chairs. Setting the candles in the Star of David Configuration, she suddenly realized for a situation such as this, she had no written incantation. *Nothing like this is documented in the Book of Spells, so … looks like there's no other choice but to make it up as I go.* Looking around the room again, she took a deep breath. *Before I begin, maybe I should consult the tarot? That's what I'll do.* She smiled to herself. *That's exactly what I'll do. I'll get another opinion on this.*

Retrieving her Tarot Cards from the kitchen cabinet, Daria closed her eyes and then cut the deck. Staring at what had manifested, she stood transfixed.

Well, I guess there's no turning back now; this just about says it all …

> *The Magician's number is One, the number of creation and individuality; his power is transformation through the use of his will. In his manipulation of the basic elements into all the substances and materials of life, he shows us that from a foundation of the mundane can emerge all that is to come. He can take the Nothing from which the Fool emerged and shape it into Something, making one out of zero. Clearly this is power of a divine sort, and it is true that the Magician is a conduit for a higher*

power, which commands all of the material world. Since all that we can see in the physical world is the conduit himself, the acts he performs often seem like magic.

When the Magician appears he shows that you are ready to become a conduit for power, like he is. The forces of creation and destruction have always been at your command but now you have the wisdom and confidence needed to use them constructively. Now is the time to act, if you know what is it you want to accomplish and why. Since the powers of transformation are at your command, change your desires into objectives, your thoughts into actions, your goals into achievements. If you have recently met with failure, now you can change that failure into success as easily as the Magician changes fire into water. The only limits you have are those you impose on yourself.

As she finished reading the text, slowly she turned the card to reveal the depiction of the Magician. "Once again, Mr. Rioux, you were right on the money." *Oh wow ... the French ... the incantation must be recited in French.* Her telephone then came to mind. *Wait a minute! I have a translator App. on my phone.* Pulling her cellular device from her purse, she set it upon the table. *Let's see ... shouldn't be too complicated.*

Engaging the application, she set the device on the table and began.

"I ask to be surrounded by the White Light of the Holy Spirit. Surrounded by his protection, I ask for dimensional reversal in order to return Shelly Levy to her rightful place in this universe. Aiding in her return, let the candles of the Star of David serve as beacons of guiding light. I ask that Shelley Levy be surrounded by God's protection and Grace as she traverses planes of subsistence her being was never meant to cross in her present state of existence. I also ask that her fragile body be coated with heavenly armor in order to safely make the transition to her natural state of being. This I pray in the name of the Holy Trinity, Amen."

Now, just choose language and press translate. Somewhere, it says the App will recite the text aloud …

Daria scanned the table configuration. "I think that's about it." She took lighter in hand and began to light the seven candle configuration. As she lit the seventh, she smiled with satisfaction. "I'm going to right this."

"You know it's not a good idea to cast these spells alone, Daria, don't you?"

Throwing the lighter behind her, Daria screamed. As she wheeled around to face the voice, she said, "Oh my God! Who are you? Why are you here? What are you doing in my house? I … I'm calling the police!"

"Wow … that's a lot of information to process at one time. Where would you like me to begin?"

"Get out!"

"Well, I'm afraid that one is not an option." Taking a step toward her, he continued. "So, were you asking God to tell you who I am or would you like for me to do so?"

Daria was silent.

"I'll go ahead and help you out. I'm Tom. No wait … here, it's Tim." He shook his head. "Never you mind, I'll answer to either one. Do you still want to know why I'm here?"

"I think I know."

"You do?"

In an attempt to engage the application, Daria bolted for the table.

"Not yet, Daria, we don't want to start all of this right now."

"How do you know who I am?"

"Oh, you're rather famous. Maybe infamous would be a better word, but how in the fuck would I know the difference between famous and infamous?" He shrugged. "Tim has a lot better vocabulary than I ever had. Kinda cool, speaking this proper grammar and all ..."

Daria said nothing.

"My sweetie thinks things are better left alone. In fact, Daria, you are almost the last detail left untended."

"Almost?"

"Yeah, that fat guy ... gotta tend to him, too." Tim pulled a cigarette from his pocket. Putting it to his mouth, he leaned toward the table. Using one of the burning candles, he lit it.

"Those candles are sacred. You just created blasphemy doing that."

"You mean committed blasphemy, and damn, it doesn't take much, does it, Daria?"

Once again, she didn't answer.

"Hey, can I have a hug?"

"What?"

"You heard me. It's chilly in here. Can I have a hug?"

Daria's glance became cold. "Do ... not ... touch ... me."

"Oh, I'm gonna do more than that, baby. We can make this as easy or hard as you want. Speaking of hard, I'm kind of gettin' that way right now."

Attempting not to be obvious, slowly she inched toward the landline telephone.

Tim laughed. "The line's cut, Daria. No dial tone, baby."

Daria knew with that being the case, it was only a matter of time before the security monitoring service called the police. She had not answered her cell and they had no signal for the landline.

"Tim, are you thirsty or anything?"

He laughed. "So which is it? Do I have a dumbass or a schizophrenic on my hands?"

In vain she struggled to clear her throat. "Neither, I just thought ... well, there's no sense in being ..." Attempting to swallow, her voice trailed away. Breathing in deeply, she tried again. "W ... would you?"

"Got any whiskey? Right about now I could use a hit."

"I just have white wine."

"No thanks, baby, that ain't too much stronger than horse piss."

Again swallowing hard, she replied, "OK …"

"I don't drink horse piss by the way, it's just an expression."

"W … what do you plan to do to me?"

Tim took another drag of his cigarette. "Daria, as I see it, you have two choices. I can fuck you to death, or just kill you right here and now. The first one would be a lot more fun and virtually painless."

"I'll bet."

"No, really. You see, doll, I need your life force. Just before I break the chakra, I can pull out, and you can go on your merry way to the afterlife. No immortal, no anything … sounds like a pretty good deal to me. I, on the other hand was not so fortunate, and have to scrounge around for energy to maintain this existence. It's a bitch …" Taking a last drag, Tim stubbed his cigarette out on her breakfast room table. "It really is." He pondered this last statement for a moment before he blew it out.

"I am asking you not to kill me. I'm begging …"

"Sorry, sugar, but that's not an option. I got orders from the boss that you're to be eliminated. Please understand that I got no beef with you, I just have to keep my lady happy. I will admit, though, I can sometimes get off on a good life extinguishing adventure."

"It's not an adventure, Tom, it's murder. If you get off on that, then you're a serial killer."

"Maybe, but I've been called worse." Breaking her gaze, he glanced briefly at his watch. "Say, it's getting late. Why don't we go ahead and get this show on the road?"

"The police are on their way. When the phone signals are interrupted, they're called automatically. You will get caught for this and you'll die in jail." She took a small step backward. "You don't have to do it, you know. You can leave now. I won't tell anyone you were here. I'll tell them it was all a big mistake. "

"Wow … with that being said, I'd better 'come and go' in a hurry." Tim closed the distance between them. "Now … how do you want me to do it?"

CHAPTER TWENTY-TWO

"Good Morning."

"Good Morning. I need to get to Florida ASAP."

"Am I missing something?"

"Excuse me?"

Looking down, she smiled. "You're the second person in two days I've had to get to Florida 'as soon as possible.' I'm beginning to wonder if there is something going on over there I don't know about."

"Well, if that's the case, I don't know about it either. I just need to catch up with a friend, that's all."

"Then let's see what we can do. I'm Theresa Davidson, by the way, and welcome to Accent Travel."

"Thank you. I'm Delia ... Delia Melancon."

As she said this, Theresa smiled again. "Where in Florida, Delia?"

"Key West."

"Oh ..."

"Is there a problem?"

"No ... no problem, but if time is of the essence, it may be easier to fly you into, say ... Miami and then get a rental."

"I'd rather fly."

"We can do that, but you may be in for a bit of a layover in Miami. If you don't mind the wait, we'll work it out."

"I guess I'll do what I have to do."

"Well, it's six of one and a half dozen of the other. Drive out of Miami, or sit in the airport waiting for the commuter flight."

"Those are my only two choices?"

"Commercially, yes … of course you can always charter."

"No, no, no … I don't have that kind of money. Let's look at a rental."

"You want to drive?"

"Yeah, it may be a good idea to have some wheels for when I get there. It'll be easier to get around."

"Realistically, you can walk almost everywhere you need to go. It's not a big place."

"Let's go with the car."

Theresa refocused her gaze from Delia toward the computer. "OK, the car it is." She then opened her top desk drawer and pulled from it a large, heavy book. Opening it to the index, she began furiously typing on the laptop which sat in front of her. "Delia, give me a couple of moments and I'll have some preliminary arrangements for you."

This brought forth a smile. "No problem."

Theresa returned the smile. "I'll have you basking in the sun of those Florida Keys in no time."

You do that, Theresa. Vince and I have a lot of catching up to do. In fact, he may finally get just what he wants … a mighty big surprise awaits my dear ole' buddy Vince …

✳✳✳

"Dans votre nom saint nous prions, le Pére, amen."

The remaining seven repeated her chant. "In your holy name we pray, amen."

"OK. The die is cast. Now do not break the Circle of Seven, understood?"

"Eight."

"Say what?"

"There are eight of us."

Mo cleared her voice. "As Arlie was so diligent to point out, the circle should be referred to as the Circle of Eight." She then turned to Arletha. "Better?"

As she turned her head in defiance, Arletha closed her eyes. "Hmmph. Anything would be an improvement, since you're the one that got us into this mess in the first place."

"Arlie, I assure you that we will confront that issue when we get home. But for now, we will leave that be, as I'm not exactly certain what is ahead of us. The die has been cast, and we all know who does not want us out of here. Assuming that we are able to get there, it may not be such a smooth ride home."

Edith turned to face them. "I ain't interested in travelin' first class, I just want to get out of wherever we are."

"Me too," Shelley added.

As she said this, the atmosphere began to diminish. Not at all like a dimming bulb, but more like a fog, an impending blackness began to descend upon them. Almost imperceptible at first, gradually, the vapor became thicker and more substantial.

Mo scanned the group. "Here we go."

Thelma added, "Lord Jesus help us."

Coretta turned toward Mo. "I don't like this Mo; I don't like this one bit. I get claustrophobic, and this is really black."

"Shut up yo' face."

Turning her face toward the opposite direction, she addressed the disembodied voice. "Verdie? Is that you?"

"It sure is, and I'm tired of you flappin' yo' jaws. This ain't—once again—about you and one of yo' many illnesses. I swear you are the biggest hypochondriac."

"If I could get my hands on you right now …"

"Well you can't, so press those lips together and quit lettin' stupid comments fly out from between them."

"Shows how ignorant you are. I am claustrophobic, Verdie." Coretta made an exaggerated effort to clear her throat. When she finished, she began again. "And the actual truth of the matter is that it ain't none of yo' business, anyway."

"Good. Then I don't have to listen to it."

"Both of you women shut the lower half of yo' fat faces and pay attention to what's goin' on around you. Right now we can't see our hands in front of us, and have no idea what the hell—no pun in-tended—is coming our way. You gals can't keep yo' teeth together long enough to realize we are in great danger? And if you do realize that, then both of you are dumber than I thought."

"And the horse you rode in on, Mo."

"Verdie, this is yo' last warning. When we get home, rest assured I will deal with you as well as Miss Jackson over there."

"Hey now, I ain't said nothin'!"

The room became silent. The blackness had managed to envelope everything. Much like an abyss, swirling away from them, the entire scenario seemed to dissipate.

"Then stay quiet, Arlie. I think our homebound hurdle is about to manifest."

Coretta grabbed her throat. "I … I can't breathe!"

"The circle, Retta, the circle! Do not break it. It's a trick to make us fail."

Coretta began to gasp.

Edith was standing next to her. "Mo! She's falling. I think she's passin' out!"

Mo felt her throat begin to close as well. *You ain't gettin' me. You think you got me over a barrel, but you ain't winning a damn thing!* Now so thick, the air was virtually impossible to breathe. Suddenly, a horrible stench filled the air. "Get up, Retta, I mean get up now!"

Edith and Verdiasee both stooped to help her to her feet. "Relax," Edith said, "try to relax. Concentrate on breathing. Slowly, now, breathe in and exhale."

Edith and and Verdiasee both held tightly onto her hands. "We still have the circle, Mo. Somehow, we managed to maintain it!" She then crinkled her nose. "Oh my God, what is that awful smell?"

Verdiasee answered. "Death. That must be what death smells like."

Revealing a vast, brown wasteland, the atmosphere had once again begun to clear. Far away in the distance, they could see a rim of fire. The rim totally encircled the horizon.

Mo turned toward them. "Ladies, welcome to the Outer Darkness. I've read about this place in the scriptures."

"We ain't supposed to be here, Mo. What the hell we doin' in the Outer Darkness?" Evidence that she was terrified, tears streamed down Thelma's face.

"We don't belong to him, baby. Keep the circle. This is just another one of her tricks to make sure we do not succeed."

"Mo, the noise is killing me!"

"Thelma, close yo' eyes and pray. I told you this was not going to be a picnic."

"Where is that hideous noise coming from?"

"I do not know. Do the rest of you hear it?"

"All nodded their heads yes."

"I don't hear anything."

"Shelley, you don't hear that? Baby, it sounds like a jet engine headed straight for us."

Shelley shook her head 'no.'

Arletha slumped to the floor. "I have to sit down. I'm about to faint."

Mo opened her mouth to speak, but was interrupted.

"Get up, Arlie. Open yo' eyes. Arlie, do you hear me?"

Mo could see the others yelling at her. Her arms fell to her side. Suddenly, she felt helpless to do anything else.

"Get up!" Sounding now more like an echo than a command, she heard this repeatedly.

She took a deep breath and closed her eyes. *Enough, already; I have done everything as I was supposed to. I need your help. I can no longer do this alone. Please, please God, get us out of here. Do not let Solange win this. We are your children. Do not let him have us.*

She opened her eyes to see him smiling at her. Shaking her head 'no,' she then exhaled,

"As if it could not get any worse …"

CHAPTER TWENTY-THREE

"What the hell are you doing here?"

"Well someone had to rescue you."

"And you are my white knight in shining armor?"

"As you wish."

"Joubert, you ain't never thought of nobody but yo'self—especially now with yo' current situation."

"Maybe I've turned over a new leaf."

"Only if there is something underneath it for you. Where am I, anyway?"

"You're in my home."

"What year is this?"

"Mo?"

She'd apparently been lying prostrate on a bed. Arising from it, she walked toward the window. After a long, pensive gaze, she realized she may have indeed made it home. She turned to face him. "I know what has happened up to this point, but what I need to understand is how I got to yo' house, and—God forbid—ended up in yo' bed?"

"My guest room, Mo, and it's a long story. Do you feel like hearing it?"

"I asked, didn't I?"

"OK, here goes, but I can assure you that you won't like the outcome."

"Spit it out, Thierry. I'm waiting. And if you took advantage of me … well, let's just say it was yo' swan song. "

"Don't flatter yourself, Mo. Even I have some standards."

"Hmmph. I used to say if it had a pulse, but these days, I'm not even so sure about that."

"Mo, you slay me."

"Not yet, but it could happen. Now tell me what you know."

"Well, we rescued you."

"Who are we?"

"No one you need to worry about."

"Oh really?"

"You will have to trust me on this one, Mo."

"We will get back to this later on. So how did you know where we were? How could you have found us in another dimension?"

"I didn't."

"Say what?"

"You have no idea, do you?"

"Apparently not, so enlighten me."

"We rescued you from the fire."

Mo turned to face him. "What fire?"

Thierry closed the distance between them. Putting a hand on each shoulder, he began. "Mo, Boliviee's burned to the ground. We found the seven of you inside; you were all suffering from smoke inhalation. A few more moments and …"

"Shut yo' face." She turned and walked away from him. When she'd crossed the room, she turned around and began again. "How? How did my restaurant burn down? Did that bitch set it on fire?"

"There's more."

"How could there be any more? You just told me there's nothin' left."

"They found a body amongst the rubble."

Oh my God … Shelley.

"Who did they find, Joubert? Who burned to death in my restaurant?"

"The body has not been yet identified. In hopes of discovering who perished, they're working with dental records."

Mo swallowed hard. *That poor little ole' thing … and that stupid, stupid Daria Landry! Her damn ignorance burned that girl up and sent her ass to Hell!*

"Mo?"

Her thoughts returned to the present. "I could kill that Daria Landry. If I could get my hands on her right now, I would barbeque her ass."

"I'm not following here."

Shaking her head in dismissal, she began again. "I may know who that body belongs to."

He focused his gaze directly at her. "Was the person there with you before the fire?"

Mo returned the stare.

"What happened, Mo? You know, don't you?"

"Let me first start by sayin' I'm a little in shock that I have no restaurant or home to return to." She then rested her forehead in her left hand. "We were tryin' to send 'you know who' back where she belongs. But the room was not sealed, because …" Suddenly, she focused her gaze past the window. "Wait a minute …"

Eyebrows raised, Thierry waited for her to continue.

"That couldn't have been Shelley in the house. She may very well still be OK."

"Who is Shelley?"

"Another long story."

"I'm all ears."

"Mmm-hmm." She paused for a moment. As if deep in thought, Mo grimaced and scratched the back of her head. "Right before our ceremony, this other bitch came over and pulled a fast one."

"How so?"

"She made sure the room was not sealed. We performed our ceremony in an open environment."

"Oh, Mo … She must have been in cahoots with Solange."

"I didn't know people from France used words like cahoots."

Suddenly, she'd derailed his train of thought. "Excuse me?"

"Sounds awfully southern if you ask me."

"I didn't."

"Well no, you did not."

A bit aggravated, Thierry continued. "Can we get back to the subject here?"

"That girl owned or managed LAPPS."

"Ariel?!"

"You know her?"

"I know her well. I've had many a reading at LAPPS."

After he'd said this, in amazement she paused for a moment. "Mmm-hmm ... You really ain't the brightest bulb on the Christmas tree, are you?"

"What?"

"You can't do any better than that? You have to go to a fortune teller ... a palm reader?!"

"I don't believe what I'm hearing. Mozetta Conerly is skeptical?"

"Let's just say my connections are a little more accurate and direct. We don't tend to make up stuff so that our customers think they got their money's worth."

"I didn't know you had customers."

"We don't. I was just tryin' to prove a point."

Point taken. It's really of no consequence now, if that indeed is the person that died.

She froze. "Where's Pierre?"

"He's downstairs in the front room. I have a hide-a-bed in the office. He's Ok, Mo, but I'm not sure about the others."

"Who?"

"I'm afraid Coretta has not regained consciousness. She's at Ochner's Medical Center."

"Thelma?"

Thierry shook his head 'no.'

"She's dead?"

"Not yet, but like Coretta, she's not faring well. They're doing everything they can for them."

Damn ... "Edith, Arlie and Verdie?"

"They're all at Touro Hospital. No, wait ... they took Verdiasee to Baptist. Her family insisted that she be transported there."

"And Shelley?"

"Who is this Shelley you keep referring to?"

"She was with us in …"

"Where?"

"That other dimension," Mo exhaled. "I need to see my husband. Thierry, if you have a phone, I need to use that, too."

"Of course."

For a moment, Mo stared at him. "You know, I never knew you were such a nice person. You have always been so disgusting."

"Thank you."

"Believe it or not, that is a compliment. It's the closest thing to a compliment you will get from me, anyway."

"I'll take what I can get."

"I'm gonna tear that bitch apart limb from limb."

"Solange?"

"No, I was talking about Mrs. Santa Claus. Whom do you think I was referring to?"

"Follow me downstairs. I'll take you to Pierre."

For a moment, she paused at the top of the stairway. *You ain't gonna have her. I will get her back. Once I do, I'm gonna pummel yo' carrot-topped ass right back to where you belong. And once I'm finished with you, you will be glad to go!*

✳✳✳

"Where' Luis?"

"I've sent him to school."

"Really, man? You're serious?"

"It'll keep his mind occupied."

"Right. That'll do it. His mom has been kidnapped or disappeared some kind of way but school will handle it for him. School's the best medicine of all, huh Tomas?"

"OK, apparent know-it-all, what would you suggest? Let him sit around here and go crazy? At least there he'll have a diversion."

"Ever thought he may be able to help us get to the bottom of this, as in three heads are better than two?"

"You mean two heads are better than one."

"You can't count?"

"Yeah, I can count, Vince, it's just that you don't count. Your brain is fried."

"Fuck you, man. I didn't deserve that."

"Then let me be the parent. I don't tell you how to raise your kids."

"I don't have any, dumbass."

"Exactly my point …You know nothing about raising kids, so don't offer any advice."

"Damn, Tomas, I'm getting a little punch drunk here. Send him to school and do what you want! I ain't sayin' nothin' else."

"Good." Turning away, Tomas walked toward the phone. Putting the receiver to his ear, he again focused his gaze toward Vince. "I'm calling the police again."

"Like that'll do any good. They don't give a shit."

"What else can we do?"

Call Mo … again. Vince reaffirmed his gaze. "Go ahead and call them. It can't hurt. Bug the hell out of 'em, and maybe they'll actually do something." He then turned and made his way toward the hallway. Before he exited the room, he looked back at his brother-in-law. "Let me know what they say, Tomas. If you need anything, I'll be in the bedroom."

"¿Qué vas a hacer?"

"I need to use the phone, myself. I'm gonna try to call home."

"When you get done, let's get out in the streets. I have to look for her. I can't sit around here and do nothing."

"You got it, man. I won't be long. Call the cops; I'll be back."

As I picked up my cell, I began walking toward the guest room. Just as I was about to once again dial Mo's number, my phone rang. The caller I.D. read Dr. Thierry L. Joubert. Joubert's calling me? What the hell would he want?

"Hello?"

"Well thank God."

"Mo?!"

"Hey baby."

"Oh my God … This is so weird. I was just about to call you."

"Great minds think alike."

Vincent smiled. "Even if they're fried?"

"Say what?"

"Out of context, never mind. Mo, I can't get in touch with any-body. Mrs. Sanders called and told me about the restaurant. I thought you were dead."

"And you were almost right."

"What happened? Who would want to burn down Boliviee's?"

"Now do you really have to ask that question?"

"No … no, I don't." He cleared his throat. Taking a deep breath, he began again. "Mo, I have some bad news."

"I know."

"No, you don't."

"Yes, I do."

"Listen to me. You don't know. Mo, my sister's missing."

"I said, I know."

"How could you possibly know, Mo? How the hell could you know anything?"

"Because I saw her."

"What?"

"One name will say it all."

Vince stood transfixed. "Surely not."

"Yep, Daria Landry."

"OK, that's not at all who I was thinking. I thought you were talking about Solange. What about Daria Landry?"

"Well, it's a long story, baby."

"And from the tone of your voice, I'm surmising that it's not a good one."

"No, honey, it's not too good."

"Did she kill her, Mo? Did Daria murder my sister?"

"I am not sure yet."

"You're not sure?"

"I know she did not mean to."

"Oh, that makes a hell of a lot of sense."

"Anything dealing with Daria usually doesn't make any sense, baby. Daria was trying to help, but, as always, created a huge mess. I'm not sure I can fix this one."

"Where is she, Mo?"

"Let's just say she is nowhere near either one of us."

"That bitch kidnapped her?"

"No, not intentionally ..."

"Who's fried, here? How do you unintentionally kidnap someone?"

"First of all watch yo' mouth. Second of all, close it and wait for an explanation. If you could somehow manage to shut that face long enough, you may actually learn something."

Noticeably agitated, Vince shifted positions. Before he began again, he cleared his throat. "Right now, I'm not much in the mood for Mo humor."

"And I wasn't tryin' to be funny, Vince. Now listen to me. I fully intend to bring you up to speed on what's goin' on, but first, I need find out how to see her."

"OK, me too."

"I'm talkin' about Daria."

"So am I. You know she lives here in Miami, right?"

"Yeah, I know that. The way things are lookin', Felton and I may have to come that way. It's not like we have a place to sleep here, anyway."

"Well, if you need my place, you know where I hide the key."

"Thank you baby, that helps a lot. Takes a big load off of these old bones."

"Should you decide to head this way, we got room for you over here, too."

"You better consult yo' brother-in-law before you decide to start inviting company to his house."

"You're not company. You're family, and I'll fix it with Tomas. Once he finds out you're trying to help—or might actually be of some help, he'll be glad you're here."

"I did not say I could help."

"Mo, you gotta help. You're our only hope. We gotta KO this Solange bitch."

"You have no idea how much I want to do that."

"Yes, I do."

As she began, she wiped her hand across her brow. "She is methodical, and thorough. I'll give her that."

"We'll smoke her evil ass … send it packing back to where she belongs."

"Let us hope so." Taking a deep breath, she let out a long, exasperated sigh. "You may need to take a good, long look in the mirror."

"Uh, yo' train of thought just took a right turn somewhere? You've lost me. Why would I need to do that?"

"Because she thinks she has dealt with everybody else, Vince. Do you know what that means?"

"Let me guess."

"No need to guess, baby, we just need to state the obvious."

"That I'm next?"

"That's right, baby, you are next."

CHAPTER TWENTY-FOUR

"Wake up, sleepyhead."

As he pulled himself to a seated position, Pierre looked about the room. For a moment, he sat speechless. "Either I don't know where the hell we are or you did some serious redecorating."

"Perhaps a little of both."

"Where are we? Who's house is this?"

"Thierry Joubert's."

"You kiddin'."

"No, I am not."

"So … do you want to fill me in on why we are here?"

"Yes, I sure do."

"Well, go on and give it to me."

"OK …" Turning away from him, she walked across the room. At the doorway, she turned back around to face him. "Let me think of how I need to begin …" Resting her chin on her hand, her eyes made their way toward the ceiling. "She burned down the restaurant."

"You kiddin'!"

Mo then refocused her gaze toward him. "That is the second time you have said that. I will answer, 'no, I am not,' again."

In amazement Pierre wiped his hand across his face. "We ain't got nothin'?"

"We were insured. We'll be OK."

"Oh really? Then where are we gonna sleep? And what exactly are we gonna sleep on?"

"Don't look as if you are doin' too bad right now."

"I have no idea even how I got here. Woman, we can't stay here. The thought of it is utterly ridiculous."

"Well, we do have other options."

"Like what? A hotel?"

"There's that and Vincent has offered us his house as long as we need it."

"For real?"

"There you go again. Do you think I just like to hear myself talk? Of course for real, I just got off of the phone with him."

"We might better call a Haz-Mat team to clean the place up before we get too settled in."

Mozetta laughed. "Yeah, you right, you old fool ..." She laughed again. "That's the first time I've laughed in I don't know when. I don't know why it struck me as so funny."

"Especially since it's true ..."

"I don't mean to interrupt."

Both Mozetta and Pierre turned to find that Thierry had entered the room.

"You were not interrupting anything. Me and Pierre were just gettin' our ducks in a row."

"Of course you'll be my extended guests."

Mo turned and took a step toward him. "Did some kind of alien abduct the real you and replace it with a faulty copy? I ain't used to this new Thierry. You ain't never been nothin' but a damned dog, and I really want to know exactly what you have up yo' sleeve?"

Thierry raised his hands in resignation. "No aliens and no sleeve."

"Then what gives?"

"A realization."

"Mmm-hmm, why don't you elaborate a little more on that one?"

"Until you were relegated to a parasitic existence, you'd never understand."

"I may understand more than you think."

"You cannot empathize with any aspect of my way of life. Life in death is not something you'd be able to understand unless you had to live it."

"And that being said, let me emphasize that not only do I not want to understand, I especially don't want to live it."

"Then we have a common goal."

"And just what is that?"

"The destruction of Madame Solange DeShotel."

"Well, go on and say her name in full and clear her mind. In that way she will be alert as to where exactly all of us are."

"My apologies, I once again forgot."

"You and Vince both need to be more vigilant."

"I'll be sure to keep that in mind."

"Mmm-hmm. Well, if Pierre will get his fat self up on his feet, we'll be on our way."

"My fat self is kinda hungry, by the way."

"We'll head down to Camellia Grill for an omelet."

"And then we may need to make our way to the department store to get you two some essentials and extra clothing."

"Thierry, while I appreciate the offer—and I really do, by the way—we will fare better in our own neck of the woods."

"But where will you stay?"

"Vincent has graciously offered his place."

"I can only imagine …"

"Yeah, it will need some elbow grease, but that may give me some mindless occupation while I sort things out."

"As you wish, but my door is always open."

Staring at him for a moment, Mozetta seemed stunned. "I sure would love to believe you are actually this nice."

"I guess time will tell."

As if brandishing a pistol, she pointed her right index finger at him. "There you go."

The smiled vanished from his face. "There is something else."

"Uh oh, I knew all of this was too good to be true. What do you want, Joubert? What is the catch here?"

"A few moments ago I received a call from Renita Jones Diggins."

"Oh thank God! What did she say? Did Nita tell you how her mother was doin'?"

"Mo, about an hour ago, Coretta passed away."

Saying nothing, she stood transfixed. A tear then began to track down her right cheek. Clenching her teeth, she took a deep breath and cleared her throat. After exhaling, she began. "I'm through threatening. I'm done with all of that. The next step is action. I will confront this head on immediately and not even seven states of Hell will be able to stop me." Swallowing hard, she turned toward the bed and retrieved her purse. She then began making her way toward the doorway. As she passed through it, she turned back to face him. Crying a bit more profusely, she attempted a thank you.

"We appreciate all that you have done for us. I assure you we will return the favor, somehow. Pierre, I am ready to leave now."

"You realize that you're now a Circle of Six. We both know how dangerous that can be."

"I understand that, Thierry, but I have not even begun to process the death of one of my best friends. I just cannot think that far ahead right now."

"So I did a bit of thinking for you, Mrs. Conerly."

In an attempt to digest the last comment, for a moment she stood staring. "And how is that?"

As if on cue, in that instant a woman appeared from the hallway. As she made her entrance into the room, Mozetta's eyes widened. She opened her mouth to speak and then closed it once again. Finally able to compose herself, she began. "Well I do say … this could not have come at a better time." Closing the distance between them, she took a step toward the woman. "I can honestly now say there is a God."

CHAPTER TWENTY FIVE

"Vera Ellen Jenkins, what in the world brings you to this neck of the woods?"

"You."

"Oh really? How so?"

"Thierry called me and informed me that my services may be needed."

"Girl, you got that right. You just have no idea."

"Yes I do."

Mozetta met her gaze and was moved by the look of conviction in her eyes. "I believe you do. How on earth did you get here so fast?"

"I was up in Monroe at a family reunion."

"For real? I'll bet it was nice. Did you see anybody I know?"

"I'm sure there was some folks there you might know, but it was mostly my husband's people. The reunion was on his mother's side."

"Mmm-hmm." She smiled and began again. "Well I'm glad you made it down here, anyway."

"Me too …"

Vera took a deep breath and then exhaled. "Mo, Thierry also told me about Retta and Thelma."

Her eyes fell toward the ground. "Yeah, Vera, Retta did not make it. I guess she was too old. All of this was too much for her."

"Well, yo' best friend is here to make sure her death was not in vain."

"Right now, you do not know how much that means to me."

"You don't think I know much of anything these days."

Mo laughed. "Get out of my face, girl! You know what I mean."

"Yeah, you right."

"Mmm-hmm, I hear yo' New Orleans accent beginnin' to resurface. Philadelphia ain't rubbed off on you too much."

"Oh, I'll always be a New Orleans girl at heart, and these days I'm gonna be yo' seventh to help you get rid of that pest."

"I wouldn't exactly refer to her as a pest. She's a lot more dangerous than that, Vera. Right about now, I really wish Mama was here; this one has washed over me like a tidal wave."

"Yo' mama couldn't handle her, either, Mo. Even yo' grandmother could not reel this one in."

"And they let it all fall on me."

Thierry stepped toward them. "Well, rest assured you're not alone."

The intrusion took her a bit by surprise. She turned back to face him. "And I'm not completely sure I trust you, either."

Putting her hand on her hip, Vera shifted her weight to her back foot. "Ditto that. We have not forgotten you're an immortal, Thierry."

"Well don't forget even though the silver chakra is severed, I still have a soul."

"And you have survival instincts, too."

"True, but that in no way overlaps this situation."

"Hmmph."

"I'm not kidding, gals, I want Solange out of the picture as much as you do."

Mo rolled her neck. "Gals?! Joubert, when in the hell have you ever used the word 'gals?' What has happened to you? Seems to me a different piece of yo' new personality reveals itself every day."

Vera cut her eyes at him. "More like every minute …"

Thierry managed a frozen smile. "And if it upsets you ladies that much, I'll make sure never to use that word again."

"And I will be gracious enough not to stand here and belabor the point, as long as you understand I got my eye on you." As she said this, she made a 'V' with her index and middle fingers. She then pointed the V at her eyes and subsequently his. Still looking at him, she squinted. "So sticky sweet I bet that butter would not even melt in yo' mouth …"

In an attempt to recapture the floor, Pierre cleared his throat. All turned their heads toward him. "Well, if we are through with 'old home week and name that Thierry,' I have a chili-cheese omelet waitin' on me at Camellia Grill."

"Always about yo' fat stomach!"

"Woman, hush yo' mouth! Vera, would you like to join us at the Grill?"

"I'd love to."

"Thierry?"

"I'll have to pass."

"You immortals don't eat?"

"Of course I eat. I just feel I'd be intruding on a reunion of sorts."

"Get yo' hat, Thierry. These women will be movin' their faces so fast I'll never get a word in edgewise. I could use someone to talk to."

"Look who is talking? By the time you finally shut yo' big, fat mouth, there ain't no air left in the room."

As Mo finished, Vera began laughing so hard she had to grab her side. "Stop it! You guys are killin' me! Let's go. That means you too, Thierry."

"Well, I guess that's an offer I can't refuse. Let me indeed get my hat."

"Now that's more like the Thierry that gets on my last nerve. I'm with Vera. Let's go. I'm kind of hungry."

Looking at her in amazement, Pierre stepped back. "Say what?! I'm the one who …"

"Shut yo' face and move it, Pierre. Quit always tryin' to have the last word."

Pierre turned and made his way through the doorway. "Hmmph" was all they heard as he stepped outside.

***

Tucked into an intersection of two famous New Orleans thorough-fares, Camellia Grill embodies the essence of Uptown New Orleans. The area is both charming and intelligent, as most of the local eateries in this locale host Loyola and Tulane enrollment. The streetcar makes neighborhood access effortless, while upscale shopping and dining render the district irresistible. A few blocks down on Oak Street sits the Maple Leaf Bar. Forever an uptown local's favorite, the Maple Leaf always draws a crowd. The tiny establishment is especially full on Thursday nights, for every week a dance competition determines what city couple truly exemplifies Cajun dance expertise.

The Maple Leaf is small. Upon entering, a long bar races away from the doorway. Giving rise to a dance floor on the right, tables and chairs are situated behind the band/dance area.

Now that they had eaten, before tackling the housing predicament, Pierre, Mozetta and Vera decided to spend an hour or so listening to some local entertainment.

"Where's the music?"

Mozetta looked about the room. "You know, I really don't know." She then spied a large calendar hanging on the wall in front of them. "Wait a minute … no music tonight, folks. It's a poetry reading night."

Furrowing his brow, Pierre looked at her. "Poetry?"

"That's what it says."

Continuing to read the calendar of events, Mo did not notice who was sitting at the end of the bar.

Vera said nothing; she simply made her way over to the woman.

As she approached, the woman smiled and began. "I see the cavalry has called for reinforcements."

Clenching her right hand into a fist, Vera did not reply. She simply drew back and struck her as hard as she could muster. Punching her squarely in the face, in a loud, sprawling clatter, Solange fell from the stool. In a fanlike pattern above her, whiskey splashed across the floor. Immediately, the alcohol began to soak into the concrete. Now lying prostrate, Solange then attempted to bring herself to a seated position. Blood poured from her nose and mouth.

"In case you wondered, I don't believe in givin' my enemies a heads up." Vera put her left hand on her hip. Pointing her right index finger at her, she began again. "I also ain't from Gentilly. You may as well refer to me as Ninth Ward ghetto, Solange, because in my neck of the woods, we address a problem by just taking the bitch out."

Before she spoke, she attempted to wipe some of the blood from her face. "Good advice from a stranger."

Vera then saw her right hand disappear into her jacket. She followed this action with a swift kick into Solange's belly. Solange immediately grabbed the affected side. In apparent agony, she began to rock back and forth so as to help mitigate the sharp, lancinating pain. Vera reached down and ripped the gun from her blazer. "How about I use this on you right now, 'ho'?"

"Go ahead. You forget I'm immortal."

"And just how much energy will you have to steal to heal up a blown out face?"

"I can start with you."

"Tough words coming from a skinny, pathetic slut sprawled all over the floor. Look at this ... you've made quite a mess!"

"I'm sure the police will take care of restitution details. They should be here soon. Your ostentatious display of force alerted every employee in this establishment. You should learn to be more subtle, Vera. It may help to keep you out of jail."

"They ain't comin'."

"Oh no?"

"These people know who we are and what we represent. That's exactly why you brought yo' ass here tonight ... you fully intended to start some shit or pull one of yo' verbose threat maneuvers followed by a carefully planned exit." Vera turned to a flabbergasted Mozetta and Pierre. Turning toward Solange once again, she continued. "We happen to be tired of that shit, Miss Deshotel, and really wish you'd get another act."

Arduously, Solange made her way to her feet. "You can count on it."

Vera took a step forward. "Well, you better not count too much, honey, because I'm ready to take you out. I have everything I need, and unlike the others around here, I have a plan. I ain't into no 'trial and error,' Solange, I know what works. I plan to use it, too—real soon. So, get ready, baby, 'cause like the song says, here I come."

Solange met her non-blinking gaze. "Learn from your enemies, right ...Vera Ellen Jenkins?"

"Dead on target ...You see, you *were* listening."

Solange said nothing else. She simply turned from her and laboriously began to walk away. As she did so, she pulled a Kleenex from her jacket.

Vera cocked the hammer of Solange's pistol and subsequently fired it into the ceiling.

As bits of plaster and metal began to rain down upon her, Solange froze.

"Just a trial run, baby, there's lots more to come."

Solange turned toward her. "You're right, Vera, there is more to come." She then turned back around and made her way out of the bar.

Mozetta moved closer to Vera. "Well, Miss Thing, you brought it all to the front. Hope you meant what you just said."

Vera cut her eyes toward her. "Girlfriend, I wasn't playin'. I know exactly what to do. Call the rest of yo' group and arrange a meeting in the morning. The six of you have some listening to do ..."

✳✳✳

When combined, oil and water will separate. Most oils form a layer on top of the heavier hydrogen-bonded liquid. Complicating an escape to safety, as an attempt is made to exit the viscous situation the oil tends to coat a fleeing entity. Many times, without heroic intervention, the end result is nothing short of disastrous.

The atmosphere was so thick, she felt as if she were submerged at the bottom of a pool. Attempting to breathe, the great volume of smoke seemed to make oxygen uptake impossible. Shelley knew that somewhere, beyond the thick air and blanketing oil layer, was a clean, breathable environment. It was so close she could almost feel it.

Bit by bit, however, at that moment consciousness began to elude her. The others had long since disappeared, and from her vantage point in the warehouse, she could see nothing else.

Interesting way to end this life … never in my wildest dreams did I ever think I'd leave alone? Never did I imagine I'd depart this existence so far away from those who love me…

In a natural order of sequential events, resignation usually comes before the end. She now had reconciled herself to the fact that perhaps in some other state of being, she'd one day again see her family. Finally letting go of this one, she was ready for the departure.

You can't yet leave! We've only just met!

So far removed, the voices served as a last umbilical linkage to this earthly existence. Shelley clung to the vocal foundation.

Breathe, dammit!

She would try, but the effort was becoming increasingly futile.

"Is she breathing?"

"Barely, but I do indeed feel respiration. There is movement in her chest as well."

"Shelley! Shelley … can you hear me?"

The voice was vaguely familiar, but nothing buried in a long, concrete past. She truly appreciated the sincere effort to save her, but the attempt stemmed from a source too foreign to be recognized as credible.

Swim up through the water. Breach the oil and fight. There is reason to survive; there is hope. Do not succumb to what has happened; it does not constitute your life plan. This must be an accident—one you did not elicit.

She drew a loud, forceful breath. At that moment, the air appeared fresh. Seemingly clean, Shelley began long, deliberate inhalations from her ambient surroundings. As she did so, consciousness began to rematerialize.

"You …"

Putting his face close to hers, he began to answer. "I wasn't sure I'd ever see you again."

Rubbing her index and third fingers against her right temple, she attempted a reply. "One can only wish that it may have been under better circumstances."

"Must not have been your time, Shelley. They barely got you out of that warehouse before the whole thing was engulfed."

She coughed a couple of times. Clearing her throat, she began again. "Who are they?"

"The Memphis police. They dragged you out at the last moment."

"Where are the others?"

"Others? They found no one else."

Forcefully, Shelley coughed again. "There were seven others in the warehouse. With me, Albert, there were seven other people."

"They must have escaped."

She then managed herself to a seated position. A furrow crossed her brow. "Surely they wouldn't have left me there … They wouldn't have left me in there to die." Refocusing her gaze upon Albert, she continued. "Would they?"

"The smoke must have been too thick, Shelley. They must have not been able to find you. They would never have left you to die in that fire."

"Then where are they?"

"I don't know."

Her gaze once again fell downward. "And I'm now here … in this place, all alone."

"The police are here, Shelly. They'll want a statement from you. I suspect there will be an investigation as to the cause of this fire."

"I can't tell them what I know, Albert. They'll think I'm insane. Either they'll think I'm insane or some sort of outrageous liar."

"You have to give them some answers. This is a serious fire. The results could have been disastrous for downtown Memphis."

"Could have been?"

"It was the most bizarre of incidents. That blaze should have spread through this district like wildfire. For reasons completely not understood, it was self-contained. It makes no sense."

"It wasn't a normal fire."

"No, it was not."

She rubbed her head once again. "Thank God for not so small favors."

"Yes, thank God."

Shelley took a deep breath and then exhaled. Looking straight ahead, and making no eye contact, she began. "I've always wondered about death. I can honestly say I never imagined it like this."

"Shelley, you're far from dead. Why would you say such a thing?"

"Well, Albert, in the first place I've been taken from my entire existence."

"You mean you were kidnapped?"

"In a manner of speaking, yes, I was. Albert, I have ... or perhaps now, I had a husband, a son and a life. I'm not from this place or this time. Through no fault of my own, I've been thrust here and abandoned. This must be some sort of afterlife ... I have to be dead. Maybe this is purgatory or something, and I have to make amends for all of my sins."

"I'd hate to think that I represent purgatory."

"Not you, of course. You're the only nice thing about this place. Think about it, Albert, I have no place to stay. I have no money, no clothes and no food. What am I going to do? Am I supposed to die again? Will I then perhaps be allowed into Heaven?"

"Let's start with some food. My mother—as we speak—has a big dinner waiting on us. We'll begin there and figure out the rest."

"I hardly think she has a big dinner waiting on 'us,' Albert."

"Well, now it's 'us.' Let me have a word with Jake Malmstrom and then we'll leave. I'll assure him that I'll bring you around tomorrow. You can answer all of his questions, then. I don't think you're in any shape for interrogation this evening."

"You're definitely right about that. I'm not sure I'll be ready tomorrow, either. I could use a visit from God, Albert. This afterlife thing is a lot to process. He did make it a rather human transition, though."

"Stop it, Shelley. I will reiterate that you are not dead."

"As you wish ..." Extending her hand, she used his strength to regain her footing. Subsequently, she managed to stand.

"Stay here. I'll be right back. Let me have a word with Jake and then we'll leave."

Shelley shrugged. Her eyes filling with tears, she attempted to manage a smile. "Take your time, I have nowhere to go."

From his coat pocket, Albert pulled a handkerchief. "Here, here. Stop all of that nonsense. We'll figure this out. Let's get you fed and then a nice hot bath. Things will look much better after that."

I want my son, and I miss my husband. I know perfectly well, Albert, that I'll never see either of them again. How could things possibly look better? I'd love for you to tell me, Mr. Janway, because right now I really need to know ...

✳✳✳

There is a stage of sleep that is as close to bliss as humanly possible. The stage lies between REM and deep sleep; a vague bit of consciousness remains before succumbing to the deep, heavily altered state. Endorphins must be released during this phase, for a feeling of total peace, relaxation and contentment comes with this brief period of rest. To abruptly awaken one from this stage is unforgiving. A brash, harsh return to reality is perceived as almost painful.

As he slept soundly, with abrupt, uncaring forethought Patrick flipped the light switch in his room to the 'on' position.

Doug immediately covered his eyes with his hands. "Aw shit! No you didn't just turn that light on. Barker, turn that fucking light back off."

"Rise and shine, Dougie! Time to get up. We have to get the bar clean and ready for the customers."

Crap ... Turning over in bed, Doug covered his head with the sheets and the bedspread. "OK, OK. Give me a minute to get awake and I'll get a shower." He then inhaled deeply.

"Sorry to disturb your beauty sleep ... although, it really didn't help much, did it? You look like hell!"

Stretching his arms toward the ceiling, he brought himself to a seated position. He then stretched once again. "First of all, shut it!

That screech owl voice is like sandpaper on my brain." Subsequently dragging himself out of bed, Doug headed for the doorway. "Second, I gotta get cleaned up, Patrick. Go ahead and leave. I'll be over there in a half hour." Scratching his bearded stubble, he then turned toward the bathroom. As if in mid thought, he stopped and turned back around. And next time, knock! I don't need a surprise 'Mr. Sunshine Asshole' as a prompt to start my day."

"So unappreciative, as well as temperamental! I was only looking out for your job, dick face." Turning to leave, he added, "Before I go, I'm headed for the pantry … that is, if you don't mind. I haven't had breakfast yet."

"Good luck with that. Vince has pretty much cleaned me out. Why don't you buy your own groceries and quit mooching?"

"Right now, I'm gonna mooch. Get in the shower and wash your stinkin' ass. We got work to do."

Making his way to the kitchen, he opened both pantry doors and began his search. *Maple and brown sugar oatmeal … well, I've had worse.* He then grabbed a handful of cereal from an opened box. *Damn … may as well bring on the oatmeal. Anything beats this. 'Stale' described this shit last year … or was it year before last?*

There was a knock at the door. Leaning toward the hallway, he attempted to swallow the hard, dry cereal. With a painful gulp, he began. "Adair! You expecting anybody?"

Realizing that Doug must not have heard him, he tried again. "Adair!"

I guess he can't hear me in the shower. Either that or he's ignoring me. Ending the thought with a shrug, he approached the door. *Hell … I guess I'll answer it.*

The opened door revealed a man standing in front of it. With a smile, Patrick began. "What can I do for you? I mean a guy can hope, can't he?"

"Sure you can, but it would probably be wasted on this one." Returning the smile, he continued. "The name's Tim. I'm looking for Vincent Jacola."

As he finished this statement, the grin vanished from Patrick's face.

"Oh." Looking about the room, he took a deep breath and exhaled. "Well, I'm sorry to tell you that Fat-ass is not here."

Tim had to stifle a smirk. "OK … Well maybe you can tell me when he'll be back?"

"If we're really fortunate, maybe never … that slob eats and drinks up everything he sees. We're going broke just trying to employ his wide load."

"Employ?"

"Yeah, my friend who lives here got him a job at a bar in town. We all work there."

"Interesting …"

The smile returned to his face. "You know, I could be persuaded to take the day off. Adair in there owes me a ton of time. I mean, it's the least he could do."

"Yeah, well …"

"I'm Patrick, by the way."

For a moment, Tim let the introduction fall silent. After clearing his throat, he began. "So, Patrick, when did you say you guys expect Vince to return?"

"Not sure. Adair says he has some business in Miami. Apparently, it's some serious shit." A look of puzzlement crossed his face. "You're good friends with Lard-ass?"

Damn …

Patrick waited expectantly. "Tim? You there?"

Tim returned his gaze to the conversation. "No, we just know some of the same people from back home. Since I was in the neighborhood, thought I'd look him up."

"This is Key West, Timster. No one just happens to be passing by." He began to laugh. "We're at the end of the freakin' country, you dumb shit."

Many times when enraged, Tim could actually feel his face turn red. This time, at the apparent stupidity of this imbecile, he was more overcome by a feeling of disbelief. Whether or not the face was beginning to sport a pissed off shade of crimson remained to be seen.

"You know, Patrick, you're right about that." Reaching into his pocket, he pulled from it a cigarette. Tilting the package toward Patrick, he raised his eyebrows in offering.

"No, man, those will kill you. They make your breath stink, too."

Tim lit his smoke. "Just one of my many bad habits." Inhaling deeply, he took a drag. As he exhaled, he began again. "Did he say where he might be in Miami? If I could, I'd like to catch up with him."

Shifting uncomfortably, Patrick began to close the door. "Are you a cop?"

Almost choking, Tim laughed aloud. He then inhaled again. "I can assure you, Patrick, that I'm the furthest thing from a cop. Me and cops don't usually tend to hang out on the same side of the law." Taking a last drag, he dropped his cigarette onto the sidewalk and extinguished it. Before looking up, he wiped his right hand across his face. "Are you a cop?"

"What do you think, Tim? Do I look like a 'man in blue?' You don't have to dig too deep around here to realize that most of us locals have some kind of warrant outstanding somewhere."

"Well then, I should fit right in. I have more than a few of those hanging around out there."

"So … we have us a bad boy here?"

"Patrick, you're too kind."

"Not yet, but that can be arranged …"

"What can be arranged?"

Lurching to the side, in an attempt to keep from falling, Patrick grabbed the door jamb. "Damn you, Adair! You scared the hell out of me!"

"I doubt it. There's plenty more where that came from. Who are you trying to hook up with in from of my house?"

"This is … uh … Tim."

Taking a step forward, he extended his hand. "I'm Tim Johnson. I'm looking for Vince Jacola."

Doug did not acknowledge the handshake gesture. "What do you want with Vince? And how do you know him?"

"I was telling charmer here that we—Vince and I—know some of the same people from back home. I work in a paranormal parlor there. Since I was in town, I thought I'd look him up."

"How'd you know he was here, Tim?"

Shifting nervously in front of the door, he thought for a moment. "Did you just forget the part about where I work?"

"For future reference, when you're trying to get the goods on someone, or find someone who's gone under, you at least need a decent lie. That transparent shit you just used was pathetic."

"Who said I was lying, Doug?"

"I don't remember telling you my name."

Patrick moved a bit closer to Doug. "Neither do I."

"You gentlemen would be surprised at some of the shit that I know."

"You are a cop, aren't you?"

Closing the door almost halfway, Doug took a step forward. "Vince isn't here, Tim—or whoever the hell you are. He isn't coming back anytime soon, either."

Patrick met this comment with a long sigh. "Looks like now that makes two of us."

"Shut your horny face, and get out of here, Patrick! And Tim, I have to get to work. If you want to chit chat any further, I suggest you drop by the bar and buy some alcohol. Otherwise, it's been real."

Giving him an insincerely sympathetic look, Patrick interrupted. "He doesn't know which bar, Dougie."

"Yeah, he does. Pull your cards out and have a good long read, Tim. Then set your paranormal GPS to White Street."

By this point, all three men were standing on the front porch of the house. Doug inserted the key into the deadbolt and locked the door. Turning toward them, he made his goodbyes. "Hasta Luego, hombres, and stay out of my fucking house."

"Nice meeting you, Doug. We'll see each other again."

Stopping in the middle of the concrete walkway, Doug turned once more to face him. "I can't put my finger on why I don't like

you, but I don't. I also can't think of a reason I ever need to see you
again. Why don't we make that a reality? May bode well for both of
us, don't you think?"

"Looks like somewhere between New Orleans and the Keys you
lost your 'neighborly,' Doug, don't you think?"

"Yeah, I do." Turning back toward the street, Doug headed for
the bike rack.

Both men watched him leave. As he mounted his bicycle and
pedaled away, Patrick turned toward Tim. "Well, I guess that's that.
The silver lining is that I'm still here."

"You know, Patrick, even though this is a little out of my usual
parameters, I am feeling a little run down. I could use an energy
pick-me-up."

"How coincidental, because I'm in the mood to be picked up."

"Can you get us back in there?"

"As luck would have it, I know where he hides the key."

*I'm not so sure you'll call it 'luck' when I finish with you, Patrick, but
you can't say I didn't warn you …*

✳✳✳

"I am so sorry."

"I'm far from home."

"I know. The event has caused many people great pain."

"You've changed everything. There is no longer anything in my
life that is familiar."

"You must understand it was never my intention to alter your
existence?"

"Oh no?"

"You had to be protected. I could not let your soul suffer the
same fate."

"Same fate as what? What kind of fate is this?"

"You retain your mortality."

"Mortality in Hell? I think not."

"You are not in Hell. Your life force has skewed onto an alternate
plain of existence."

"One that I did not ask for."

"Yes, that is correct."

"I miss my family, Daria."

"Yes, that is an appropriate response."

"You had no right."

"One day you will thank me."

"Oh, you do think so? So many loose ends, and so many facets of life are forcibly left incomplete. It is not right."

"It must be, Shelley."

"And you are allowed this? This does not interfere in your outcome?"

"It has."

"How?"

"As I speak to you, my words penetrate the veil."

"As do mine. Both of us were allowed the transition."

"True, but you retain an earthly presence. There shall be closure. You must take comfort in this."

"Bitter … angry … confused and disturbed are the descriptives which service my emotional state. There is no room for comfort. I shall not find it, ever."

"You will find it."

"I hate you."

"I understand."

"I hope you're burning in Hell."

"I am not."

"Rot in Purgatory, then."

"No."

"You must leave. You must leave and never return."

"As you wish. I only ask that you pray for the hardened heart. It would not bode well for you to maintain it."

"How dare you ask me to pray for anything! Get out. Reap what you've sewn, Daria. Take solace in the fact that you've destroyed the lives of three people. You've wrecked an entire family,"

"I shall heed your wishes."

Through gritted teeth, Shelley muttered, "Somehow, someway, you'll pay for what you've done."

As she began to fade from view, she replied only, "I have."

She took a deep breath and then opened her eyes. Exhaling, she wiped her right hand across her brow. *It was a dream. Thank God* ... Her relief, however, was short lived. Looking about the room precipitated the stark realization that nothing was familiar. The bed in which she'd slept was polished mahogany. A spread sewn from champagne colored chenille had been neatly folded and draped across the foot of her mattress. To her left was a chest of drawers made from the same mahogany wood as the bed, and beside this piece of furniture was the doorway into the bedroom. In front of her was a battery of closet doors which literally spread from one side of the room to the other.

The room as well as all woodwork was painted white. This austere color palette was broken only by the colored bedspread and a pair of floral drapes adorning the room's single window. The floors were of stained oak. Resembling the first September honey harvest, their color was lighter than most.

On a table beside her, light emanated from a lamp. Still in bed, she had begun to hoist herself to a seated position when she heard a faint knock on the door.

"May I come in?"

Turning to address the knock, she began. "Please, by all means do come in."

An older woman made her way through the opening. Smiling, with a tray in her hands, she paused at the threshold of the room. "You retired so I early, I had a sneaky suspicion that you may awaken a little hungry. I thought I'd leave a glass of buttermilk by your bed."

"How sweet! Thank you so much, Mrs. Janway."

The woman smiled. "You're very welcome. And just in case you decide you want to read a bit, I've brought you a couple of books as well. If you like, I can bring in today's newspaper, too."

"That would be ... swell." *May as well arm myself as best that I can.* "I assume Albert went home?"

"He sure did, hon. He has an early day at the hotel, but we'll see him again around lunchtime."

So, I have a few hours this morning . . . A bit frayed around the edges, she decided to revitalize her smile. Clearing her throat, she attempted to continue. "Is there a Catholic church near here?"

Malva Janway managed a smile. "Yes, as a matter of fact, not too far from here is St. Peter Catholic Church. I believe it's on Adams Street—near the river."

"Not too far from the hotel, either. Mrs. Janway, a little later this morning I think I'll head over there."

"I'd be happy to drive you."

"That would be really nice."

"Do you want me to check and see what time church services are held?"

"Of course . . . yes, please. She paused for a moment. Redirecting her gaze, her facial expression changed to one of anxiety. But more than that, I will need an audience with the priest."

"Oh . . ."

As she said this, Shelley managed to exhale. Looking down, she began once again. "Yes, well, perhaps an early start would be best. If I'm to get all of this accomplished before noon, I'd better get dressed."

"Shelley, I took the liberty of hanging some clothes for you in the bathroom. I hope you don't mind; I usually do wash on Saturdays. I'd be glad to do your wash, then."

"Oh, just throw it into the washer. I don't buy anything that I have to hang dry."

"I'm sorry?"

Returning her gaze to Malva, Shelley realized that Albert's mother had no idea as to what she was referring. "I'm the washer, dear, and laundry tends to take up much less room if it's hung. It also dries much faster."

Oh, my God . . . "I see. Forgive me for being ridiculous, and thank you for the clean clothing."

"Now don't you give it a second thought. I have another surprise for you, too."

"I don't think I'm up for too many more surprises."

"Not to worry, as this is a good one. Tomorrow afternoon I have a hair appointment at Nell's Salon. She said she'd be glad to see both of us. I thought you may enjoy a wash and set—my treat of course."

"I … I don't quite know what to say."

"How about, yes?"

"Well, alright then."

"And don't worry, dear."

Shelley cut her eyes toward her. "About what?"

"She'll have no problem doing *something* with that peculiar cut."

"I see."

Putting her hand on Shelley's arm, Malva leaned toward her. "I hope I didn't offend you. It was the furthest from my intentions."

"No offense taken."

"Then it's a date." Walking over to the bedside table, she set down the tray and the glass of buttermilk. "If you decide you're hungry, we'll be downstairs listening to a bit of radio. You're welcome to join us."

"Thank you so much. For now, I think this buttermilk will do just fine."

"Of course … Now make yourself at home, dear, and I'll be ready around eight."

"Perfect. I'll go ahead and grab a bath." Shelley followed Malva toward the bedroom door. "Thank you again for everything, Mrs. Janway."

As she said this, Mrs. Janway turned around to face her. "Call me Malva. We may as well become good friends."

We may as well, Malva. From the looks of things, I'll need all of the friends I can get.

CHAPTER TWENTY-SIX

"It's amazing how something so simple can be so good."

"Ain't nothin' but crescent rolls, cream cheese, powdered sugar, and butter. Oh and there's two tablespoons of lemon juice in there, too."

"Well, girl, you sure did do a good job with nothin'."

As she said this, Vera helped herself to another pastry.

Mozetta watched as she swiftly ate the second confection. "Might better slow down with that. Too much of that nothin' and yo' pants ain't gonna fit, Miss Jenkins. I tend to think that one of those may have been enough."

"And I'm not sure two's gonna be enough." Returning her fork to her plate, she then dug around in search of her next bite. Smacking just a bit, she continued. "It's the little things in life, Mo. You gotta enjoy 'em. Life is hard. We have to have some little something to lighten things up."

"Those ain't gonna lighten nothin' up. As I just told you, they are goin' straight to yo' ass, Vera."

"And as we speak, my mouth is givin' them directions."

Mozetta laughed. "Well, I'm glad you are enjoying them."

"Get everybody in the den and tell them to have a seat. Before we get started, I'm gonna fix myself one more cup of coffee."

"Fix me one, too. All I like is a splash of cream. I just bought some, so it should be good and fresh."

Diligently carrying two steaming mugs of cream-laced chicory coffee, Vera maneuvered her way into Vince's living room. She then proceeded to lower one of them onto the end table beside Mozetta's chair.

"Thank you, baby."

Vera smiled. "My pleasure."

Cutting her eyes toward them, Arletha irritably shifted positions in her chair. "I'm glad you two are all up in each other's face making nice, but I do have other things to do. If we can get past the etiquette lesson, I'd like to begin."

Mozetta turned toward her. "Arlie, we can always count on you to put a black cloud over everything. Why don't you stuff another doughnut in yo' mouth and bite down?"

"I probably would do that if they weren't three days old."

Mozetta then arose. Putting her hand on her hip, she began again. "I don't need attitude. Especially from you …"

"Don't get all high and mighty on me, Mrs. Conerly, I'm just speaking the truth. This ain't no 'bridge club' meeting and we ain't here to socialize."

"Do you really think I would socialize with the likes of you?"

"No, I don't. I don't think you would socialize with much of any-body, 'cause nobody can stand yo' ass!"

Vera then stood as well. "Arletha, all of this over a damn cup of coffee? If being left out chapped yo' ass that bad I will get you one right now."

Mo turned toward her. "You ain't getting her nothin'. At the urg-ing of our colleague, let's go ahead and get started."

Turning her head away from Mozetta, Arletha exhaled. "Oh yes, by all means … once again the mighty Mozetta has spoken."

Clenching her teeth, Mozetta made her way across the room to-ward her. With her left hand she grabbed a handful of hair from the back of Arletha's head. As she did this, she suddenly realized she was left with a wig and several dangling bobby pins. She had inadvertently ripped off Arletha's hairpiece.

Immediately, Arletha's hands were on top of her head. Seeing that Mozetta had her wig in hand, her eyes widened. "You bitch!"

Stunned, all of the ladies in the room fell silent. A moment later, one of them began to snicker. Breaking the ice, the laughter in the room became contagious. The room became an uproar. The atmosphere becoming infectious, Arletha began to laugh as well. Waving her hand at Mozetta, she stood up and said, "I ought to beat yo' damn ass."

Now, too, laughing with the rest of them, Mo handed her the wig. "You sure should. Here you go, and I'm sorry, baby." Lowering her gaze, she began to remove the pins from the wig. "Give me a minute and I'll fix it."

"Oh hell, Mo, it's too hot for all of this, anyway." Taking the wig from her, she proceeded to stuff it into her purse. "Let's not worry about none of this and let Vera go ahead get started. Next Saturday you can pay Rozella for my wash and set."

Mo shook her head in resignation. "OK, Arlie, whatever you say. Serves me right, anyway."

"Miss Vera, are you ready to enlighten us?"

"I am." Straightening her dress and smoothing the wrinkles, Vera arose. "I can honestly say, ladies, that on this one, I've done my homework. The main issue at hand is how to deal with an immortal? You can't kill them, as they're protected by some kind of evil magic."

Edith now arose and straightened the back of her skirt as well. Returning to her seated position, she began. "Well that's comforting. Not only can you not kill them, they're protected by magic."

Vera cleared her throat. Turning toward Edith, she cocked her head just a bit to one side. "Edith, correct me if I'm wrong, but didn't I just say exactly that? I do thank you, however, for the reiteration." Turning her attention toward the rest of the group, she continued. "Ladies, at the end of the meeting, there will be plenty of time for comments. I'd like now to finish—unless the rest of you ladies need to hear everything twice, too."

Shifting in her seat, Edith refocused her gaze. Looking beyond the window beside her chair, she answered her. "Well excuse the hell out of me …"

Vera ignored the comment. "Immortals will be here on earth—alive and kicking—until Judgment Day. Therefore, the way to handle this sort is to render them inactive. In other words, we have to make sure that Solange is powerless to wreak any more havoc."

After she'd said this, Thelma leaned toward her. "And just how do you suppose we do that?"

"I've done a good bit of research into her background. I kind of got to know her past life."

"And?"

"It wasn't too good."

"Tell us something we don't already know?"

"I plan to use that against her."

"And how do you plan to do that?"

"Listen closely, ladies, for you're about to learn how the demise of Solange Deshotel will come about."

*** ***

"Nice place."

"It's a dump and you know it."

Standing in front of the threshold, with his hands in his front pockets Tim looked about the room. He then took a deep breath and exhaled. "It's a roof. Keeps out the rain and cold."

"We don't have cold here."

"We'll see …"

"But if we did, I could sure warm you up."

"You sure you're up for this, Patrick? Last chance to back out …"

"Oh, I'm up for it. Believe me."

"Well, there's a first time for everything … and this certainly is."

I guess food is food …

Slowly, Tim leaned over and put his lips to Patrick's. Feeling his touch, Patrick grabbed Tim into an embrace. Pausing for a moment, more forcefully, Tim began to kiss again.

Patrick pulled away. "Damn … I have goose bumps."

"That's all?" Tim leaned in and kissed him once again.

Beginning somewhere in his lower back, Patrick felt a shiver run across him. For a short moment, violently, he shook.

"You OK?"

Breathing deeply, Patrick wiped his forehead. Feeling a bit clammy, he was not even aware he'd been sweating. "I'm not sure."

Tim grabbed him again.

"Wait! Wait just for a moment."

Grabbing him by the back of the head, Tim once again forced his mouth onto Patrick's. *You asked for this, Patrick, and now you're fucking gonna get it.* "Too late to back out now, baby, we're just getting started good." Deeply Tim drew against Patrick's breath.

Patrick felt his arms fall to his side. Rapidly, his strength was leaving him. "Please don't."

"Oh, no, Patrick, I insist—just as you did." Tim laughed. "Kind of reminds you of that old adage, be careful what you ask for, you just may get it?" Locking him in a strong embrace, Tim once again forced his mouth over Patrick's. Breathing in deeply, he continued. "Now I could stop now and you'd just fucking die. But I don't think you deserve that privilege, Pat. Right now I'm about to suck the rest of your fucking life force out and tear apart that little ole silver chakra of yours. Then, just like me, you can hang around forever. Hey, it's not all bad ... you won't age anymore. You should love that."

Too weak to utter anything else, he merely replied, "Don't ..."

"Patrick, Patrick, Patrick ... we can't waste what's left of that precious life force, now can we? I could really use it." No longer able to hold his head erect, Tim moved Patrick's mouth closer to his own. "Here, let me go ahead and take care of that for you. And don't worry, it won't hurt a bit." For the last time, Tim shoved his face onto the man beneath him. This time he inhaled so deeply, Patrick's ribcage actually descended toward his backbone.

As he did this, Patrick's eyes fell vacant. Smiling, Tim then tossed him aside and started for the doorway. As Patrick's head hit the floor, near the corner of his mouth, a pool of blood began to form. As if in final protest to the assault, he managed a raspy exhalation.

Noticing the stark contrast between crimson red and bleached white maple wood, Tim smiled. "Looks kind of nice together ... and one hundred percent organic, too. You know, Patrick, I kind of miss those lumberjack days. Maple was always such a beautiful wood to mill." Taking a deep breath, he exhaled once again. *Should I leave his ass feral? Hell, he'd probably wipe out half of the island population within a week.* Reaching into his pocket, he pulled from it a pen. On the back of Patrick's left hand he then proceeded to write a name and telephone number. "Thierry seems to be our new immortal mentor. We'll let him handle this one." Laughing aloud once again, he added, "Don't worry, Pat, you'll awaken soon enough—hungry as hell! Or should I say hungry as Hell?" *'Cause from here on out, that's what it is for you, Patrick … Hell.*

＊＊＊

"Hey Doug, we got ten cases of beer to go in the cooler. Also, while we're empty, I need you to get over to the supply house for pineapple and olives. And whenever Patrick gets his ass over here, have him mop the floor again. It doesn't look worth a damn and feels sticky."

"Yeah, yeah, Chris, I'll tell him. You also better stock up on Cab, there ain't but seven bottles in the back."

"Who comes to Key West to drink red wine? I can't sell the shit."

"You're wrong on that. Around dinner time, I sell a butt load of it."

"Alright then, go ahead and get me a case, but keep it around seven."

"You mean keep it around nine, don't you?"

"Seven dollars, Doug."

Doug sighed. "As I'm in no mood to argue, I'll see what I can do."

"Then get me a beer. What do you have on draft?"

Realizing this address came from his left side, he turned toward it. "You … What the hell do you want, now? Back at the house, I thought I'd made myself clear."

"You said if I wanted to chit chat any further, to drop by the bar and buy some alcohol. Here I am, and now I'm buying. So let's chat."

Saying nothing, he turned away from him. He walked over to the spigot and poured a beer. Returning to the place where Tim was sitting, Doug handed him a frosted mug. "Here, try this. It's one of Louisiana's finest."

"That just boggles my mind. How'd ja know, Doug? Are you a psychic or something?"

"Cut the bullshit." Leaning in a little closer, he continued. "Why are you here?"

Taking a long drink of the beer, Tim set the mug onto the bar and swallowed. Inhaling deeply, he began. "It's not complicated. As I told you back at the house, I want to see Vincent Jacola."

"For what?"

"That's between me and him."

"I ain't telling you shit. Finish your beer and leave, Tim. Chit chat is over."

"It's not over, Doug ... not even close."

"Unless you want your fucking ass beaten, it is."

"You know, some guys—like your friend Patrick—may actually like that. I tend to be the type that gives a lick if I have to take one. There may be more than one ass beating, Doug, and when I get done, not too much left of this nice establishment, either. You want to risk that?"

"If I have to, yeah, I'll risk it."

"Well then how about this. Over in Dallas you have a sister named Marissa, right?"

"How do you ..."

"Oh, I make it my business to know lots of things. I also know all about your little niece Callie, too."

Clenching his right fist, with his left hand Doug grabbed the collar of Tim's shirt. "I'll take you out right here and now. Don't fuck with my family or I will kill you!"

Using both hands, forcefully Tim shoved Doug away from him. He then pulled his cell phone from his pocket. Breathing deeply, he began. "Before you start swinging, you better hear me out."

"I ain't hearing crap!"

"Then they're about to die."

Saying nothing, Doug froze.

"Glad that got your attention. We're gonna do a little test here, and you're gonna keep your mouth shut. After we finish, you'll be convinced I'm not whistling Dixie."

"I'll bet you don't even know the words."

"Maybe not, but I thought I'd better use a metaphor you'd understand. You don't strike me as the cerebral sort."

"Whatever that means."

"Point taken. Now have a look through that doorway over there. Across the street do you see that white compact car?"

"Yeah, so what?"

Tim then again focused his attention toward his cell. "So that I'll only have to press one number, I remember having this App on speed dial. Let's see. I think white compact was number eight ... at least I hope it was."

Doug gave him a puzzled look.

Looking around, in a mock attempt to make sure no one was listening, Tim continued. "Here goes, Dougie, and remember: It's our little secret."

On the virtual keypad of his phone, Tim then pressed the number eight. As soon as he'd done so, the white car exploded. Sending shrapnel everywhere, bits and pieces of glass and metal cascaded through the open French doors.

Covering his head, Doug crouched to the floor. "Mother of mercy! What was that?"

"My new toy! With a little prep work and some plastic explosives, I can blow up anyone from anywhere ... and with free long distance, too!" Looking at his cell phone, he continued smiling. "I just love this thing!" He then returned his attention to Doug. "Man, this new millennium is swell!"

"Swell? Dude, you just blew up someone's car. You could have killed somebody! What if someone was in there or walking by?"

"Uh, Doug ... that's the general idea. It's called, murder? And on that note, I want to make sure that you understand that on my speed dial, Marissa's car is number six. I also had some friends get me a copy of Callie's dance schedule. As luck would have it, as we speak, they're on their way to the studio. Now, if I press this button ... well, you know what happens. And you know what the best part is? I've hacked into your information. Now this phone is listed in your name, under your social. They'll think you made the call!" Uncontrollably, Tim began to laugh. As he did so, with his right hand he slapped the edge of the bar "I just kill myself sometimes." After he'd said this, the smile suddenly vanished. "In a manner of speaking, of course …" Unsuccessfully attempting to stifle a smirk, he then chuckled once again. "So you want me to press the button?"

Doug froze.

As if a switch were turned to 'off,' his face once again became serious. "I thought not. You know, Dougie, I really have nothing to gain by offing Marissa and Callie. So, if you'll just give me what I need, we'll call it a day. I'll even take them off of speed dial."

"What about the explosives attached to the car?"

"I'll make sure all of that disappears."

Beginning to tremble, Doug cleared his throat. As he began to speak, his words were drowned by the peals of police sirens careening toward the fiery wreck. He waited a few moments for the sounds to dissipate. Upon the scene, three police cars suddenly descended. From the opposite direction, a fire truck made its way to the event.

Cupping his hands around his mouth, into Doug's right ear Tim began to yell. "We'd better make our way to my car. I suspect it'll be noisy here for awhile."

Making his way around the bar, Doug followed Tim outside. As soon as the two of them had reached the street, they encountered Patrick headed inside. By now the sirens had abated and the street was abuzz with activity.

Looking toward Patrick, Doug began. "What the hell happened to you? You look terrible. And where have you been?"

Patrick focused his gaze directly toward Tim. "I'm not sure exactly what happened, and I feel about as bad as I look."

Turning toward Doug once again, Tim whispered, "A little friendly advice: Probably wouldn't be a good idea to hang around him right now. He looks kind of hungry. Besides, we have work to do. Let's go."

Looking away from Tim, Doug addressed Patrick once again. "Chris needs olives, pineapple and red wine. Find a Cabernet Sauvignon for around seven or under, and put those cases of beer into the cooler. I'll be back later."

"Much later," Tim added.

"You planning on fucking him up, too, Tim? What do you have, some sort of aromatic drug? Well, it ain't worth a shit."

Craning his neck a bit to have a look at the back of Patrick's hand, he managed a half smirk. "Don't lose that number on the back of your leftie, Patrick. You're gonna need it sooner, rather than later."

His eyes momentarily falling toward it, he then glared at him. "Suck it, asshole."

Taking a step in his direction, Doug also cut his eyes toward Patrick's hand. "Just get over to wholesale, Patrick, and tell Chris I'll be back to work as soon as I can. It's a family emergency."

"What happened?"

Tim answered him. "Nothing, yet … we hope. Let's go, Doug."

"And what's with all the fire and metal everywhere? Did someone blow a hole in the side of that building?"

Once again, Tim answered. "Probably happened when that car blew up, Pat. Scary thing … just happened right out of the blue." He turned toward Doug. "What kind of car was that, anyway? I'm thinking a recall may be in order."

Not answering, Doug just stared at him.

"Well, Chao, Patrick. In case you didn't know, that's the Hispanic version of 'later'."

"Gee, you're just a wealth of cosmopolitan knowledge today, Timothy. Doug, call me later. I'm headed in to talk to Chris. He's probably gonna fire your ass for walking out on him like this."

For the third time, Tim answered him. "Can't be helped."

"Shut your stupid face, Tim. Let the man answer for himself. I've had enough of your cocky bullshit."

Doug merely replied, "I have to go."

The two men then turned and began to walk away from the bar. As they walked down the block, Patrick stood and watched them disappear. *None of this adds up. Something's wrong.* Breathing in deeply, he exhaled. *But then again, right about now that applies to a lot of things.*

✳✳✳

"Here, Douglas, you drive. It'll be easier to hold a gun on you. And why don't we take the rental? It'll attract less attention."

"It's Doug, not Dougie or even Douglas, Timothy. You got that?"

"So sensitive ... No need to be irritable, Doug. There, is that better?"

"We need gas."

"No problem. I can usually make it up to Miami and back on a full tank. We have over half. We'll be fine."

Probably not gonna make it back alive, Doug. You better find a way to get some help or he's gonna kill all of us. "You have to be careful with that on the Overseas Highway. If there's a lot of traffic, it's a crawl up to Miami."

"Just drive. Once I get to your buddy Vince, I don't really give a shit who's where or how they got there. It won't matter, anyway."

"Hope he's home. He doesn't know we're coming."

"We can wait. We have all the time in the world."

You may have all the time in the world, Tim, but if I'm gonna get my ass out of the crapper, I'm gonna have to act fast. Let's just hope that between here and Miami I can come up with a plan ... and it better be a good one.

CHAPTER TWENTY-SEVEN

She found St. Peter Cathedral to be nothing short of breathtaking. Obviously a historical as well as an architectural masterpiece, the Cathedral stands as a lasting tribute to the talented Charles Keeley. Entering the church, Shelley took a moment to drink in the beauty and splendor of the stained glass windows. Built into perimeter of the structure, the intricate works of art narrate the life of Christ as well as several saints.

Nine years prior, the French-Canadian firm of Casavant Freres oversaw the construction of the choir loft Sanctuary organ. From its day of completion, it was considered one of the premiere recital instruments of the area. With its vaulted ceilings and Gothic characteristics, the church is nothing short of a glorious accolade to the Lord.

Immediately upon entering the building, she felt comforted.

It's safe here.

As she stood in awe, a man approached her. "It is beautiful, isn't it?"

"That's putting it mildly."

"I'm Father Welton Brindham. Welcome to Saint Peter Church."

"Thank you so much." Shifting a bit, she refocused her gaze toward him. "So you're the resident priest here?"

"As a matter of fact, I'm the Pastor."

"You're just the man that I wanted to see."

"What can I do for you?"

"Father, my name is Shelley Levy."

"Very nice to meet you, Shelley. What brings you to Memphis?"

"Well, it was not by choice, I can tell you that."

A look of concern washed over his face. "I'm sorry to hear that. Your husband was transferred here?"

"No, Father, my husband and son live in Miami, Florida."

"I see." Sensing that a long conversation may be ahead of them, Father Brindham turned and walked toward the pews. "If you have a few moments to talk, why don't we get a little more comfortable? Here, have a seat and rest for a moment." Breathing in, he refocused his attention toward her. "Are you and your husband divorcing?"

"No … although our future together doesn't look too bright."

"I'll take the liberty of being presumptuous and tell you that you must learn to forgive. If the marriage is in trouble, both of you must learn to forgive. You must learn to forgive and also to be flexible. Be sensitive to each other's needs and desires."

"If it were remotely possible, I would do all of the afore mentioned."

"And it is not?"

"Father, I was brought here against my will." Shifting positions in the pew, she leaned closer toward him. "And not under natural circumstances, either. I need God's help and didn't know to whom else to turn. I figured if anyone could help me, it would be a man of God."

"If I'm to put any of the pieces of this situation together, you'll have to continue."

"I'm not from here."

"We've already established that."

"No, Father, what I'm trying to say is that I'm not of this time and place."

Father Brindham said nothing.

"There were others here with me, but now they're gone. Somehow, I was left behind."

"What others?"

"Well, there was Mozetta, and … well, you see it was a group."

"Seven others, Shelley?"

"Yes, seven, how on earth did you know?"

"Shelley, I'm beginning to get a handle on the situation at hand, and it's serious, I might add."

"You're kidding … really?"

After that statement, he gaze fell downward. "Accompanying that last statement, I was not anticipating sarcasm."

"Father, think about what I've just told you, and then about what you have revealed to me. Don't you realize that I'm well aware of the severity of this situation? I mean I've died and gone to freaking Purgatory for Christ's sake. That's pretty darn serious, you know?"

"Had you died and gone to Purgatory, it would have been for your own sake, not Jesus.' Purgatory is a place which enables one to serve, after one's death, the appropriate penance for venial sin that remains attached to the soul. You're not in Purgatory, Shelley. This place is real."

"I'm not in-between worlds?"

"No, you're not."

"Then what has happened, Father? Why did God let this happen?"

He opened his mouth to speak, and then closed it once again. Looking straight ahead, in an attempt to complete a thought, he fell silent. After the moment, he returned to the conversation. As he arose, he began. "Would you excuse me for just a second, Shelley? I'm in need of a drink of water—my mouth is so dry. When I return, I'll do my best to explain everything to you."

"Of course, thank you."

"Would you care for some?"

Her glance was diverted. "Um, yes … please. That would be fine."

Saying nothing else, Father Brindham arose and walked toward the rear of the church.

Well that was odd … such an abrupt exit. She then turned to see if he was returning to the sanctuary. *Maybe he didn't have the words; maybe he didn't know what to say."* She turned around once more. Still, he had not returned. *"Basically, what Father*

Brindham is telling me is that the phenomenon of time travel is possible, and apparently, there are rituals, which can catapult one though time. How wonderful that I've managed to get caught up in some netherworld fistfight.

"Here you go."

Her train of thought broken, she turned to address the voice. "Thank you."

"I will now attend to your question and bring you up to speed on this situation. As I've just told you, you're not in Purgatory. You're not dead and you're not in-between worlds."

"So I've managed some sort of time travel."

Pausing for a short moment, he took a deep breath and exhaled. "It's a bit of a stretch. A long stretch, actually, but for the sake of simplicity, we'll begin by describing it that way."

Lowering her forehead to her hands, she answered him. "This is too much. I was afraid you might agree with me."

"Shelley, have you ever heard of Father Donovan?"

"Sounds familiar ..." For a moment she fell silent. "Wait a minute ... of course! He wrote the book. Yes, that's right. Daria gave that book to me, and I gave it to Vince to read."

"I wasn't aware of a book. You are referring exactly to what? "

She exhaled. "Right ... Well, for the mean time, maybe I'm putting the cart before the horse."

"Father Donovan wrote a book?"

"He did ... or will ... about Solange Deshotel."

"Who you must realize is at the root of this entire evil equation."

"You make it very easy, Father, but you'll get no more derision from me."

"I thank you for that. You mentioned time travel, Shelley, and I'll attempt to weave that phenomenon into an explanation of your predicament. A moment ago, you asked me why God let all of this happen."

"I did ask that."

"God had nothing to do with any of this. It is not of his work."

"He could have prevented it. He could have fixed it. This is impossible." Swallowing hard, she forcefully clenched her teeth. "And not supposed to happen. It cannot be real."

"I've talked with Father Donovan at length, and you're right. This was not supposed to happen. First of all, Shelley, for Solange Deshotel time had stopped. She was imprisoned in it. God took her out of the running and left her in an endless time loop of sorts."

"Looks to me like she's moving forward at the speed of light."

"Literally." After taking a long sip of his water, he then swallowed. Clearing his throat, he began again. "Something happened. Something occurred that should not have and allowed her to escape. Father Donovan knows of the occurrence; we've discussed it, but not in depth. Something penetrated that time-line continuum and destroyed her prison."

"OK, Father, you're now talking miles above my head."

"If you give me your word that you'll leave off any semblance of cynicism, I'll attempt to simplify."

Raising her hands in resignation, she bid him to continue.

"Imagine a horse race."

"A horse race?!"

"Bear with me, Shelley."

"I'm … I'm trying …"

"The horses are racing on a circular track, right?"

Expectantly, she cut her eyes toward him. "OK …"

"Now tear down a section of that fence, which subsequently allows the horses to escape. Once the track is breached, in a linear fashion they all run through the break."

"And now we'll attempt to weave all of this together, right?"

"Although time is linear, Shelley, it has no beginning nor does it have an end. Therefore, God is everywhere. He's here for you in the past and he's waiting for all of us in the end of days as well. In order to take an entity as powerful and evil as Solange Deshotel out of circulation, she was relegated to her own form of Hell—also described as an endless time loop. That loop branched off of linear time much like a cul-de-sac connects to a main road. Solange had finally reached her own dead end. The loop then ceased to be reality and became an imprint—a memory if you will."

Looking at nothing, she whispered the thought aloud. "An imprint …"

"Once that loop was destroyed, Solange was able to escape. That timeline then directed itself toward the linear, and merged with it."

"Moving forward once again?"

"Exactly."

"So this is not some other dimension?"

"In a manner of speaking, yes it is. In ordinary life circumstances, there should be no way to access the past. The timeline continuum should remain intact."

"And if what you're saying is true, Father, then I am back on track. I'm gonna catch up with my old life in say … some thirty odd years or so? And then what? Do I watch my mother carry me or do I find some way to crawl back into the womb?"

"I thought we had a discussion about sarcasm, Shelley."

Her voice rose almost an octave. "Father, please! Please … please … please! I mean, what's a girl to honestly believe here?"

"I just told you that time is linear. I'm not saying that it cannot be bent, but it does tend to move in a forward direction. That being said, all of us pass through this existence only once. Therefore, I cannot see you reaching your previous existence. I'm not God, but somehow I don't feel he'll allow the paradox to materialize."

"Let us hope."

"You must have faith."

After he finished, she took a deep breath and let out a long sigh. "So, there is no hope for me."

"The Lord still has a plan for you. It may not be his original plan, but obviously he has work for you to do."

Shelley began to cry. "I was hoping that you could help me."

Reaching into the inside front pocket of his coat, he pulled from it a handkerchief. Handing it to her, he began. "I'll help in any way that

I can, Shelly. I'm sorry that I don't have the answers that you wanted to hear, but if you like, I would be glad to help you get settled. "

Dabbing her eyes, she attempted a smile. "That would be nice, thank you. The Janways have been most kind to me as well. I spent last night with them."

"Malva Janway is a good woman. Between the two of us, we'll get you onto your feet."

Looking directly into his eyes, she placed her hand atop his. "Father Brindham, I am in so much pain. I never imagined it was possible for one person to be so unhappy."

"We'll pray together for resolution. We'll pray for healing, Shelley. In that respect, perhaps we can help you find your way."

She stood up to leave. "My way? I don't even know where I belong."

"Perhaps now you belong here."

The tears began to flow once again. "I must leave. I … I have an appointment at the beauty shop. I'm sure by now Mrs. Janway is wondering what on earth has happened to me."

"God bless you, Shelley."

"I could use that, Father, I really could." She turned to leave and walked a few steps. She paused and turned back to address him. "God could have stopped this, you know. He could have left me with my family."

"We'll make an attempt to look forward. Ironically, for you it'll be a little easier than most."

"On that you are wrong. Nothing will ever be easy again."

With both sadness and compassion, he attempted a smile. He merely replied, "I understand."

Saying nothing else, she then turned once again and walked toward the doorway.

You did the best you could do to help me understand a shattered existence, Father Brindham. Unfortunately, there are times when someone's best is just not good enough.

✻✻✻

"Hey Patrick, where's Doug? He was supposed to get some things from wholesale for me."

"I dunno. About a minute ago, he left."

"What?! What the hell?"

"Said it was some sort of family emergency."

"Did he leave by himself?"

"No, he didn't. He got in the car with some dude by the name of Tim Johnson. Says he's from New Orleans."

Looking toward the street, Chris wiped his hand across his face. "Something bad must have come up. He didn't say goodbye, kiss my …"

"I don't know what's going on, but it didn't look like Doug wanted to leave."

"Really …"

"Yeah, man, the whole scenario was kind of strange."

"You ever see that Tim guy before?"

Looking downward toward the number written on his hand, he swallowed hard. "Briefly. He showed up at Doug's house this morning."

"Who is he?"

"Said he's an acquaintance of Vince's, and he wants to catch up with him."

"So he drives all the way down here from God knows where to find him? I don't think so. This ain't no 'just passing by visit,' Pat. He is up to something."

"He has to be." Taking a step away from him, Patrick cast his glance toward the floor. "Chris, this guy's not right."

"So you do know him."

He returned his glance toward him. "No, I hooked up with him."

"Oh, smart, Patrick. A stranger shows up and you fuck him." Shaking his head in disgust, he continued. "You're such a whore."

Patrick said nothing.

"Must've not been too good, though. You guys didn't seem too chummy."

"It wasn't like that, Chris."

"Really? Then how was it?"

"We didn't do anything. I hugged him and then he kissed me. He kept on and on and he wouldn't stop."

"You've always been a sucker for a hopeless romantic, so what was the problem?"

"The problem was that it wasn't a normal kiss."

"A normal kiss …" Pausing for a moment, he contemplated Patrick's last statement. "Besides the fact that you were sucking face with a strange guy, what exactly wasn't 'normal' about it?"

"The best way I can describe it, is that I felt he was literally sucking the life out of me."

Chris laughed. "You wimp … I can't believe we're having this stupid conversation. Here I am worried that Doug may be in some real trouble and you're complaining that your hookup kisses too hard." As he finished this statement, he turned away from him and walked toward the bar.

Patrick took a step forward. "He did something to me, Chris. I don't know what, but I'm not the same."

"You're in love? Or should I just say in lust?"

"Neither one, man, but during that kiss, I passed out. I passed out cold." He took a deep breath and then exhaled. "I'm thinking that he used some kind of shit on me, and it was potent as hell. He may have been trying to rob me, and I didn't have anything."

Making eye contact, Chris began again. "Alright, I'll give you that one."

"He could do the same thing to Vince."

"I hardly think Vince would voluntarily kiss him, Patrick."

Ignoring the comment, he continued. "What if that shit could be lethal? What if I was just lucky?"

Swallowing hard, Chris began to shake his head, 'no.' "You think we need to call the police?"

"Maybe …" As he said this, he noticed a small, black box atop the bar. "Hey, is that your phone over there?"

"Nope, I have mine in my pocket."

"Me, too. I wonder if Doug forgot his cell?"

Walking over to it, Chris picked it up. "I think this is his phone."

"See if it's locked."

After touching the appropriate markings on the face of the device, it sprang to life. "It's not locked."

Walking over to Chris, Patrick then took the device from him. "He left it here for us. I think Doug intentionally left it here for us to use."

"Should we call him?"

Squinting his eyes in a mixture of scorn and disbelief, he began again. "Now who's being stupid?"

"What?"

"We gotta call Vince, Chris. That's why he left his phone here—it wasn't by accident." Looking downward toward the device, he attempted to access Doug's list of stored telephone numbers. "We'll call Vince and let him in on what happened. He needs to know that guy is looking for him. After that we'll call the cops."

"Patrick, Doug is the one who's now missing. We need to first call the police."

"I didn't see Tim put a gun to Doug's head, Chris. He voluntarily got in that car. Vince, on the other hand, is blindsided. He doesn't know shit about this. What if they're headed to Miami? We gotta at least warn him."

Chris inhaled deeply and let out a long sigh. "Then see if you can find Vince's number. Let's just do it."

Concentrating intently on the device, Patrick diligently manipulated the electronic keypad. "Here it is."

"Call him and tell him we think Adair may be on his way—with company."

As he dialed the number, Patrick again glanced at the written number on the back of his hand.

And then I have another call to make. I'm gonna find out what exactly went down and what I have ahead of me, too. This Tim is some seriously bad news ... and there's a lot more bad shit in store for all of us.

✴✴✴

As he glanced at his watch, he noticed it was 12:50 P.M. Seeing that it was time for Senior Clinic, he arose from his desk and turned toward the door. *A mere four more hours on my feet ...* As he reached for the doorknob, his cellular device began to vibrate. The display read, *Private Caller.*

He debated on whether or not to answer it. Finally, after the third vibration, he touched the button area demarcated by a green telephone receiver. "This is Dr. Joubert."

A doctor ... "Yes, my name is Patrick Barker, and ... um ... I believe a friend of yours gave me this number."

"A friend? What friend gave you my personal cell number?"

"Well, Sir, his name was Tim Johnson."

"I see."

"You know him?"

"Did he tell you why you needed to call me?"

"No, he just said to make sure I didn't lose the number."

A feeling of dread began to spread through him. "Mr. Barker, exactly how do you know this Tim Johnson?"

"Well, Dr. Joubert, I really don't know him at all. I know to you that must sound pretty crazy, but I actually have an explanation."

Thierry sighed. It was a long, weary, exasperated sigh. "In reality, it doesn't sound in any way outlandish. This may sound senseless to you as well, but I suspect that I have a good idea why you're calling."

"You do?"

"I didn't know Tim slept with men."

"I don't think he does. If he did, I would have been his first—at least that's what he told me."

"So you didn't."

"Not exactly."

"What exactly constitutes 'not exactly', Mr. Barker?"

"Doctor, do you have a few spare moments for a story? Things in my life are very different than they were a few hours ago." As he finished the statement, his voice began to crack. Simultaneously wiping tears from his eyes, in an attempt to start again, he cleared his throat.

"Maybe you could answer some questions?"

As Patrick finished the statement, Thierry's shoulders sank. "I'm sure they are. And when I'm done answering your questions, Mr. Barker, you'll realize how different your life actually is."

And will be forevermore …

CHAPTER TWENTY-EIGHT

He had no sooner left his office and walked into the hallway when his cellular device vibrated once again.

"This is Dr. Joubert."

Vince froze. "Joubert?!"

"This is Dr. Joubert. To whom am I speaking?"

What the hell...? "Joubert, this is Vincent Jacola."

For a moment, Thierry was speechless. "Vincent? Where in the world are you?"

"Just where I said I was. I'm in Miami, Doc."

Guardedly paused for a moment, he began again. "What can I do for you?"

"I don't know."

"Well, that's an odd response, and it's certainly not the one that I was expecting, either."

"Believe it or not, I'm telling the truth. I don't know why I'm calling you."

"Well then let me approach this a little differently." As he said this, he leaned against the wall of the hallway. "What I really want to know is why you dialed my number, Vince."

"I called you because I received a text message containing this number. It's as simple as that. I had no idea whose number it was, nor did I have any idea why Doug sent it to me. So I called it, and here I am ... and there you are, too."

He swallowed hard. "Have you by any chance spoken with Patrick Barker?"

"Patrick Barker ...You're referring to Key West Patrick Barker?!"

"I am."

"How the hell would you know him, Joubert?"

"It's rather complicated, Vince." Breathing deeply, into the cell device he exhaled. "I need you to level with me. Have you recently spoken with Patrick Barker?"

Scratching his head in bewilderment, Vince continued. "No, I haven't spoken with Asshole lately, but I did just get off the phone with Adair."

"So Adair told you to call me?"

"No, he didn't. I said that wrong. He's the one who sent the text message."

Realizing this conversation may be of significance, Thierry turned and made his way back into his office. Closing the door behind him, he continued. "That's impossible. I don't know a person by the name of Adair."

"You don't? This is so fucked up. Then why would he send me your number?"

"And how would he get hold of it?" Taking a seat into the high-backed leather chair in front of his desk, he continued. "Does this Adair by any chance know Patrick?"

"Yeah, he does, but what does that have to do with anything?"

He must have somehow gotten hold of this number from him.

"Vince, I'm afraid you have some changes on the horizon and they're not good ones, I might add."

Déja vu ... where have I heard that before? "Like I need more change. Doc, you have no idea what's going on here."

"I know much more than you realize. I think I now understand why your friend may have sent you my number."

"Then by all means, enlighten me."

"If you receive a call from Patrick Barker, you must answer it. Your friend Doug Adair is in danger—as are you. Through some sort of persuasion—of which I'm not quite aware—he's been coerced into revealing your whereabouts to a man named Tim Johnson."

Déja vu. You need to watch your back. You have some deep water in front of you. You don't need to make a change anytime soon. It won't be a good one.

"Of course … It was LAPPS! Tim is the paranormal from LAPPS."

"Then you're aware of how dangerous this man is?"

"I thought he was a palm reader."

"Word has it this man does the dirty work for Solange Deshotel."

Vince's pulse began to race. "Oh God …" *He's headed here. Adair is bringing him here.*

"Vince?"

"So, Joubert …" Pausing for a moment, he attempted to swallow a large, seeming lump in his throat. Pulling a tissue from his front pocket, he then wiped his brow. Attempting to refocus his attention toward the telephone, he answered him. "What do you suggest I do next, Dr. Joubert?"

"Talk to Patrick Barker, first. Perhaps it would be wise not to wait for his call. The sooner you talk to him, the better prepared you will be. Patrick can give you an accurate chronology of recent events."

"I'll call him."

"After you've spoken with him, I'll need you to gather a rather bizarre array of protective armamentarium. You have to hurry as you do not have much time. Once you've assembled the items I've listed, you'll need specific instructions on how to proceed. You'll probably have only one window of opportunity to survive this situation, so you will have to listen closely and pay attention to every detail."

"It is what it is, Joubert. I'll do what I can."

"If you succeed, you'll be eliminating a most dangerous adversary. Many lives will be saved because of your actions. Do you have a pen?"

"Just text the list to me, Thierry. I'll call once I'm on the hunt."

"As you wish."

As I wish? If I had a wish, it sure as hell would not be for this. Who would wish for every man's worst nightmare?

***

Located on Prentiss Avenue, St. Raphael the Archangel Church has served the Gentilly neighborhood since 1947. After the end of the Second World War, the Elysian Fields corridor saw an exponential boom of growth. To accommodate this surging area development, Archbishop John Francis Rummel brought into existence what is today referred to as St. Raphael Parish. The existing church was constructed in the year 1958. With use of the finest Botticino marbles, and rich oak planks for both ceiling and woodwork, the building served as tangible testimony as to the vitality of the district.

The St. Raphael choir is somewhat famous among Gentilly locals. Mostly composed of women, the five men in the choir stand on the highest tier and handle most of the baritone and bass accompaniments. The choir director for St. Raphael is none other than Mrs. Mozetta Conerly. Born with perfect pitch, her gift insures that the group is always on key and singing neither sharp nor flat. Coincidentally—or maybe not—all of Mo's 'Voo Crew' sings in St. Raphael's choir. Almost always, this makes for interesting banter at practice.

"Ladies and gentlemen, let us all give a hand of welcome to this week's guest solo artist, Ms. Vera Ellen Jenkins."

Putting her hand on her hip, Arletha turned from the front row toward the choir. "Hmmph. I thought it was my week to sing solo."

Mo then turned to face her. "Oh, here we go again. Maybe you need to be front row center aisle every week? 'Cause that's what you seem to think."

"Every week? Seems to me a certain Mrs. Blankenship sang the last two solos. And that being said, Yo' Majesty, I'm not quite sure how that adds up to me singing solo every week." Raising one eyebrow, she then met her glance. "Perhaps it's just that yo' math is not too good."

"Call me 'Yo' Majesty' again and yo' voice might become a little muffled."

"Oh, I don't think so."

"Well, you might better think again, 'cause we're soon gonna see how well you sing with yo' head stuffed up yo' …"

"You two both shut up those big, damn mouths! Here we are in church—standin' in front of the altar, I might add, and still you women cannot behave."

"Well, Pierre, then how about you tell Miss Astor over there that the Queen is not in the mood for sarcasm?"

Taking a step downward, Vera rested a hand atop Mozetta's shoulder. "Let Arlie sing the solo, Mo. It is her week, after all, and I'm good with just being able to perform with all of these fine folk."

"Well now … that is so nice. Are we not so lucky to have myself the Queen, Miss Astor and Mother Theresa all in one choir?" Mimicking Arletha, Mo put her hand on her hip as well. "Well, the Queen just issued her edict, and Mother Theresa is gonna sing the solo. And if any certain someone does not like it, she can just get her 'Astor' out of here."

Shedding her choir robe, Arletha turned toward the door. "I sure can. I think I'll just tell all you ladies 'Astor la vista,' and like Her Majesty said, I'm out of here."

Stepping off of the platform, Vera quickly made an attempt to intercept her exit. "Please don't leave."

"Oh, I'm leavin' alright. I don't have to take that off of anyone!"

"It is always drama with you, Arlie. You cannot ever just let it be, can you?"

Turning to face the address, she began. "It's just a damn shame we all are not perfect like you, Mozetta. I'm gonna have to do my best to work on that."

Rolling her neck, Mo simply told her, "You do that. The sooner you get started, the better."

Saying nothing else, Arletha turned back around and made her way toward the door.

"Ok, Ladies and Gentlemen, this may be a good time to take a break. We still have to get the refrain harmony in sync on the recessional, so be back in ten."

Walking over to Mozetta, Vera began. "Do you think that she left?"

Glancing toward the window, she replied, "Looks that way. I don't see her car on the street."

"Mo, we have to go after her."

"For all I care, that 'hot mess' can stay gone."

"You don't mean that."

"Oh do I not?"

"No, you don't. Come on, Mo, let's go and get her."

"I ain't goin' nowhere."

"Yes, you are. You two are too good of friends to fall out like this. I don't care if Arlie is a 'hot mess,' she's our 'hot mess.' And Lord knows we need her big fat self around here to aggravate the daylights out of us. I don't want Arlie upset because I'm singing solo, Mo; I'm just a visitor."

"You ain't no visitor, Vera, you're family."

"Well, this relative is asking you to make this right."

Staring at her, Mo sighed in resignation. Breaking eye contact, her focus migrated toward each individual Station of the Cross. "I guess that would be the Christian thing to do." Her glance then fell to Vera. "I'm parked out back." Walking toward the vestibule, she began to wave at two women standing near the door. "Thelma, we are going after her fat ass; please lead them through the recessional."

Thelma smiled. "OK, honey. Go unruffle her feathers—once again!" She began to laugh.

"We'll be back in a few."

Mo and Vera made their way toward the back door. Once outside, turning toward the parking lot, they began to walk in the direction of the car.

"It's over here."

"And so am I."

Focusing on the interruption, Mozetta and Vera stopped abruptly. Taking a step forward, Vera addressed the intrusion. "You have some nerve to show up on a church parking lot. For the likes of you, even this is sacred ground."

"I'm following some good advice from an adversary, Vera."

"I know you don't want me to whoop yo' ass again."

"No, I don't, and you're not doing that."

"Again?"

Pulling a gun from beneath her blazer, she pointed the weapon at the two women standing in front of her. "Right."

"You are kidding me."

"Do I look like I'm kidding you?"

Immediately allowing the song books to fall to the ground, Vera stood frozen.

"What could possibly be wrong, Vera Ellen Jenkins? Could it be that this weapon evens the score just a bit?"

"It could be …"

At that moment, Vera slightly raised her elbows. Within a moment, almost in a flash, she'd spun around and kicked the gun from Solange's hand. Quickly, this was followed by a sharp blow to her face. Still in a martial arts stance, Vera began again. "Or it could that you are too stupid to learn from yo' mistakes. I guess you don't remember the last time?"

"Oh, I well remember. I don't forget anything."

"OK, then, well here is yo' lesson for today. First of all, you need to find someone else to handle yo' weapons, because you can't seem to hang onto them. Second of all, you should not have pulled a gun on a black belt, bitch. We're trained deal with shit like that."

As she then lunged for the weapon, Vera deftly swept Solange's feet from under her. Awkwardly, Solange fell to the ground. Vera once again continued. "Third of all, keep yo' skinny ass on the ground before I really hurt you." Shifting her focus from Solange toward Mozetta, she continued. "I've had enough of all this, and I think it's past time to deal with it. Mo, get the gun, and get that bitch in the car." Breathing in deeply, she simultaneously exhaled and sighed. "Unfortunately, it looks like this time Arlie may be on her own."

Quickly, Mozetta recovered the gun. Seeing Solange splayed upon the ground, she simply replied, "I think so …"

And I'm kinda thinking that right now you and I may be that way, too. Get in the car? Let's just hope that you know what the hell you are doing, Vera Ellen Jenkins.

✳✳✳

"Hold the gun on her, Mo."

"It might not be a good idea to put this in my hand, Vera. The fifth commandment says, *Thou shalt not Kill*, and I'm gonna have a hard time obeying that one."

Smiling, Solange answered her. "Considering I'm immortal, you certainly will. Destroy this body and I'll simply look around and find another one."

"Maybe so, but while you're in this one, I can make yo' life a living Hell."

"Like I did to you ... twice?"

Pulling back on the hammer, Mozetta cocked the gun. "You did not do a damn thing. You get credit for nothing, Solange."

"Oh, didn't I? Let us try to think of where your little friend Shelley may be at this moment? You remember her, don't you? She's the one you left there ... alone."

"I did not bring her there and had no way of getting her out. You made sure of that."

Following this statement, Solange began to laugh. "You're all such fools to think you are worthy opponents. I'll let you have your little fun ... for now."

"You better hope to God nothing happens to her, either. If it does, believe me, I will find out."

"Well I'm certainly not planning on wasting any hope on God, Mozetta. Why bother?"

"You blaspheme him any further and I will blow yo' fucking head off."

"And would that not be an interesting, eclectic sequence of events? I blaspheme, and then you murder—in his name, of course. You kill for God to protect his name even though rule number five says not to do so."

"You can make it as difficult to understand as you like, but the bottom line is this: I ain't listening to the likes of you blaspheming the Lord. If I have to eliminate yo' nasty face to shut you up, then I will do just that. I will settle up with him later on, because he knows where my allegiance lies, Solange. You, on the other hand, are a source of constant evil irritation to him."

"So loyal to such a distant source of comfort, Mozetta … a sign of real weakness on your part."

Gritting her teeth, Mozetta reared back and swiped the pistol across Solange's left cheek. The sight of the gun sliced a long narrow trench down the side of her face. Immediately, the wound began to bleed. "White trash, you better shut it before I beat yo' damn ass here and now. I ain't listening to no more blasphemy from you. And just to set the record straight, whore, he's a lot closer than you might think. With all of yo' experience in Hell, one would assume you would know better."

Still holding the gun on her, her glance fell toward Vera. "You're beginning to drive awfully fast. Are we in that much of a hurry?"

Vera smiled. "As a matter of face, we are."

CHAPTER TWENTY-NINE

"C'mon, c'mon … answer the phone." Pacing from one end of the living room toward the other, with his cell device pressed to his ear, Vince awaited anxiously for a response.

The call was then forwarded to Doug's voicemail. Pressing the button on which a red telephone receiver had been inscribed, without leaving a message, he ended the call. As soon as he'd done this, his ringtone was activated.

Wow … mediocre minds really must think alike. "Hello?"

"Vince."

"Man, I just tried to call you."

"You need to listen closely, and don't say anything. All of this is gonna sound crazy, but some bad things are about to happen."

Vince took a deep breath and exhaled. "Shoot."

"Not a good choice of words, Vince."

"Cut the humor and spill it, Patrick. I ain't in no mood for a play on meanings."

"Vince, I think Adair is headed your way."

"I know."

"You know? How would you know?"

"I talked to Joubert."

Standing silent for a moment, Patrick attempted to process the sequence of events.

"I guess my next question is why would you call him?"

"Patrick, it's like this. Someone—and I think it's Adair—texted a phone number to me. I called it and Joubert answered. He seems to think I'm in danger and that a palm reader from New Orleans is the reason. He also thinks somehow Adair is in danger, too, and has been coerced into bringing him to Miami."

"Adair is the only one who would know where you are, Vince. I was there, and I don't know why Adair agreed to go, but he looked nervous—almost afraid."

"This guy is up to no good, Patrick."

"You don't have to tell me that. I've experienced it firsthand."

"How?"

"Too long of a story, fat ass. Listen, you need to call the police. All of your lives are in danger. This guy is freakin' crazy."

"Tell me."

"He acts weird, Vince, and bizarre shit happens when he's around. This Tim guy shows up, and suddenly, in front of the bar, a car bomb explodes."

"Did you report him to the Key West Police?"

"No."

"Then let me use one of my favorite phrases. Are you just dumb as shit, or what?"

"Vince, I think he's some kind of hired killer. Deep down inside, I felt I could do some serious harm to Adair if I reported what I suspected. Adair acted as if he were being blackmailed or something. There's more to this than you and I know."

"Which would explain why he's bringing him here ... This Tim is holding something over Doug's head, and if he did blow up that car, he's probably threatening to blow something else up, too. That's how he forced Doug to reveal our whereabouts."

"Do you think you should call the cops on that end?"

"I think that I have a couple of calls to make." Taking his phone from his ear, he looked at the screen. He then returned it to the side of his head. "Patrick, I have to go. I'll be in touch."

"I'm dying here, man. Don't leave me hanging."

"I won't. You have my word on that."

"Be careful, Vince, some heavy shit is about to go down."

"Let's just hope I'm not about to go down with it. Later, Patrick."

Vince then ended the conversation and scrolled though his telephone list. Bringing the number in which he'd dialed Thierry Joubert to the screen, he placed another call to him.

"Hello Vincent."

"I called Patrick, and everything you said was true."

"You probably have about two hours to gather a list of items that I have for you."

"All I need is a gun."

"It won't do you any good. It will only get everyone involved killed."

"Doesn't sound like you have too much confidence in my abilities, Joubert."

"It has nothing to do with your abilities, Vince. You're not dealing with a normal situation here. You must stop talking and listen to me."

"I'm all ears."

"I'm texting you a list of items that you have to do your best to procure. You will need help as there is not sufficient time for you to do all of this by yourself."

"I have a brother-in-law and a nephew here. Maybe they can help."

"Vince, make your way immediately to Nuestra Madre, La Reina del Cielo Catholic Church. Ask for Father Alberto Cardoza. Mozetta has given the Father specific instructions on how to help you."

"Wow ... so you've been talking to Mo, too?"

"Time is of the essence. If you're successful, this whole disastrous chapter could be behind you."

"God help us all."

"Let us hope so."

"Hey Joubert ..."

"Yes, Vince?"

"I haven't heard from Mel, lately. Is she OK?"

"She's not at work, Vince. She's taken some time off ..."

"What?"

"That's all I know." *For now, that's all you will know as well ...*

Rubbing his chin in bewilderment, he only answered, "Strange …"

"At this moment, Delia is the least of your worries. Get over to the church immediately."

"On my way, Joubert."

"When they arrive, you must be ready."

"Oh, one way or the other, I will be." As he said this, he shifted positions. Reaffirming his train of thought, he continued. "After I have a talk with the good Father, I'll call."

"Make sure that you do. I'll be waiting, Vince, as you will need my help."

I need a lot of things, Joubert. Why? I don't know, but at this point, asking that is a waste of good air.

✳✳✳

Located a mere five minutes north of Miami International Airport, Hialeah, Florida holds the rank of Florida's sixth largest city. Predominately Hispanic, since the 1920's, Hialeah has grown into a district whose residents not only embrace their cultural heritage, but assimilate it into their everyday lives. The abundant mom and pop stores of this effervescent area have remained viable to such an extent that national chains, in order to be competitive and meet the demands of the local community, have had to alter their traditional business strategies. Proud of its ethnicity and family oriented neighborhoods, it is a hard working, diverse community.

As Tomas made his way into the house, Vince met him at the front door. "Where's Hialeah?"

"Hialeah? It's not too far from here, just a little bit north. Why do you ask?"

"I need you to take me there."

"Right now?"

"Yeah, now."

"OK …" As he pulled his keys from his pocket, he turned back toward the door. "What business do you have in Hialeah?"

"I need to get to Our Mother Queen of Heaven Catholic Church."

Pausing in thought for a moment, Tomas attempted to recollect the place of worship. "If my memory serves me correctly, that church is close to my Aunt Lidia's house. It's on NW 186th street."

"Then let's go."

"You still haven't told me why we're going there."

"I have to meet with a Father Alberto Cardoza."

"You know him?"

"No, I don't." Shifting his weight, Vince shoved his hands into his pockets. Taking a deep breath, he continued. "He has some items for me … some items of great importance."

"Are we headed on another wild goose chase?"

"I hope not … God, I hope not." Then pulling his keys from his pocket, he then also turned toward the doorway. "Look, if you don't want to take me, I'll go by myself."

"And you will stand out like a sore thumb."

"You seem awfully sure of yourself. Why the sore thumb?"

"Well, Vince, because Hialeah is almost one hundred percent Cuban and virtually no one there speaks English."

"I can handle the English thing—or the lack thereof. That won't be a problem."

"Trust me. It'll be much easier if I'm with you. Let's go—you can fill me in on the rest in the car."

***

The color turquoise helps to open the lines of communication between the heart and the spoken word. Creating emotional balance and stability, in color psychology, turquoise aids in both healing and controlling an emotional state of distress.

On the color scale, turquoise is situated between green and blue. Radiating the peace, calm and tranquility of blue, as well as the balance and growth of green, turquoise also provides the uplifting energy of yellow. During times of mental stress, this rich hue recharges our spirits. In an emergency situation, the color may also be of great aid in the decision-making process.

Assisting in the development of organizational and management skills, rather than to demand, turquoise merely influences. A good color to enhance concentration and clarity of thought, it exerts a calming effect upon the central nervous system. Giving control over speech and expression, this encouragement also helps to build self-confidence.

At times quite discriminating, the color turquoise has strong powers of observation as well as perception. Balancing the pros and cons, in any given situation, it has the ability to identify the way toward success. If one is unsure how exactly to proceed, this color is a good one from which to draw strength.

His glance migrating toward the horizon, Doug began to take note of all that was around him. Far ahead of him, demarcating the horizon, was a line of indigo. Above it was a soft, almost cottony shade of sky blue. As his eyes climbed upward, this whispering hint of azure seemed to intensify.

Below that line of course, was his reassuring, favorite effect. Giving them an appearance of almost navy blue, the thick, syrupy, oceanic shade seemed a constant source of replenishment to the shallow, underlying rocks. Enabling him to think, surrounded by even the nastiest of circumstances, this cool color palette provided a tranquilizing effect. Right now tranquilization was good thing, as this truly was a worst case scenario.

"Not sure I care for these long bridges."

"You'd rather take a boat?"

Still pointing the gun toward Doug, Tim continued. "I guess not. It's just that we're five hundred feet up in the air, and surrounded by nothing but green." His eyes then momentarily diverted toward their surroundings. "Water as far as the eye can see ..."

"It's turquoise, Tim, and don't worry. Before you know it, we'll be back in the everglades."

"Everglades ... I like the sound of that. A good place to hide shit ..."

Doug cut his eyes toward him. "Nothing stays hidden for long. You ought to know that by now."

"You can't drive any faster than forty-five miles an hour?"

"You want to get stopped by the cops?"

"Only if you're ready to die ..." Rubbing the side of his nose with his left hand, he cleared his throat. He then began again. "Wouldn't make much difference to me."

For a moment, Doug looked toward him once again. "You realize Vince is a big, fat nothing. He ain't worth much to anyone."

"So I've heard."

"So why the hell-bent effort to get to him?"

"Just settling the score for my lady."

"You don't even know him."

"And that matters, how?"

"Why don't you be a man and think for yourself? Her thing ain't lined with gold, Tim. What's with the obsession?"

"I admire your persuasive powers of reasoning, Doug, but you're wasting your breath. I intend to finish this."

"So noble of you, Sir Pussy-Whipped."

Cocking the hammer of the pistol, Tim raised the barrel of the gun. "Coming from someone who's about to have his face blown off, those are some mighty strong words."

"Go ahead. Hope you can swim."

Sitting frozen for a moment, he contemplated the last statement. Un-cocking the hammer, slowly, he lowered the barrel.

He can't swim. "I thought so."

"You haven't thought anything, Douglas. Just like the others, I plan to take care of you—a little later on."

"Shouldn't tip your hand, Timothy, it's not too bright. When your captives realize that they really have nothing left to lose, it tends to make them go for broke."

"Yes, they do." Holding up his cellular device, he then pointed toward it. "Have something left to lose, that is. Remember speed dial number eight?"

"So it would seem that basically, the only things standing between you and me are that gun and that piece of equipment. If I had them, the situation would be reversed. Vince, his family, my sister, and my niece would all be safe, right?"

"Wrong."

"How so, Timothy?"

"You seem to have forgotten one variable."

"And what variable is that?"

"Solange." *Who should have called with instructions by now.*

"You don't think that maybe some measures have already been taken to circumvent this situation?"

"Probably, but as you and I both know, those measures are most likely futile."

"You seem pretty sure of yourself."

"I've been around for awhile now, Douglas." Glancing downward toward his cellular device, he began concentrating intently upon the keypad.

We'll see. Saying nothing else, Doug returned his attention to the journey ahead of him. Mentally preparing himself for the battle to come, he decided to let the turquoise ambience work its magic. Hopefully it would be enough, but deep down inside, he knew that an off shade of blue was no match for certain, predestined ruin.

CHAPTER THIRTY

Looking down the barrel of the pistol, she fell silent. Hurdling past the car at great speed, Mozetta was peripherally aware of a band of trees beside them. The scene was almost mesmerizing.

The piece you possess has the ability to lift the thin veil between our world and the spiritual one, allowing passage from one to the next. Unfortunately, Madame knows this and is well aware of how to use it. God himself only knows what havoc she might wreak upon the ages if she were to have access to this portal. It was not meant for her hands. I firmly believe it was meant to aid you in your journey home.

"She sure did know what she was talking about."

Still dabbing her cheek, Solange turned toward her. "Who?"

"My Aunt Angelique. She had yo' number—right from the start."

"She was a fool. She could have had everything. Instead, well … you know the rest."

"What do you mean everything? She could have ended up like you—an immortal headed for Hell? Believe me, she is a lot better off."

"Why should I believe you? You know nothing. You have no idea about what you're speaking, Mozetta. Just as she was, you're an idiot."

"You must like blood smeared all over yo' face, 'cause if you don't shut it, I'm fixin' to take care of the other side." Maintaining her aim on Solange, she focused her attention toward Vera. "Take yo' damn foot off of that gas pedal. That speedometer needle is not what we are supposed to bury, Vera. You get us stopped and we are all in deep trouble."

"I don't have any intentions of slowing down, Mo." Extending her right foot toward the floorboard, the car subsequently went into passing gear.

"Well, that's just great. Either you are fixin' to blow my car completely up, or we're gonna end up in jail. Either way, we're through, so I am telling you for the last time to get yo' size eleven shoe out of my gas tank!"

"Maybe Mozetta should take the wheel, Vera. She seems a bit anxious."

Raising her arms a bit, Mozetta refocused her aim. "Just anxious to get this over with, Solange."

"Absolutely, I'm sure that by now, your arm is quite tired."

"It is, and my trigger finger is getting itchy, too." As she finished the statement, a smirk made its way onto her face. "To say every damn one in the world is afraid of you, you sure are easy to apprehend. Without yo' gorilla bodyguard, you are downright defenseless." As she finished the statement, both she and Vera began to laugh.

"Circumstances would indeed appear that way." Taking a deep breath, she exhaled and returned her gaze toward her lap. It then seemed as if she were she were searching for something. "Would you mind if I placed a call?"

"Say what?"

"I should probably use my cellular device. I will only be a moment."

"Solange, you got to be kidding. We have you at gunpoint. You have no idea what's in store for you—or the outcome—and you ask to place a phone call? I will say this again. I just don't know if you are dumb as hell or … well, just dumb as hell." She then refocused her attention toward Vera. "I really don't know."

Not removing her eyes from the highway ahead of her, Vera began. "I do. You were right on both counts."

As Vera finished the statement, a loud, vibrating buzz began to permeate the atmosphere. At the prompting of the interruption, Mozetta turned to face Solange once again. "And what a coincidence that at this very moment, yo' phone just happened to start ringing."

Momentarily, Vera's eyes left the road. "Mo, that sounds like yo' ringtone."

Looking downward, she saw the device illuminate. "So it is." Touching the button area demarcated by the green telephone receiver, she answered the call. "Hello?"

Sounding almost breathless, the disembodied voice began. "Mo? Oh my God, Mo!"

"Arlie?"

"Where in the hell are you!"

"Well, right now I really can't say."

"About the way I acted a little while ago … Girl, if I hadn't left …"

"Look, I don't have time for this right now, Arlie. We'll have to finish it later. Right now I'm …"

Abruptly interrupting the statement, Arletha began. "Mo, you have to get over here quick."

"If you would have let me finish, I'd have told you that right now I'm in the middle of something that cannot wait. You, on the other hand, will have to do just that."

"There's been a horrible accident."

"What? Who?"

"There was an explosion at the church."

"St. Raphael?"

"Where in the hell do you think I'm talking about, Mozetta? Of course St. Raphael!"

"How bad, Arlie? How damn bad?"

Her voice beginning to quiver, she attempted to describe the situation. "Real bad, Mo. On the back side of the church, the roof caved in. Baby, when the explosion occurred, the choir was practicing."

Feeling the blood drain from her face, her eyes met those of Solange. "Was anyone killed, Arlie? I want to know who was hurt."

Beginning to sob, Arletha pulled a cotton tissue from her purse. Dabbing her eyes several times, she took a deep breath and loudly exhaled. Breathing in again, she continued. "They don't know. They don't know how many are buried under the rubble."

"Pierre?"

"Mo, I'm not sure. There are cop cars everywhere and the whole block is roped off." Beginning to cry again, she finished. "This is terrible!"

"Arlie, I am putting Vera on the phone. I need you to repeat all of this her."

"I heard everything. You inadvertently put the phone on speaker. Did you hear it, Solange? Are you aware of what has happened?"

"Vera, did you say Solange? What in the world are you doing with her? What in the hell is going on?"

"We'll get back to you, Arlie. Keep us informed, baby; we intend to help."

"Ain't nobody here from our group but me, Vera. As soon as possible, you two need to get over to the church. I need some backup ... Please!"

"Hang in there, baby. We got yo' back." As she finished this statement, Mozetta ended the call. Looking away from the device, she refocused her gaze. "Well, well, well, Solange ... this time you really put on quite a show."

"You may actually find it beneficial to allow me to place a call when asked, Vera. Had it not been for your pig-headed, cavalier attitude, perhaps the total annihilation of your church, as well as your pathetic choir members, may have been avoided."

"Oh my God ..."

Looking into her rear view mirror, Vera addressed the exclamation. "What is it now, Mo?"

"Standing under that overpass back there was a cop. He had a radar gun, and he pointed it right at us." Continuing to focus her attention on the rear window, she paused for a moment. "And here he comes. Do you see those blue flashing lights screaming up behind us?"

"I sure do."

"Well, it's all over now, Miss Lead Foot. You just wouldn't listen, would you?"

"Believe it or not, there is a method to my madness."

Interrupting the conversation, Solange began. "And what might that method be, Vera?"

"This looks like as good a place as any. OK, gals, it's show time."

"Say what? Show time? What do you …?"

As Mozetta began the last question, Vera gave the steering wheel of the automobile a significant twist toward the right. Careening in the direction of the wooded area beside the highway, immediately, the compact car awkwardly left the interstate. For a few moments it was airborne, after which it began crashing its way through the mire and brush. Once the front tires again arrived on solid ground, the car began to flip end over end until finally smashing roof-first into a large oak tree. Upon impact, the car exploded and burst into flames. Around the vehicle, the dry brush ignited as well. At the edge of the accident scene, close to the point of highway departure, flashing blue lights emanated from the roof of a Louisiana State Police patrol car. In amazement, from inside the automobile, the State Trooper looked onto the accident site. Apparently, the driver had managed to attain a high rate of speed before deliberately aiming the sedan toward the wooded area. Provided there was more than one occupant in the vehicle, the event was nothing more than a premeditated murder-suicide.

Putting the radio microphone to his mouth, the officer began to speak. "This is Officer Dennis Christman. Just past the Interstate Ten mile marker number forty- seven, I have a single car accident. Vehicle left the road, crashed into the woods and burst into flames. There are no apparent survivors, and I'm not sure how many occupants were in the vehicle."

"Roger, Officer Christman, we have assistance on the way.

As he watched the scene disintegrate into a fiery mess, he exhaled. *The only assistance we'll need is a cleanup crew. At this rate, it shouldn't take 'em too long, either.*

***

"This is crazy! The whole thing is nuts!"

"We have to do it, Tomas. We don't have any other choice."

"What have you done to my family, Vince? Look what has happened since you showed up. That Balancia boy was murdered—someone slit his throat. My wife has disappeared and now you and this priest say we have to commit murder to fix everything? I won't do it. I won't be relegated to the status of a killer." Taking a step closer toward Vince, he continued. "I have a son. At least I still have a son and a mother to take care of. You need to leave this to the Miami Police Department, Vince. Get out of it while you still can." Swallowing hard, he finished. "We're not murderers; I don't want to hurt anyone."

"When you closed your fly, did you zip up your balls or what? Who wants to do this shit, Tomas? I certainly don't. We have a dangerous criminal on his way to kill us. Our demise—that's his agenda. You want to let the police handle it? Go right ahead. They don't even have a single lead on the Balancia murder. We know who did it, and why he was killed. You're right, Tomas, I should have never come here. But even that is no guarantee you guys would have been safe. I didn't do shit and am about to be offed by some serial psycho murderer. Before she does you in, this Solange apparently likes to eradicate everyone close to you. She must get off on it—I don't know. I do know that I'm not rolling over and playing dead. Father Cardoza has the means here to get us out of this and I plan to utilize them. You're either in with me or can take your chances against Serial Tim. Makes no difference to me, but if you want to help eliminate this impending doom, we gotta move fast."

As Vincent finished the statement, Father Cardoza stepped forward. "Behind the church is an unmarked moving truck. All of the items Mrs. Conerly requested are in the back of the vehicle."

"See, Tomas, it's already loaded. We're ready to head back to your house."

In apparent resignation he hung his head. "Entonces, nos vamos."

"Then you're with me?"

"Yes, Vince, I am with you."

"Mrs. Conerly has specific instructions on use of each item. For a successful outcome, they must be followed to the letter."

Turning toward the priest, Tomas began. "And how do we obtain these instructions? Vincent cannot seem to make contact with her."

"I don't have to, Tomas, all we need to do is call Joubert."

As Vince finished the statement, he noticed Father Cardoza seemed to lose a little color.

"If you are triumphant with this, I would then terminate my association with this man. No good can come of his friendship."

"We're not friends. I can't stand his ass." *Oops . . .*

As he finished the statement, he then realized what he'd said. Obviously blushing, Vince began again. "Pardon me, Father Alberto. I was merely saying—perhaps a little too emphatically—that he and I are nothing more than acquaintances. There is no bond of friendship."

This brought forth a smile. "No offense taken. Now, be on your way and may God bless both of you."

Turning to face the priest, Tomas interjected, "We'll need more than that, Father. Perhaps he could just come and take care of this for us."

"It is written that God never gives us more than we can handle, Tomas."

Leaning forward just a bit, as the priest finished, Vincent began. "It also says 'an eye for an eye,' Cuñato."

"Then I guess we'll have to use both of those as inspiration. Let's go."

As they began to head toward the car, from his hip pocket Vince pulled a flask.

"What's that?"

"Liquid courage."

"This way when you're done, we both could use a little of that."

✳✳✳

Security: freedom from danger, freedom from fear or anxiety, measures taken to guard against espionage, or sabotage, crime, attack or escape.

Since childhood, the reassuring comfort of security had eluded him. Finally, reaching adulthood he then realized that in fact it did not exist. With no guarantees, life is taken on a day to day basis. In a mere instant a life may be forever altered, or even terminated. What comes next? It's the best kept secret of all, but surely offers more in the way of comfort than this existence.

Replaying the sequence of events that have recently transpired reads more like a movie than reality. Bad things do indeed happen to good people; he is living proof of that. He may have not done such a great job with his life, but he never hurt anyone else in the process of screwing it up. That alone would label him as good, wouldn't it?

As of late, too many irreversible things have come to pass. Where is his sister and what has happened to her? And why has he plummeted into the path of a serial locomotive? In a matter of days, this evil destructive force has managed to plow through every facet of his ordinary life. His family, his friends, his job, and even his favorite restaurant have all fallen prey to a driven destructive force—a new found nemesis that literally appeared out of nowhere.

Most devastating is that one way or the other, the culmination of this horrible sequence of events will end in murder. The determining factor of the outcome? Who will die. Who succeeds in extinguishing their intended target is the determining factor of the outcome.

This time, being labeled a loser was not the issue. Even if he managed to succeed, the label of winner was not appropriate. What murderer is identified as a winner? Sadly, this time, even if he wins, he's still a loser. This victory would brand him as a killer. Even for him, that was a new low.

CHAPTER THIRTY-ONE

Our Lady of Grace Memorial Park Cemetery is nothing short of beautiful. Upon entering the sanctuary, visitors are immediately captivated by a majestic acknowledgement as to the trials and tribulations of the Cuban people. Acres of meticulously maintained tropical landscaping stretch past the striking monument; if one must be interred in Mother Earth, this would surely be the most beautiful garden in which to be laid to rest.

Toward the back of this idyllic setting is a stately, imposing wall of granite. Nameplates bolted onto these thick stone slabs label those who eternally rest behind them. Much like an apartment house for the dead, the mausoleum structure stands almost two stories high. Architecturally beautiful, the splendor of this edifice hopes to somehow mitigate a bit of the pain which accompanies the finality of eternal rest.

"I'm not sure we didn't do something illegal here."

Working for the perpetual care facility for more than ten years, Rogillio Alvarez was acutely familiar with interment protocol.

"No te preocupes, as it's none of your business. Polish any traces of excess calking off of the front of that plate and let's move on." Sweeping the sidewalk below the crypt, Jason Ullman began an assessment of what tools remained alongside the burial site. "Let's get this stuff back in the van before it rains."

Pausing for a moment, Rogillio pressed his ear to the stone. "I swear I heard something. It sounded like tapping." Turning toward his co-worker, he began again. "I'm telling you something's not right about this, Jason. Everything is so secretive and there was no ceremony for this body."

"And I'm telling you that it's none of our business, so cállate!"

"Don't tell me to shut up! You know this is not right."

"What I know is that I'm drawing a paycheck and doing what I'm told. I do not want nor do I need to be aware of any details."

After a moment in thought, Rogillio began once again. "And what's with the funky cloth around the casket, Jason? What do all those symbols mean?"

Setting down the broom, Jason turned to address him. "Rogillio, my family has been in this industry a long, long time. My grandfather Cecil started with a monument company in rural Arkansas and built it from there. We have cemeteries in Tennessee, Florida and South Carolina. Everywhere a branch of our family migrated, a branch of the business seemed to follow. Lots of unexplained shit followed every branch as well, Rogillio." Swallowing forcefully, he then took a deep breath. After he'd slowly exhaled, he continued. "In this business you learn to take your money, keep your mouth shut, and do as you're told. If there is an issue, let the authorities handle it. We don't know nothin', got it?"

"That casket is sealed with silver chains, Jason." As if he were making sure no one was eavesdropping, he paused for a moment. After a reassuring look from side to side, he continued. "You know what else?"

"No, I don't want to know what else."

"Inside the crypt, someone poured a ring of salt around it. I saw it."

"And your point is?"

"I've never seen that before. That's not normal."

"What is normal, Rogillio? Is embalming a corpse normal? How about painting the face with all different colors in order to make it appear like the living—is that normal?" He then turned and walked a few steps away from him. Turning toward him once again, he continued. "Dust to dust ... that's normal. That's the way God intended, not pumping them full of formalin so they'll never rot. And now you have a problem with a little ole ring of salt around the coffin? Well that, Sir, is none of your business. If it makes the family feel better and brings them comfort then what of it? Why should you care?"

Shaking his head, he turned to answer him. "You know, you're right. I don't care. In fact, I don't care about none of this and don't have nothing else to say."

"Good … and neither do I. Let's finish up and get out of here." *And leave this immortal to ponder his eternal entrapment. He'll have plenty of time to come up with an explanation to the almighty for his actions … a futile effort, but as of now, his only option …*

✳✳✳

Someone must lead. To do so, they must be strong and in control of every given situation. Always in the shadows lurks an undermining force.

Left untended, small details may result in the ultimate demise of leadership. In order to preserve and maintain status, the one in command must be multifaceted. No matter how minute, all particulars must be tended. To become negligent or sloppy means a loss of control.

She was careless. She became too comfortable. No one is that powerful; letting one's guard down is not only stupid, it's lethal.

Crossing the room, Thierry made his way toward the coffee pot. Pouring hot, steaming coffee into his cup, his gaze fell across the room. *I'll have no problem with detail management. I'll have no problem with leadership as well. Now that Solange's goon is bound and forever absent, there will be no impediments to my leadership assumption.*

Taking a long, slow sip, his attention was diverted toward the doorway. *Someone has to lead. Someone has to educate. Me, I'm an educator by nature. With that in tow, I'll soon be powerful … very powerful.*

Breathing deeply, he once again took a sip of the strong, black beverage. *As for Father Cardoza? His ultimate goal is to meet his maker. As long as that happens, all is well.*

As he finished the thought, he smiled to himself. *I'm all for maintaining accord. After all, there is much to be said for harmonious existence. Those who oppose it? They must be eliminated.*

His train of thought was broken by activation of his cellular device. Realizing Vince was calling, he pressed the activation button.

"Hello, Vincent."

"It's done."

"Did you follow to the letter the instructions I gave you?"

"To the letter."

"Then you're correct in your assumption that it is done."

"Is he dead, Joubert?"

"Technically yes, Vincent, but realistically, that answer is no."

"What kind of fucked up explanation is that?"

"Of course the physical body of Tim Johnson cannot survive the conditions you've brought forth. You've basically buried him alive."

"Great. I'm a murderer."

"If you followed protocol exactly, then you've also trapped the essence of Tom Banks into that space as well. Barring unforeseen circumstances, he'll forever have to remain in that rotting corpse."

"Now I feel even better, Joubert."

"You should, Vincent. There was no possible way to save Tim; he was lost to this life. His soul had already moved onto an alternate plane of existence. Had we somehow been able to extract the essence of Tom Banks from his body, he would have immediately died. Nothing could have been done to save him. The occupying consciousness was the life force sustaining his physical self. In a way, Vincent, he'd already been murdered, and his corpse had been hijacked. Does that make sense to you?"

"Yeah, about as well as any of this other bizarre crap adds up."

"Then you should feel better and realize that you're not a murderer after all. You've simply protected countless others from a grim serial killer entity."

"If you say so, Joubert. What's up with the blessed garments, the salt and silver chains? How was all that shit supposed to work?"

"Why did you not ask this before?"

"Because, asshole, we didn't exactly have a lot of time, remember? And for some strange reason, we trusted your ass, that's why. Now answer my question without the smartass inquisition."

"If you care to continue this conversation, Vincent, I'll ask that you contain yourself. You managed to call me an ass three times in that one retort and I meant nothing by the preceding interrogatory."

"Just answer my freaking question, Joubert."

"As the title would indicate, an immortal cannot be killed. They may, however, be eternally contained. To do this, a protocol exactly as you have performed must be executed. The body must be subdued and placed in a coffin for eternal rest. The spirit must be contained by a surrounding of blessed garments worn by a priest on the feast of All Souls Day. The color of the vestment is usually white. The casket is then wrapped in chains made of pure silver. The chain does not have to be substantial in nature, just pure in content. Re-establishing a connection with mortality, this silver wrap in some manner bypasses the tear in the silver chakra. In this way, the spirit may be contained in the space. Finally, to be sure evil is not able to enter or escape the space, the casket is surrounded by blessed salts from the Sea of Galilee. As long as the circle remains intact, this salt forms yet another impenetrable barrier." Taking a deep breath, he exhaled and continued. "Now I have a question for you. How did you manage to subdue him?"

"It wasn't exactly rocket science, Joubert. It was a fairly predictable situation. As you're well aware, we knew he was coming. There were three of us and one of him, so we ambushed him. What's so hard to figure out?"

"He's a dangerous man, Vince."

"First of all, Tim's not particularly stout. I outweighed him by more than fifty pounds. Second of all, I tased his ass a few times and rendered him unconscious. Apparently, he's never heard of a taser, because it surprised the hell out of him." Vince chuckled after he'd said this. "After that he was fairly manageable. I guess the tricky part was getting the body into the back of that truck without any of the neighbors seeing. And I didn't, by the way, particularly enjoy having to strip him naked in order to wrap him in that religious shroud. Seems like there could have been an easier way."

"No, I didn't figure you would particularly enjoy that part, but it had to be done." Before he began again, Thierry swallowed hard. "You weren't spotted by any of the neighbors, were you?"

"I don't think so."

As he'd said this, his conversation was interrupted by a beep. "Hey Thierry, I may need to take this call. It's from New Orleans."

"Who would be calling from here? Do you recognize the number?"

"No, I don't. Let me call you back."

"I'll await your call."

Pushing the button demarcated 'accept' on his device, he answered the call. "Hello?"

"Vincent?"

"Yes, this is Vincent. Who is this?"

"Vincent, this is Arletha Jackson."

"Wow, Mrs. Jackson ... OK ..." Taken aback, he breathed in deeply and exhaled. "This is really a surprise." For a moment, he stared straight ahead. Although saying nothing, he instinctively put his hand over the mouthpiece speaker. *Why in the hell is she calling me ... and how did she get my number?* His train of thought then returned to the call. "But it's nice to hear from you. Umm ... how are you?"

"Vince, honey, I'm not so sure you're gonna feel that way much longer."

"I'm sorry?"

"I have some news for you, and it's not too good."

"OK ..."

"Honey, before I begin, I think you might better sit down."

"Mrs. Jackson, I'm not really liking the tone of this conversation. What has happened? What's going on?"

"Vince, I know you and Mo were like family."

"We are. Right now she's the closest thing I have to a mom."

"I can assure you this is the last phone call I wanted to make."

"Did you just say *were* like family?"

"Vince, I'm afraid I have some bad news. For you it's probably the worst of news."

Leaning back against the wall, his head began to spin. "Don't do this to me, Mrs. Jackson. I can't take it. I can't take another thing." As a lump arose in his throat his voice fell off. Struggling to regain it, all he managed to utter was, "Please ... don't ... do it."

"I'm so sorry, baby. I really don't know what to say. I just thought you needed to know."

Beginning to cry, he could feel himself losing control. He'd held up pretty good thus far, but this last straw was more than he could take. There were no more details from Arletha as his emotions had broken down into a series of halting sobs. With cellular device in hand, he slid to the floor. As if in prayer, he bowed his head and began to cry. His entire emotional base was gone; all of his emotional anchors had been destroyed. He wasn't sure when she'd hung up, as a loud, piercing, land line style ringtone abruptly returned him to consciousness. When he finally was able to focus upon the clock face, he realized he'd been incoherent for more than two hours. The sad part of it all was that this was the tip of a very deep, painful iceberg. No one understood, and no one was around to help. He'd have to go this one alone, and frankly, the prospect of doing so sickened him.

Heading toward the shower, he decided that before attempting any more telephone calls, a concerted effort to pull himself together was in order. Once he was clean, he'd again be able to think clearly. A shower would help; some steaming hot water would help even more. It would take a hell of a lot more than hot water to get his life back together, but this was a start. After all, he did have to start somewhere, didn't he?

✳ ✳ ✳

Most often 'black' describes a color. Labeling mood or evil intent, the word actually covers a multitude of expressions. Frequently used in reference to a loss of consciousness, it may also describe race or formality. Black can be slenderizing, charring, defining or even the decisive end of a spectrum. Symbolizing the ultimate void, time and again black will have the final say so. However the word is used, categorically, this color—or lack thereof— represents an extreme.

Resembling thick, dark ink from a well in which as a child she used to dip her pen, so presented the black that surrounded her. Her grandmother had always insisted on perfect penmanship. To her a ballpoint pen was nothing more than a waste of time. Every entry, as well as every documentation, must be worthy of calligraphy status; therefore, a well and fresh indigo ink were mandatory. During the time of her childhood, the well had long been obsolete. This made no difference to her grandmother, however, as she insisted on strict protocol adherence.

Much to her dismay, some fifty years later, the protocol had manifested once more. As the blue-black before her mimicked the rich, dark indigo color of the well, she could not see her hand before her face. She sensed there were others beside her, but essentially could see nothing. Acutely aware of background noise, she could not make out voices or distinctive sounds. Somehow, though, she knew the up and coming scenario was familiar.

Instinctively, she was aware the surrounding void was fast losing its stronghold. A glimpse of lemon yellow confirmed the ink was now ruined. Resulting in a dissipation of the darkness, light both infects and disrupts the transparency of nighttime. The very moment sunlight appears on the horizon, darkness becomes more dilute. Before giving way to the vibrant cornflower blue of the daylight hours, the blue-black color of infinite star speckled space must first dissolve into beige.

As if regaining consciousness, daylight returns. The only difference in this instance was that before the infestation of blessed relief, there was no lucidity. With the loss of the night came the reassurance of successful continuance.

She'd been here before. The smell was the first trigger. Where and when had she already seen the tiny, cramped flat?

"What a dump."

Mozetta jumped. "Vera, you scared the hell out of me."

"Don't be too sure."

"Where in the world are we?"

"I'm not exactly certain."

"You want to know something strange?"

"I'm not exactly sure of that, either."

"I've been here before."

Putting her hand on her hip, Vera turned to face her. "Lucky you. With that being the case, do you have any idea how to get us out of here?"

"No, because I have no idea how we got here in the first place ..." Taking a step forward, she began to look around. "The last thing I remember …" In mid-sentence she abruptly paused. As if an answer had suddenly occurred to her, she once again turned toward Vera. "Wait a minute. The last thing I remember before that pitch black darkness was a horrible car accident. You turned my car in the direction of those woods." Inhaling deeply, her eyes became wide. Making her way back to Vera, she continued. "Ms. Jenkins, I can assure you we're not in Kansas anymore."

"How would you know? You've never been there."

"Look around, Vera. We're on the front steps of some flat. This doesn't even look like the United States. There is a street, but have you seen a single car drive by? There is no one walking around out here. It feels almost as if we have been dropped into a 3-D postcard. In this whole scenario, we're the only things animated." Waving her hand in front of her face, she attempted to dissipate the persistent fog. "And what's with this smoky air?"

"It hasn't gotten hot enough out here to burn it off."

Sensing movement in her peripheral vision, she turned toward it. "Is that someone up the block?"

Craning her neck in an attempt to better see the distant figure, Vera then turned back toward Mozetta. "It appears to be that way."

"They're walking toward us."

"Ain't no they, it's just one person. I think it's a woman."

"You assumed correctly."

Mozetta returned her hand to her hip. "And now I know we've died and gone to Hell, because look who just prissed her ass up to greet us."

The woman replied, "And you're surprised?"

"Not happily …"

Smirking wryly, she continued. "Maybe you should have thought of that possible outcome before you decided to take matters into your own hands."

Taking a step back from her, Vera continued. "Oh, I thought of the possible outcomes. This outcome is exactly what I expected. In fact, Miss Deshotel, it's right on the mark."

"You think so?"

"I know so."

"You seem very sure of yourself."

"Well, it's like this: We wanted you to have all the time in the universe to contemplate what you have done. It was bad enough that you wreaked havoc on one lifetime, Solange, but to wreak havoc on two—and create a whole new race in the process—is a bit much. I believe it was time for a break. You have done enough."

"Oh, I've just begun."

Taking a step toward her, Vera continued. "No, bitch, you are through. You hear me? It is over, and it ends here … Right in yo' own back yard."

As if a light bulb were switched to the 'on' position, Mozetta came to life. "I was sure that I knew this place, and I remember it now. We're in her past, aren't we, Ms. Jenkins?"

"Yes, we sure are."

Turning toward Solange, Mozetta continued. "You know, I've beaten yo' damn ass more than once, but you kept coming back again and again. You just wouldn't listen. We finally had to send you back to Hell in order to shut up yo' big, fat face." Breathing in deeply, she then exhaled. "So enjoy it, Solange, and take the pain."

"As will you … Circumstances seem to point to the fact that you've landed here with me. You will learn a lot, however, and perhaps have the opportunity to be an unwilling recipient as well."

Regaining the step she'd recently taken, Vera stepped between them. "I doubt that."

Now smiling, Solange merely answered, "We'll see."

"Mmm-hmm." Turning away from her, Mozetta continued. "Well, Ms. Jenkins, I think that it is time that we be on our way. Good luck with yo' new gilded cage, Solange. And this time, enjoy Hell … over, and over and over."

"You know I will find a way out. I made my way out once before and will do so again."

"And we, too, will see."

Turning her attention toward the flat, she continued. "I'm not afraid of him. I'm not afraid of you, and I'm surely not afraid of your God."

"Well you see now, that's where you made yo' big mistake, missy. You just do not know when to keep yo' mouth shut, do you?"

"I only said what I believe."

"Honey, if you even remotely believed in, 'my God,' you would have kept that dyed red- headed mouth of yours in the closed position."

"I speak the truth."

"Baby, you don't even know the truth anymore. If it came up and bit you right on the end of the nose, you would not recognize it."

Solange began to laugh. "So where will you two go? From past experience I can assure there is not much diversity in an endless time loop." Her train of thought was then interrupted by a scream, which emanated from the door beside them.

As a look of sadness made its way across her expression, Mozetta answered her. "This brings new meaning to the expression 'help yo'self.' Even on the likes of you I don't wish something that brutal, but this is yo' eternal damnation ... although it's probably a lot less than most of the lives you have destroyed." She took a deep breath and then sighed. Looking at Vera, she began again. "I guess one of the worst things about Hell is that it truly is a no win situation. Things never get any better."

In past conversations Mozetta had never seen an emotional shift in Solange. This time was different. This time she'd apparently struck a nerve.

"You pathetic display of insignificance ... Don't you dare feel sorry for me! You think because you've stumbled into some haphazard en-snarement that you've won? I think not. This is but a pause in which I'll gather momentum. In order to hone my skills, I'll torture that monster in there. Loop after loop, I'll refine my technique. When I'm done—and I will be soon enough—I'm coming after both of you. No matter what plane of existence houses you, I will find you. Look around, girls. Compared to what is in store for you, this will seem like paradise. Enjoy your little accidental victory, as it will be your last."

"Strong words coming from the damned."

Mozetta then took a step forward. Leaning toward Solange, she added, "The *damned*, damned, that is, because you sure were a pain in my backside. And just so you know, you may want to think twice about threatening me." Drawing back her right hand, across the face she then slapped her.

Gritting her teeth, Solange drew back and returned the assault. Knocking Mozetta down the three steps, she descended upon her to continue. "You may want to remember that things are different here, Mo, and no … we're not in Kansas anymore. I no longer have to put up with your alpha female tactics as I am now the alpha."

Attempting to arise, Mozetta answered her. "Then bring it on, Alph. Bring on everything you got."

At that moment, Vera stepped between them. "Stop! Both of you will cease."

Turning to meet her gaze, Solange began. "I will no longer answer to you, either, Vera Ellen Jenkins. Get out of my way. I have work to do."

Remaining steadfast, Vera simply replied, "No, you do not."

Continuing to stare at her, she fell silent. Slowly, a light of recognition began to manifest. "Ah … I see now. To do his bidding, he's sent a lackey."

"If you wish."

"My shortcoming for not recognizing this sooner, as things may have turned out differently."

"Things turned out exactly as they were destined. You should have realized that as well."

"How kind of him to leave us here … Maybe your friend should have been a bit more faithful? Apparently, she was not truly devout."

"I ain't stayin' nowhere, Solange. This is yo' rodeo."

"And how quaint to express oneself utilizing such rudimentary language …" Leaning toward Mozetta, her eyes narrowed. "Now shut up and speak only to when you are spoken."

"I hope yo' favorite color is bald, because we fixin' …"

At that moment, Vera once again interrupted. "We must now leave, Mozetta."

Pausing, Mozetta turned toward her. "Oh, so now you are finally taking my advice? Who would have thought?"

"Walk with me, Mozetta. There will be no more conversation with Solange."

As she said this, Solange began to laugh. "Oh there will be plenty of time for conversation, Vera. Remember what I have told you: We'll soon meet again." Standing with her right arm clutching the wrought iron railing, she watched their silhouettes disappear. As her two rivals faded from view, the smile never left her face.

✳✳✳

Rounding the corner of the first block, Vera paused. "Well old friend, I guess our work here is done."

A streak of panic ran through her. "So I am left here alone?"

Vera smiled. "Of course you are not left here." Taking a deep breath, she then exhaled. "With your right hand, reach into the pocket of your dress."

"Why? Ain't nothin' in there."

"Just indulge me."

With an expression that was both bewildered and non-trusting, she did so. As she removed her hand from the pocket, she pulled from it a coin. "What is this?"

"Have a look."

Examining the coin, she discovered it was a 1907 twenty dollar gold piece. "Well I do say. This looks just like the dollar Dr. Staten gave me back at the restaurant." Returning her gaze to Vera, she began again. "What am I supposed to do with it?"

"Symbolically speaking, that's your ticket home."

"Miss Thing, since we are symbolically speaking, maybe you ought to enlighten me as to how I use this?"

"Your destiny is planned for you, Mozetta. You don't have to do anything."

"I have another question."

Continuing her gaze, Vera simply replied, "OK."

"Back there with Solange, as she was looking at you, suddenly, something made perfect sense to her. After that occurred, she said, 'to do his bidding, he's sent a lackey.' What did she mean by that?"

"Condescendingly, she was referring to me as the Lord's minion. She dismissed me as nothing more than a runner or a messenger, if you will."

"You should have let me beat her down."

"That is no longer in your genetic makeup, Mozetta. For now, you're a lackey as well."

"Oh really?"

"Yes ma'am."

"Well, I don't feel much different."

"Let's just say you have some orientation and training ahead of you." Vera smiled once again. "The sooner you get started, the better."

"Am I gonna get me some wings?"

This brought forth a laugh. "Now you know, I really don't know … because it wasn't that 'Wonderful of a Life'."

"Mmm-hmm … Well, maybe you ought to speak for yo' self."

"Are you ready?"

Mo let out a long, exasperated sigh. "Yeah, I guess I am."

As the two of them began to walk forward, Vera extended her arm. Acknowledging the gesture of friendship, Mozetta smiled. Arm in arm they made their way down the street.

CHAPTER THIRTY-TWO

"How's it going, man? I think they did a good job on the service."

Looking downward, Pierre replied. "I guess it was as good as it was gonna be. A service for five dead people either blown to smithereens or burnt beyond recognition is not too much reason to celebrate."

"Yeah, that was a pretty stupid comment. Sorry, man." Putting his arm around him, Vince continued. "You know I love you."

"Wasn't stupid, Vince. I know you mean well."

"I've missed you guys. Never thought I'd be returning for something like this."

"Me neither. Looks like I've damn near lost everything … my wife, my friends, my business and even my church. What on earth did I do to deserve all of that?"

"You didn't do anything, man. None of this was your fault. It wasn't any of our faults, Pierre, it just happened. But hey, I'm your friend, aren't I?"

"You damn right you are."

"And my little house should make a pretty good restaurant, don't you think?"

"It'll do in a pinch."

Vincent laughed. "Man, that's the first laugh I've had in I don't know when. Feels good to actually smile for a change."

"What do you think we ought to name it? I was thinking of Vincent's Place?"

"Pierre, we gotta call it Boliviee's. Nothing else but that."

"Ain't gonna be Boliviee's, boy, 'cause Mo ain't there. It won't be the same."

"That's OK. A new motto I've adopted is to 'embrace change.' Things change so rapidly that nothing ever stays the same anymore. A new Boliviee's is OK."

"At least for awhile, Arlie's gonna help me in the restaurant. Ain't but the two of us left, so I guess she needs the diversion as well."

"I think that's a good thing."

"Good therapy, maybe, but the food won't taste the same."

"Embrace change, remember? I'll bet Arlie is a kick-ass cook."

"We'll see. She has a hard act to follow."

As Pierre said this, a lump formed in his throat. Swallowing hard, Vince attempted to continue. "There is no following that act, Pierre. She'll have to find one of her own." Letting out a ragged, raspy sigh, he arose. "On that note, I'm gonna have to step outside. I think I need a cigarette."

"You need to quit that shit."

"I know, I know … God, how I know. But have a look at my life the past couple of months. It's a wonder I'm not a chain smoker by now."

"Yeah, you know that's right." Shoving his hands into his suit pockets, Pierre paused for a moment. Taking a deep breath, he raised his eyebrows in apparent resignation and exhaled. "Go on and have a cigarette." A crowd of well wishers talking and visiting in the adjacent room then captured his attention. Turning away, he began to walk in their direction. Stopping for just a moment, he returned his gaze to Vincent. "I think I'm gonna head in there for a few. When you're finished, just come and find me."

"Sounds good."

After Vince had acknowledged Pierre, he headed toward a set of double glass doors located at the front of the gymnasium. Since the church building was in such disarray as a result of the explosion, the congregation had set up temporary quarters in the gym. When all was said and done, it was actually a nice conversion. As he stepped outside, he pulled his lighter from his pocket. Attempting to light his smoke, a fairly sizeable gust of wind managed to extinguish the flame. Before he was able to try again, his cellular device began to ring. Checking his caller identification, he realized that Tomas was attempting to get in touch with him. Instead of letting the call go to voice mail, he decided to answer it.

"Hello?"

"Cuñato."

"Hola brother-in-law, what gives?"

"How is New Orleans?"

"Kinda sad and blown up to Hell and back. How are you?"

"Depends on the day, sometimes the hour. Right now I'm making it."

"No one sniffing around down there, huh?"

"No, nothing. How about there?"

"Cool as a cucumber."

"You coming back here? I meant what I said when I told you that you were welcome to live with us."

"No, man, I think I'm headed back to the Keys. Adair found me a dental lab job on one of the islands, so I may do that for awhile. Even in the islands people need crowns and dentures."

"We could find you a job here. You're family, Vince. Come live with us."

"Tomas, you have no idea how much that means to me. Except for Pierre, I don't really have anyone left up here, but right now without my sister, Miami would be too painful." Trying again to light his his cigarette, he was successful. After taking a deep, long drag, he exhaled. "Maybe one day … we'll see."

"The offer stands. It's always open."

"I'll be up there on the weekends to bug the shit out of you and Luie."

"Luis could use some support right now. He's having a hard time comprehending what has happened."

"Tell him to get in line, Tomas."

As Vincent finished the sentence, he heard the doorbell sound. "Hey Vince, let me call you back. Someone just rang the doorbell."

A feeling of concern washed through him. "You're expecting someone?"

"No … I'm not." With telephone receiver in hand, Tomas turned toward the ring. "Luis, see who's at the door."

Upon opening it, Luis found an older woman standing in front of the doorway. Approximately five foot nine in stature, she was elegantly dressed and perfectly coiffed. As he looked at her, she smiled.

"Hello, I'm looking for the Levy residence."

Cautiously, Luis returned the smile. "This is the Levy residence."

"Is Mr. Levy at home? If so, I'd very much like to speak to him."

"Who may I say is at the door?"

"I'm Anne Janway McDonald."

"Does he know you, Mrs. McDonald?"

"I don't think so, but I feel as if I already know all of you."

"Umm, hang on a minute and I'll get him." Luis turned to give his father the message and then stopped. Turning back around, he addressed her once again. "Mrs. McDonald, we've never met, have we?"

"I don't think so."

"I don't think so either, but something about you looks so familiar." Staring a bit longer, he began again. "I can't put my finger on where I've seen you before."

"Probably here, son."

"What did you just say? You just told me we've never met, right?"

"Yes, I did tell you that."

"And you've never been here before, right?"

"No I have never been here before."

"Then how could I possibly feel like I've seen you before today?"

"Perhaps for the same reason people tell me that back home. I don't particularly see it, but everyone says I look just like our mother."

CHAPTER THIRTY-THREE

"Vince, hang on a minute. There is some crazy person at the door with Luis." As he was finishing the sentence he walked toward the door. Once there, he stepped in front of Luis and began. "May I help you?"

"Mr. Levy?"

"Do I know you?"

"I don't think so. I'm Anne Janway McDonald."

"You look very familiar, but I don't think we've met. What can I do for you, Ms. McDonald?"

"Well, there's really nothing you can do for me, I've just come to fulfill a promise that I made a long time ago."

"And how does that involve us?"

"Before I begin, Mr. Levy, would you care to maybe step outside? I'd hate for you to run up the utility bill standing in that doorway."

"I'm fine."

"As you wish. Mr. Levy, my mother's name was Shelley."

"What a coincidence, so was my wife's, although my family called her Aracely."

"It's no coincidence, Mr. Levy. My mother's full name was Anne Michelle Jacola Levy Janway."

"Is this some kind of sick joke? Who are you? What did you say your name was again?"

"My full name is Alberta Anne Janway McDonald."

"And how the hell do you know my wife's full name?"

"Growing up, I always knew there was something missing in my mother's life. There were certain dates on which she'd become very sad and moody. She never told us why, but during the Christmas season, she always hung an extra stocking over the fireplace. My father and grandmother were in on it as well, but no one would ever elaborate. My brother and I decided it was a mystery that would just die with her. I thought she'd maybe lost another child and it was too painful for her to talk about. As it turns out, I was right."

"A very interesting and heartwarming story, Ms. McDonald, but again what does that have to do with us and why you're here?"

"I wish you'd call me Anne."

After she'd finished, he said nothing.

"My mother was old when she had my brother and me. In fact she was almost forty-six years of age. In that day and time it was virtually unheard of. So as you can see, I had older parents. Toward the end of her life, my mother decided that there were loose ends that must be tended. One fall day—I remember because it was quite cool and my brother had just built a fire—she sat both of us down and told us a chronology of her life. To say the least, it was an interesting litany of events. Like you, I refused to believe it. The sort of things to which she referred defied all logic. My mother never suffered from dementia, Mr. Levy, and was of sound mind right up until the moment of her death. Her story never wavered; my father remained steadfast in his beliefs as well. As time went on, I decided to do some research and see if these people to which she fervently referred actually existed."

She paused for a moment to give him time to digest the story thus far.

"Those people did exist, Mr. Levy, and everything she described about them was painstakingly accurate. Many also thought my mother was a seer. She dismissed that, always insisting that she had no special gifts. She knew the future only because she'd been there."

"So if what you're saying is true, Ms. McDonald …"

"Please call me Anne."

Slightly annoyed at the interruption, he started again. "So if what you are saying is true, Anne, then there are intimate details you should know that would not be accessible by any other venue than my wife."

"I feel that my mother anticipated that, yes."

"Who do you think caused my wife's disappearance?"

"Daria Landry."

Tomas fell silent. After a stunned moment, he then regained his momentum. "What did she have to do with anything?"

"The seven group of Mozetta Conerly was attempting to recapture Solange Deshotel. Without their consent, Daria cast your wife as the misfit number of eight."

A tear began to track down his cheek. "Where do I have a tattoo?"

"Between your shoulder blades and just below your collar, you have a zigzag. You also have a four leaf clover on the left cheek of your behind, Mr. Levy. You got that during spring break in Daytona Beach, Florida. That particular night, you were so drunk that you don't remember who, when, where or how you got it."

After she'd finished, he was speechless.

"Anything else, Mr. Levy?"

"Yes. Call me Tomas, and please come in." Stepping away from the doorway, he allowed her to enter. "This is my son, Luis."

"Hi Luis, I'm Anne."

Managing a smile, Luis said nothing else.

"I thought it was about time that I met my big brother."

Turning to face them, Tomas began. "That sounds so bizarre."

"Well it is bizarre considering I'm an old lady of almost seventy-nine. I don't have too many good years left, Tomas, so I thought it was high time I met what was left of my family. I wanted Luis to get to know me as well."

"You look like an old version of mom."

"A little while ago, I told you that, remember?"

"Yeah, I remember."

Taking a step forward, Tomas interrupted. "You must understand this is hard to digest, Anne, as my wife's only been gone a short time. For you, on the other hand, it's been a lifetime."

"My mother died in 1959, Tomas. She was seventy four years of age."

"And she began her life in 1965, Anne, six years after she died. How do we make sense of that?"

"There's no way to logically make sense of that, as this was not remotely a normal situation. Luis' mother and my mother is the only individual who has ever lived a single lifetime in two different eras. She raised and educated her youngest children first, and she died before she got her oldest child grown."

"Do you have any kids?"

"I do. I have two boys and a girl."

"Did she know them?"

"She knew my oldest two. I had my first in '55 and my second in '57, so Momma was able to enjoy those two grandchildren. Of course both of them were very little when she died."

"Did Mamí ever mention me?"

"Luis, after Mother finally divulged her past, I think she told me every single detail about you. Losing you was a wound that never healed; part of her died the day she was ripped away from this family."

Looking at both of them, Tomas continued. "Then I guess it's now safe to say that she's not coming back. For us we can consider the day she disappeared the day that she in fact died."

"Sadly, I think that's a correct assumption, Tomas. I can't see Mother ever coming back."

"Then it is done." He took a deep breath. "And you are now family, Anne."

"Well, I consider that a great honor."

"You have a place with us whenever you want. Having you here somehow makes my wife feel a little bit closer. Perhaps it's the strong physical resemblance."

Luis took a step toward them. "I feel the same way."

"Well, I'm certainly not Mother, but I, too, feel her presence. I think she'd be happy that we're finally all together."

"And what about your brother? Where is he? Did he come with you?"

"No Tomas, my twin brother died several years ago from heart disease. My husband is gone as well, so now it's just me."

"And your children?"

"They're spread out everywhere. The oldest and the youngest live in Washington, D.C., while my middle child lives in California. He just loves Los Angeles."

"And your way cool teenage big brother lives in Miami, Anne."

"That certainly tops it off, Luis. I just don't think anything could beat that."

"Except a cup of Cuban coffee. Follow me into the kitchen. I want to make a toast to family."

"I can't think of a better toast."

Neither can I, except for the fact that I don't have any freaking Cuban coffee, asshole.

"Who said that?"

Me.

Tomas held the receiver to his ear. "Vince?! You're still there?"

"The fact that you're hearing my voice would indicate a *yes* on that one, Tomas."

"So ... you heard everything?"

"Everything."

"Estas muy metiche, Cuñato."

"I'm not nosey, Tomas. You just forgot to hang up the damn phone, and I found that conversation quite interesting. But hey, now you don't have to recant the whole thing because I heard it all first hand."

"That you did, Cuñato."

"Tell my little niece Uncle Vince can't wait to meet her."

After he'd said this, Tomas handed her the receiver. "And I can't wait to meet my Uncle Vince, either. I've heard all about you, Uncle Vince. Momma told me every story. So don't try and pull a fast one on your old lady niece, you hear?"

"Damn ... Even with all of this, Shelley still makes sure I don't have any fun."

"Oh we'll have fun, don't you worry."

"Night, night, niece Anne, I'll soon be in touch. Give all of your contact info to your step daddy. I'll make sure you get mine as well."

"Will do. Night, night, hon."

With that, he pushed the device's *off* button.

Could this whole thing get any more bizarre? No way in Hell ... but lately, who knows?

CHAPTER THIRTY-FOUR

With the television on, he'd fallen asleep on the couch. At first, the knock on the door fit into his dream. As the knock became more furious, he realized there was indeed someone at his front door. In a sleep induced fog, he arose to answer it.

"Well, well, well, the fat-ass has returned to Key West."

"Glad to see you too, asshole. Move, as I have an armload of crap to put in my room."

"Your room? I thought you were just a guest."

"Permanent guest now, Adair."

"OK ... I see how it is ... then you better get your permanent fat self on the payroll. You can foot the light bill this month."

As he reached his room, Vincent dropped his things to the floor. "Is that any way to treat a long, lost friend? You'd begrudge me a few breaths of cold air?"

"You want free cold air? Move to Alaska."

He laughed. "You really are a jerk, Adair. That was funny, but you are such a piece of shit."

"I only call 'em like I see 'em."

As he said this, Patrick walked out of the bathroom. "Barker, what are you doing here? And don't tell me you've moved into my room and have been using my stuff."

"I merely came by to visit a friend. Occasionally, I have to pee, too. Is that OK? Mind if I use a little bit of your water from time to time, Fatso?"

"You know, it just warms *my heart* to see your *gay heart* the instant I get into town, but now that our reunion moment is behind us, don't you have things to do? I'm sure there is someone else's toilet you might need to piss in?"

"I never knew you felt like that about me. You can warm *your heart* with my *gay heart* anytime, Tubbo. I get into fat guys sometimes."

Vincent laughed. "You know something, Patrick? I haven't missed your queer ass at all!"

"And I was just being nice, Sir Blubbalot. Actually, I really don't get into fat guys."

Stepping forward, Doug interrupted. "Now that we're through with 'old home week,' why don't we go up the street and find some good seafood. I could use a beer, too."

Nodding his head in approval, Vincent grabbed his keys. "Sounds good to me."

"Guys, it's still a little early for grub. I understand, with both of you being on the portly side, that you have to 'feed that beast' inside of you. I, on the other hand, do not have that pressing need … especially when the sun hasn't even made it halfway up into the sky."

"No, you just have that pressing need to get 'other things' inside of you."

Both he and Doug began to laugh. Starting to crack up as well, Patrick continued. "OK, I give up. So that I'm not the brunt of every insult, let's treat your hypoglycemic butts with some sugar and fat. After that, maybe you'll be nice to me."

"And then to the beach. You look like hell. When's the last time you've been out in the sun?"

"Comes and goes, O Fat One … just an affliction I have these days."

"Maybe you need to start taking vitamins or something."

Cutting his eyes toward Vince, he answered him. "Or something is probably more like it." Shoving his hands into his pocket, in order to face them, he readjusted his stance. "You know guys, I love how we're picking right up where we left off and everything, but I have an issue with the fact that we've not discussed a grave situation that occurred a few days ago."

Turning toward him, Doug held up his hand in protest. "Don't use the word grave, please."

"Well you can fluff it up or gloss it over any way you like, but it is what it is. The word 'grave' fits."

Taking a step toward him, Vince began. "Barker, I'm gonna say this one time and one time only. Some shit went down that we hope stays buried forever. It's not something we can ever discuss, and if you're a real friend—which by your recent actions I think that you are—you won't bring it up around anyone ever again."

"And that's it? You will not tell me what happened?"

"I will tell you this. If everyone dragged into this keeps his mouth shut, the man who tried to murder us probably will not resurface. Most likely there will be folks snooping around and asking questions, but we don't know shit. Got it? Our minds are blank slates."

"Wow ... Ok." As if deep in thought, he stared straight ahead. After a moment, some stray thought, some sound or maybe some other stimulus broke the train. Looking again at Vincent, he continued. "I'm not sure I want to know anything else, Vince. In fact, I know I don't want to."

"Trust me; you're better off not knowing."

Doug turned to answer them. "Man, you got that right."

Shifting uncomfortably, Patrick turned toward the door. "I think I will pass on the seafood, guys. Suddenly, I feel the need for some fresh air." After he finished saying this, he began to walk toward it.

Taking a step behind him, Vincent put a hand on his shoulder. As he did this, Patrick froze. "Not one word, Patrick ... I'm serious. You could bury a lot of folks with loose lips. For a myriad of reasons, the consequences would be disastrous."

Turning around to face him, he replied, "Things are a hell of a lot more complex than even you realize, Vincent. I probably know more than you could imagine. There's no need to elaborate, or to worry. I'm well aware of the disastrous costs of leaked information. As far as I'm concerned, it stops here."

Doug chimed in. "Me too. That last round of shit almost got my family blown up. Thank God for my niece's bronchitis, or they'd have been in that car. As far as I'm concerned, it stops here, too."

'Unfortunately our church was not so lucky." Pausing for a moment, Vince took time to look at both of them. "We're all in agreement?"

All nodded their heads 'yes.'

"Then it's settled. Barker, you sure you don't want to come with us?"

"I'm sure. It's all good. I'll see you guys a little later on."

With that, he turned back around and made his way out of the house.

After he'd left, for a moment both of the men stood silent. Vincent then began. "Boy, I didn't see that coming. I've never seen that side of Patrick before; he was so solemn and serious. For a moment I had to remind myself who I was talking to."

"Did you get the feeling that he knows a hell of a lot more than he let on?"

"Yeah, it was pretty obvious."

"Scary fact."

"I'm not too sure about that. A minute ago, I saw a deep founded wisdom in Patrick that I never knew existed. Between then and now, something's happened, Adair. Something big has happened."

"I wonder what it could be?"

"Judging from the expression on his face, I'm not sure we'd really want to know."

As Vincent finished the sentence, there was a knock on the door.

Both of the men looked at each other and shrugged. "He must have forgotten something."

Vincent walked toward the door. Upon reaching it, he turned the handle and pulled it open.

"What?! I don't believe this… Are you for real? What are you doing here?"

CHAPTER THIRTY-FIVE

"What? You aren't glad to see me?"

"Hell yeah, I'm glad to see you! Adair, this is Mel! You know, the girl I used to work with at LSU."

Delia took a step forward. "Hi, I'm Delia Melancon."

"How's it going? I'm Doug Adair, Fatso's best friend."

Beginning to laugh, as she extended her hand she continued. "Nice to meet you."

"So, Mel, what gives? Why didn't you let me know you were coming?"

"Obviously, Vincent, I wanted to surprise you."

"Well, you sure as hell did. Where are you staying?"

"Don't know yet."

"We got room on the couch." As he finished the statement, he turned toward Doug. "That is, if it's alright with you, Adair."

"I got no problem with it. If she's brave enough to sleep in this stinkin' rathole, it's OK by me."

"Believe me; I've slept in a lot worse."

"You still haven't told me why you're here."

Looking around the room, she then turned to answer him. "Is there somewhere I might put my things?"

"Yeah, just set them over there in that corner. You hungry?"

"I could eat."

"We were headed over to Sunset Docks for seafood."

"And beer," Doug interjected.

"You want to come?"

"OK, sounds good. I'll get settled when we get back." As Delia finished the sentence, her cellular device ringtone activated. After checking the caller ID, her gaze again met Vincent's.

"Vince, I have to take this call. How about I just meet you guys at Sunset when I'm done? It's not far from here, is it?"

"No, not at all, just a few blocks away. It's at the end of Duval. You can't miss it; just call me if you can't find it. We'll save you a seat. Want me to order for you?"

"Don't worry about that; I'll wait until I get there. I need to look at the menu." On her device, she then pressed the answer button. "I'll see you in a few." Putting the cellular phone to her ear, she turned away from them and began to walk toward the bathroom. Vincent and Doug subsequently made their way toward the door.

"I can't believe Mel is actually here."

"It's a hell of a coincidence, huh Vince?"

"A good one … Man, she's a sight for sore eyes."

"Did you notice how she didn't answer you? We still don't know what brings her down here."

"She didn't, did she?" Breathing in and then exhaling, he raised his eyebrows in defeat. "Well, I guess we'll find out at the restaurant. Lock the door, man. I don't want anyone walking in on my next piece of ass."

This brought forth a laugh. "You ain't right, Fatso. I swear your mind is warped."

"And it's taken you this long to figure that one out? Not too bright, Adair … No siree, you ain't the sharpest tool in the shed."

* * *

"Why are you calling me?"

"I'm so sorry if I disturbed you, Delia. I just wanted to make sure that you arrived safely."

"Can the bullshit, Joubert. What do you want?"

"As you wish, no more bullshit. I need for you to take care of someone for me."

"Take care of someone? Who?"

"A priest by the name of Cardoza."

"As if we're not already enough on God's bad side, you want me to off a priest? You want to make damn sure that I end up in Hell, don't you?"

"Where you end up is really none of my concern."

"Oh but yes it is, Joubert. It is none other than you that extended my stay here on earth by a few thousand years. So, yes, I think you can assume responsibility for that one." Feeling her face beginning to flush, she grabbed a tissue from her purse. Dabbing her neck, she continued. "I ought to fly home and beat your fucking ass for that comment."

"You'll have to wait a bit on that, as I need you to take care of Vincent and Douglas as well."

"What?! Are you out of your freakin' mind?"

"They know too much, Delia. They know too much and are also potential targets. With that much dangerous knowledge, we cannot afford to have them fall into the wrong hands. I need them on my side."

"Then come and get them. I will not do your dirty work. Better yet, let Patrick take care of this for you. He may actually enjoy it."

"What happened to Patrick is indeed unfortunate but also a mute point. On a much brighter note, we can return Patrick to the trio and restore the three stooges in their entirety."

"Like that's a brighter note, Joubert. Rob them of their mortality, but as long as they're together, everything is just peachy keen. You make me sick."

"I'll make you sicker if you don't shut up and do as I say. I'm through with the Mr. Nice guy act, Delia. I have the recipe—and the means—for a nice, long mausoleum snooze. If you would like to focus your attention on the upholstered inside of a wooden box for … say … the next millennium or so, then cross me. If by some chance you don't believe me, make your way up to Miami and have a chat with my friend Tim. He'll fill you in on all of the details of what lies ahead of you. Just say the word, and I'll give you directions."

The flush continued upward. She now felt her face getting hot, too. "You bastard."

"Get it done, Delia, and call me when you're through. We'll both know they'll all have to be trained on how to properly sustain without attracting attention."

"Go to Hell, Joubert …Take your ass to Hell and stay there!"

Pushing the off button on her device, she leaned against the wall behind her. Taking a deep breath, rapidly, she exhaled and looked toward the doorway. At that moment, *damn it all* were the only words that went through her head.

✳✳✳

"It's about time you got here. Adair and I are about to starve to death. Did you get lost?"

"Judging from the … let's see … seven beer mugs in front of you, I hardly think you two were starving to death. You ought to be full by now."

"We're just getting started. Hey Mel, I have a job at a dental lab in Marathon. It's an hour away, but they have a really good crew there. The lab does a kick-ass business, too. If you're serious about staying down here, I may can get you on."

"Vincent, I am more than serious. I've decided I'm staying right here in Key West with you, Doug and Patrick forever."

Eyes lighting up, a smile crept across his face. "Really?"

He didn't see it. Perhaps she wiped it away soon enough, or he may have thought it was brought on by the wind. He may have even thought she was just that glad to see him, when a tear began to track across her right cheek.

She merely answered, "Oh yeah, really."